Cutting It Fine

A strand of hair is all it takes

Sheena Billett

Also by Sheena Billett

The Woman Who Wrote In Green Ink

Eagle Court

From Manchester To The Arctic

Shifting Horizons – a collection of short stories

For Adele and hairdressers everywhere

Chapter One

The scissors hovered motionless for a few seconds above Em's head.

Rose pressed her lips together, resisting the urge to cut chunks out of her client's expensive extensions.

'Everything all right, Rose?' Em looked at her in the mirror, eyes wide. 'You look like you just saw a ghost.'

'Yup, all good.' Rose forced a smile and, relaxing her grip on the scissors, went back to the task in hand. 'So tell me again about this guy.'

Em didn't need any further prompting. 'Like I said, he's a personal trainer at that gym, ProFit, and he's really fit! I can tell all the women fancy him – and some of the men, I'll bet.' She smirked. 'He can't keep his eyes off me, though. He's made it crystal clear how he feels – if you know what I mean'

Rose didn't know what she meant but couldn't bring herself to ask. Moving round the side of the chair, she concentrated on trimming Em's fringe, creating the new look, swept to one side, conscious of how close she was to those startlingly blue eyes. Rose wondered, not for the first time, what natural colour was hiding behind the contact lenses.

Em waited until Rose stood back before continuing. 'And he's got such a cute dimple – right here on his cheek.' She pointed with a carefully manicured fingernail. 'Don't you just love a dimple?'

Rose held on to the back of the chair and held her breath, steadying herself. Ignoring the question, she asked, 'How does that look, or do you need a bit more off?'

Em studied her reflection, turning her head from side to side. 'I think maybe a teensy bit more thinning?'

Rose stifled a sigh and cut into the fringe, thinning it out a little more.

'Great. That's better.' Em surveyed herself in the mirror, turning her head this way and that.

Rose held up the mirror so that Em could see the back of her head and the blonde extensions cascading over her shoulders. 'I think these extensions are going to need replacing soon – maybe next time?'

Em hesitated for the briefest second. 'Sure. I'm sure I'll be able to manage that.' She gave a dazzling smile.

'What's he called?' Rose asked as Em stood up and Rose untied her gown.

'He calls himself Jay – to me.' She pointed theatrically at her chest with a long, slender finger. 'It's a special name, just between us. I think some of the others call him Olly or something.' Em shook her hair out and ran her fingers through it. 'I think I might have persuaded him to give me a little bit of personal training in-between times.' She made air quotes as she accentuated the word personal.

Rose tried to swallow the hard lump that had been forming in her throat. She couldn't stop herself from asking one more question. She had to know. 'So, have you got a pic? Let's see.'

Em's forehead puckered into a frown. 'He won't let me take any photos of him. But that's quite exciting really...and mysterious. Maybe he's famous for something I don't know about.' The high-pitched giggle made Rose want to slap her. 'Maybe he's a spy!'

'Or maybe he's married!' Rose was unable to sweeten the acid tone.

'Oh I don't care about that! Nothing to do with me. But I'll get the truth out of him and talk him round sooner or later. My followers are dying of curiosity. I'm enjoying having a mystery boyfriend.'

'Wait! You're actually going out with him?'

'Well, kind-of. We've only met once outside the gym. But he's taking me out next week on a proper date. She scrunched her shoulders and gave a squeal, bringing her fists together.'

Rose walked her over to the till.

'Hang on.' Em scrolled through her phone as she walked. 'I have got a pic. He doesn't know I took it. Yes, here. He's on the rowing machine, looking all manly and athletic. I can't wait to show him off to my followers!'

Rose studied Olly for a moment. Her husband had his I'm-going-to-do-this-until-I've-got-to-a-hundred face on. She tried to see him through Em's eyes and had to acknowledge he did look athletic these days. She had never thought of him as 'fit' though. In her head, he was just Olly, still the skinny, asthmatic boy she'd known at school. When had he turned into this man that other women desired?

Rose didn't trust herself to speak.

'*You* should try extensions. Let your hair down and make more of it.' Em studied Rose, head tilted to one side. 'Don't you think so?' Em directed this question at Abby on reception. Abby presented the card reader without responding.

The conversation was familiar territory. Em never failed to make a suggestion about how Rose could improve her appearance. Rose always nodded, or said, 'I'll think about it,' before rapidly dismissing the idea. She always kept her shoulder-length brown hair up in a clip at work. Partly because it was easier and cooler in the summer, and partly because, generally, it avoided comments and suggestions about her appearance. Not with Em though. Em was on a mission to make Rose look more like her – complete with filled lips, sculpted brows and immaculate make-up. She had told Rose too many times that it took at least two hours of work to look this good, but that she wouldn't be seen dead not looking her best. There was no way Rose was going to give up that two hours in bed. She was happy with the way she looked – a quick smattering of mascara, lip gloss and that was it.

Realising there was no response forthcoming, Em turned and left, leaving the door swinging open behind her.

'Who does she think she is?' Abby's eyebrows lowered into a frown. 'I wasn't going to give her the pleasure of answering that question.'

Rose sighed. 'Thanks Abby, but at the end of the day she's still a client.'

Abby was on work placement but was old beyond her years. Rose admired her confidence and wished she'd been like that at nineteen. Or even now, when it came to it.

She loved her job at Cutting It Fine but the one thing that did rile her was the way clients felt entitled to comment on her appearance. 'You look as if you've put a bit of weight on, Rose. Glad to see you're looking after yourself.' Added as an afterthought in case the observation could be taken the wrong way.

The worst culprit in this department was Em, which was why she was already Rose's least favourite client, but now Em had taken things to a whole new level.

Rose, her stomach churning, saw the next client was already waiting. She wouldn't think about any of this this now. Maybe if she put it out of her head it would go away – as if somehow she could unknow what Em had revealed. Turning to Diana, she said, forcing a smile, 'So what are we doing today?'

Rose half-listened, nodding here and there as Diana chatted about her latest cruise. 'You'd love it Rose. Honestly just being waited on hand and foot and watching the scenery glide by...it's bliss.'

Rose felt it would be her worst nightmare to be cooped up on a ship with hundreds or even thousands of other people, a large percentage of whom were half-cut most of the time.

Much as she tried not to think about it, her head was full of Olly. Em had only started talking about him today, so it couldn't have been going on for much more than a month. She thought back. Had there been any changes in her husband's behaviour? Other than his increasing obsession with the way he looked she couldn't think of anything. And this fitness thing had been going on for much longer than a month. It had been developing over the last few years. At first she'd encouraged it, thrilled that at last he was feeling better about himself, putting the bullying years at school behind him. She had supported him as, eventually, he had given up his job at the supermarket and trained as a fitness coach. Rose had loved seeing him blossom and grow in confidence. He always worked a few evenings a week at the gym, but that went with the territory of being a personal trainer and was nothing new. A niggling worry had developed over the last months, however, about his increasing obsession with his self-imposed fitness regime and his use of powder shakes. But that was just Olly. When he got into something, he gave it total commitment. And he was married to her – totally committed.

By the time she had finished Diana's hair, Rose was feeling less shaky and had convinced herself that Em was making it all up. Olly would never do something like that. She knew him too well. She would know if he was... She couldn't form the words, even in her mind.

She also felt better knowing that it was Wednesday, the Sugden weekly family meal night – jokingly known as 'family date night'. It was always on a Wednesday when Olly was working. Rose had fallen into the habit, not wanting to eat on her own at home, and in true Sugden tradition with anything that happened more than once or twice, it soon became routine. It was a win-win because Olly was allergic to cats and dogs. Her family had always had animals – currently two Jack Russell terriers were in residence – so they always met at Rose's or out somewhere if Olly was around.

Rose looked forward to it – not just because of her mum's cooking but she always felt safe with her family around her. Almost as if she was a child again. And tonight, more than ever, she needed to be cocooned in the warmth of her family to drive the threatening nightmare away.

As soon as she had finished Dora's weekly shampoo and blow dry, Rose was anxious to head home and get changed.

She waved to her next-door neighbour, Walter, standing by his lounge window as she went in through the gate. He came to the front door.

'Hello Rose. Good day? Time for a cuppa to put the world to rights?'

Walter always greeted her when she came home from work and sometimes Rose sat and had a drink with him, but tonight she couldn't face it.

'Sorry Walter, got to rush, I'm a bit behind.' She gave an apologetic smile.

'I know you young ones have busy lives. Oh it's Wednesday isn't it? You'll be going to your mum and dad's. Give them my best wishes.' Rose noticed a tremor in his hand as he held onto the door handle and there was an uncharacteristic fragility about him.

Rose had a thought. 'How about I bring back some of my mum's casserole? You can re-heat it for your dinner tomorrow?' Why hadn't she ever thought about this before? Maybe because he'd never seemed so frail and vulnerable before.

His face lit up. 'Oh my! That would be wonderful!'

Walter was well used to Mrs Sugden's cooking as she had been the school cook at the primary school for around twenty years when he had been the headmaster.

'If she doesn't mind,' he added.

'Of course she won't. You know Mum.'

She put the key in the door. 'Okay must dash, Walter. I'll bring the casserole around in the morning.'

Rose had never imagined herself living next door to her old headmaster – her ten-year-old self would have been horrified. But many years had passed since then and she had got used to it.

A quick shower and then Rose planned to be off out again. She had to keep moving so that the nightmare didn't catch up with her – she especially didn't want to be in the home she shared with Olly. But the sense of the place they had created together caught her off balance, like a tidal wave, forcing her to clutch at the banister and sit on the stairs as she caught her breath.

There was no escaping their relationship – the photos lining the walls in the hall and up the stairs detailing important events, like when they had got engaged when they were both eighteen (her parents had insisted they wait until they both had secure jobs) to their wedding three years ago when they were twenty-one. She lingered by a family photo from when the Sugden clan had gone on holiday to Crete when they left school. Olly had always been part of her family as he had none of his own, having been brought up in care. His parents had died when he was young and a series of fostering placements hadn't worked out. When the subject came up with friends or others that didn't know him well, he changed the subject saying said it was the present that mattered, not the past.

It had always been Rose and Olly since they were in Year 9 at school. Surely this all had to mean something? Their bond was easily strong enough to withstand the likes of Em. Rose nodded in agreement with her own thoughts.

She studied a primary school class photo. There was Mr Powell on the end of the row, (when she thought about school he was always Mr Powell) and next to him, Olly, his thin arms and legs like matchsticks. He looked as if the smallest gust of wind could blow him over in spite of the fierce scowl he was directing towards the camera. He'd never liked having his photo taken. Moving down the hall, she picked up another one of their wedding photos – even here when she knew he was happy – the smile was hardly there, his glance directed over the shoulder of the photographer.

It had been the happiest day of Rose's life and she had loved every minute as they had celebrated their love and commitment to each other. It had been like the best fairytale ever and had resonated with every romantic fibre of Rose's being.

She caressed Olly's face with her forefinger, realising how much more craggy and chiselled it had grown since then as his body had developed its muscular bulk. The advent of new inhalers when he started high school had made all the difference to his health but the bullying hadn't stopped. Rose had defended him with all her might along with Poppy, Olly's friend Euan and a few others. She felt fiercely protective of him, and that had never gone away. She felt it now.

If Em was telling the truth – and she very much doubted it – she would get Olly back and see her rival off. That was what true love looked like.

Chapter Two

Olly was already home by the time Rose placed the casserole dish on the stairs, threw her keys into the bowl and shook her wet coat, hanging it on the banister to dry.

'Everything okay?' he called from the lounge.

Rose realised, too late, as she carried the dish into the kitchen that she hadn't called out her usual greeting, 'I'm home.'

All through the evening with her family, she had managed to push all thoughts of Olly to the back of her mind, refusing to give them space to grow, convincing herself Em was making it all up. But now she couldn't avoid thinking about it any longer as, for the first time since Em's revelations, she was with him in their home.

She ran her hands over her hair, tucking stray strands behind her ears and went in to Olly, planting a kiss on his lips. 'Sorry, I was soaked and just wanted to get my wet coat off. Everything alright with you?'

'Yeah, just another day at the gym,' he stretched and yawned. 'I'm knackered now, though.'

No matter how much she had persuaded herself that it wasn't happening Rose couldn't unhear the things Em had said. Now she was face to face with her husband, it all came flooding back with a force that hit her in the very core of her being. She looked at him and knew that she just didn't feel the same. Something had shifted.

'Any new clients?' Rose hated herself for asking the question, a question that would never have occurred to her twenty-four hours ago.

'No, just Mandy and Gareth. Same old, same old.' He stretched again. The movement reminded Rose of a cat stretching in the sun or in front of the fire, and a flicker of anger crept through her body. How could he not have a care in the world?

Olly had been Mandy's running partner in a few marathons, and Rose and Mandy's wife, Tina, had always been there to cheer them on.

'It's the Weldon half-marathon next month, so we both need to be on top form if we're going to get in the rankings – well Mandy, anyway.' He grinned ruefully. Rose knew that Mandy had her sights set on becoming part of the GB team and was proud that Olly was her trainer.

Again, that flicker of anger – what on earth was he doing? Messing about with an airhead like Em? Was it really that easy to throw everything away? Rose reminded herself that she didn't know anything for sure yet. She would hang on to that thought.

Olly turned his head and looked at Rose. 'Everything alright, babe?

'Yes, why?' Rose turned away to straighten some books on the coffee table.

'I don't know. You just seem a bit...on edge. Did something happen at the famous Sugden date night?'

Rose was taken aback at how easily he could read her. But surely that was a sign of a close relationship. She felt the tension in her body soften. They knew each other so well. Olly tilted his head and raised his eyebrows in question. The expression in his eyes still had the power to make her insides quiver.

'Oh Mum and Dad have been having a dig at Finn for not getting a 'proper job'.

Olly sighed. 'It's not like them to come on all heavy. They've always been happy to let you all find your own way.'

Rose felt ashamed of the lie about her evening. Where had that come from? Why had she done that?

She knew without looking at him that Olly was thinking how lucky she was and how he would have given anything to have any family at all. Rose's parents had welcomed him into the Sugden clan – he was almost another son and brother, but Rose knew that nothing could replace that yearning for a family of his own. For people who looked like him and with whom he had a shared history. It was a conversation they'd had so often that it no longer needed to be spoken aloud.

She leaned into him and Olly put his arm around her. 'Mum's sent home a casserole for Walter. He looked so frail when I saw him earlier. I thought he could do with some home cooking.'

'Mmm. That's good.'

Rose snuggled her head into his neck. She inhaled his scent – familiar for so many years, now tinged with a hint of the gym. She hadn't noticed that before.

'Come on, I'll get you a glass of wine. Let's watch a bit of telly and unwind.'

As he headed for the kitchen, Rose didn't have the heart to refuse. She'd had several glasses and already had the beginnings of a headache. Also, Olly hadn't drunk any alcohol since New Year saying that he didn't want toxins in his body and that real athletes never touched the stuff. Rose doubted that was true if some of the shenanigans footballers got up to was anything to go by. And even though she had been vocal about not joining him, she had never got used to drinking on her own – even though he always joined her with a tonic water, it just wasn't the same.

As they settled on the settee, cuddled up, as usual, Rose covertly studied Olly as he watched the screen, the dimple in evidence when he smiled. She caressed it with her forefinger. If Em hadn't said those things, she would never have guessed that anything had changed. He looked just the same, throwing his head back as he laughed at something in a way that he had done since he was fifteen. Rose had never forgotten their first trip to the cinema – alone together, and their first kiss. The way he laughed when he was relaxed with her, had been one of the things that had made her fall in love with him, that and the way she could lose herself in his chestnut eyes.

But something had changed. Everything had changed.

She needed to find out for sure. Once she knew that it was all just a ruse by Em to give her followers a frisson of mystery, then she'd feel better and things could go back to normal. Maybe she and Olly could have a laugh about it. But she had to know for sure. Tomorrow she would talk to Poppy. She would know what to do.

Rose felt herself being gently shaken awake. 'Come on, babe. Time you were in bed.'

'Oh God! What did I miss?'

'Only a whole episode of Game of Thrones.'

'You liar.' She looked at her phone. 'It's only been a few minutes. She threw a cushion at him. For a moment everything had righted itself and they were just Rose and Olly again.

Olly steered her up the stairs and they went through their usual bed-time ritual, taking turns in the bathroom and checking their phones before turning out the lights. Rose loved feeling like part of an old married couple – it felt safe and the routine was reassuring. And it wasn't as if they didn't still have their moments. They weren't that old!

But once she was lying in bed listening to Olly's breathing, sleep eluded Rose and when she did doze, she was plagued by dreams of Em and Olly together in various scenarios that seemed all too real.

Chapter Three

As she was heading out the following morning, Rose remembered the casserole. Hurrying back indoors to fetch it, she was just leaving once more when Olly appeared on the stairs, yawning.

'Have a good day, babe.' He tapped his cheek with one finger leaning forwards. 'Surely you're not leaving me without a kiss.'

Rose moved to the stairs and gave him an awkward peck while trying not to tip the casserole dish.

'It's alright for you, not having to be in 'til eleven,' she teased.

Turning to look at Olly as she hovered on the front step, her heart softened at the love in those chestnut brown eyes. No, nothing had changed. She would know.

Impulsively, she put the casserole down and strode over to Olly and held him tight, turning up her face to give him a deep kiss.

'Wow! That was worth waiting for.' Olly smiled and gave her a gentle push. Shouldn't you get going? All your old ladies will be waiting for you, to say nothing of Walter.'

Rose gave him a playful shove and, picking up the casserole, headed up Walter's path with a lighter heart. Everything was just as it should be.

Rose was grateful that Walter had the door open just as she reached it. 'Morning, Walter. One casserole delivery, as promised.' He stepped aside to allow her to pass. 'Get in the dry, Rose. This rain is going to ruin my seedlings if it doesn't stop.'

Rose went to pass the dish to him but, noticing he was using one of his hands on the wall to steady himself, thought better of it. 'I'll just take this through to the kitchen, shall I? Tell you what, if you just open the oven door, I'll put it straight in.'

'Thank your mother very much. I'm certainly looking forward to my lunch today!' Walter smiled and Rose noticed his eyes were wet.

'Mum says, put the oven on 180 degrees for about an hour. That should heat it through.'

Walter did a mock salute. 'Understood.'

Rose looked at the clock. 'I need to get going. Have a good day.'

'Yes, yes, you go, Rose. I'll maybe see you later.' There was an unsettling quaver in his voice.

Dodging the growing puddles along the way and keeping well away from the kerb and splashes from passing vehicles, Rose was in sight of the salon within ten minutes. In the past she would have driven, especially when the weather was bad, but over the last few months she'd been making an effort to keep her New Year's Resolution to walk more. And since Chrissie had joined the team there was one less parking space. Now that she was used to it, Rose no longer thought of taking the car even when the weather was bad.

Queenie was already waiting under a purple umbrella as Rose approached. She unlocked the door and smiled at her client. 'Sorry I'm a bit late. You're right on time as usual, Queenie.'

'You know me, I hate being late, always have.' Rose hung Queenie's coat up and shook out the umbrella. She reached for a gown. As she slipped her arms in, Rose knew exactly what was coming next. 'My old dad used to say, "If you can't be on time. Don't bother turning up." And I've always followed his advice.'

'Quite right, too.' Rose seated her client in the chair and fluffed her hair as they looked at each other in the mirror. 'So what are we having today?' I'm thinking purple with green tints, and this side shaved.'

Queenie collapsed in a fit of giggles which led to a fit of coughing. 'Oh, you are a one, Rose Sugden.' She blew her nose on a tissue. 'You know very well that I'll have the same as usual. Trim and blow-dry.'

Rose smiled. 'One day, I'll just do it, without even asking.'

'Over my dead body!'

As Rose carefully washed Queenie's thinning hair, she thought about how much she loved her job, things like the same banter with Queenie every week and the familiarity of routine. She had always loved being around people and felt she had the perfect job. It wasn't without its niggles of course but Rose felt the salon was like a second home.

Shona bustled in a few minutes later, banging the door open with her behind and dropping an enormous umbrella on the floor.

'Oh God! When is this rain every going to stop! Pleease can we have some sun.' She made a praying gesture towards the sky.

She retrieved the umbrella and shook the drops off out of the open door before letting it close with a bang.

'Tell me the kettle is on, Rose,' she puffed as she struggled out of her coat.

'Yup. Only boiled a few minutes ago.'

'Right. I need coffee.' Shona grinned at Poppy as she hefted an enormous handbag over her shoulder. 'Morning, Queenie.'

Rose smiled and winked at Queenie in the mirror as they heard Shona crashing around in the kitchen, getting her drink.

'I know you're talking about me out there,' she called.

'In your dreams,' Rose returned cheerfully. 'Good day off, yesterday?'

'Shopping. Shoes.' Shona shouted through a mouthful of biscuit. 'What else can you do in this weather?'

Shona was the life force behind the salon – literally. She had opened Cutting It Fine after the early deaths of her parents in a car accident and had used her inheritance to create a business they would have been proud of. Her bubbly and sometimes mad personality had created a loyal customer base as well as making it a positive and fun place to work. Not that they didn't have difficult customers – but somehow Shona was able to take them in her stride and the others followed her lead.

It was Abby's day at college, so Rose left Queenie for a few minutes to answer the phone.

She returned to find Shona cooing over photos of Queenie's latest great-grandchild. 'I can't ever imagine getting to that stage with my two.' She got her equipment ready at the next station. 'I have to prise Aaron out of his bedroom to do anything remotely sociable.'

'I expect he's got lots of friends online though.' Queenie put her phone away. 'They all have friends on these games they play.'

'That's what I'm afraid of. I don't know what he's doing up there.' She sighed. 'And as for Lottie...all she's worried about is her socials.'

The door opened letting in another blast of cold air.

'Hi Bobby. Come and take a seat.'

Shona beckoned him over. 'You don't know anyone who wants to give a home to a couple of teenagers do you?'

Bobby shuddered. 'Not likely. I've done my time.'

Adele arrived and headed straight for the kitchen. 'I need coffee,' she muttered.

'Heavy night, last night?' Shona called.

Adele reappeared, mug in hand. 'You could say that. A whole gang of us ended up in Starz. It was great fun even if I am paying the price today though.' She checked the appointments and heaved a sigh. 'Thank goodness. No one until half nine. I'll be sitting quietly in the kitchen if anyone wants me.'

Shona and Rose exchanged smiles. Adele was a party girl but also one of the best stylists in town. She always knew about the latest styles and her clients were mostly under forty. Rose loved that about the salon – that so many ages and characters came through the door.

'So sorry I'm late, everyone!' Chrissie closed the door carefully behind her. 'Tom decided he was ill this morning until I discovered he had a maths test!'

Shona groaned. 'Yup. Been there! Still there!'

'In the end I had to take him to school, otherwise I'd not have known whether he'd actually gone. I had to see him walk through the door. He's hated having to move and leave all his friends behind. I just hope he'll settle soon.'

'What year is he in? I'll tell Aaron to look out for him.'

'Year 9,' Chrissie replied, opening the door for her client.

Shona gave a thumbs-up in response.

As the salon settled into its day, thoughts of Olly and Em elbowed their way into Rose's thoughts again and hovered in the back of her mind, refusing to be banished. By the time they were closing, Rose's earlier positive frame of mind had all but vanished as doubts returned. There was only one person she could share her fears with.

'So what do you think?' Rose circled her glass on Poppy's kitchen table, watching the wine sway with the movement.

'Well, you've got to admit, it's a possibility.'

Rose stilled the glass and gave Poppy a sharp look. 'You're joking!'

'Oh come on, Rose. Take off those rose-tinted spectacles for once. Olly is an attractive man, and all men are susceptible to flattery. I should know,' she muttered as an afterthought.

'But not Olly...'

'Why not Olly? He's not the skinny kid from school anymore.'

'But he's still Olly inside though...isn't he?' Rose tailed off.

'People change – he looks different now, so he must feel different, surely. I think he's much more confident than he used to be. You don't see him at work like I do. He's quite...' she paused, searching for the right word, '...assertive, in a way.'

Rose was confused. This was not what she had expected from her best friend.

'But *I* haven't changed.'

'No darling. You haven't changed.' Poppy drew Rose into a hug, before holding her at arm's length and holding her gaze. 'But maybe you might have to now.'

'I don't want to. I don't want anything to change. My life is perfect just as it is.' Rose felt her voice trembling as she was overwhelmed by a wave of fear and foreboding. It had not occurred to her that Poppy might think Em's revelations were actually true. But then, she couldn't expect Poppy to be unbiased – not after the way Vic had left her for Cas the previous year. That was different though – everyone knew he'd been playing around ever since they'd got married.

She took a large gulp of wine. 'I need to know...one way or the other. Em says he's taking her out next week. That can't be true. She must be making it up. I need to get it out of my head.' Rose shook her head as if she might be able to dislodge the thought, like shaking a stone out of a shoe.

She turned to Poppy. 'Do you know this Em? She comes to the gym at least two or three times a week, apparently.'

Poppy took a deep breath. 'Long blonde hair, lips like a goldfish, boob enhancements. acts as if she's an A-list celebrity?'

Rose couldn't help a snigger at Poppy's description of Em. 'Yup. That sounds like her.'

'Yeah I know her. Everyone at ProFit does. Hard to miss.'

'So?'

'So have you seen her around Olly?'

Rose broke the silence. 'Well, have you?'

'Not that I've noticed because I haven't been looking.' Poppy sounded evasive.

'Can you start noticing then?' The tension was tight in Rose's voice.

'What? You want me to spy on your husband? I'm not a private eye, you know. I charge by the hour.'

Rose wasn't in the mood for Poppy's joke, and she felt tears forming that her best friend wasn't taking her seriously. She stood, drained her glass and put it in the sink. She should have known it would be like this.

'Oh Rose, I'm so sorry. I'm such a clumsy idiot.' Poppy held her as the sobs escaped Rose at last. 'Come on, it'll be okay. I'm sorry. I know I'm a bitter and cynical old witch. Not every man is like Vic. And if Olly is messing about with that Em, he'll have me to answer to.'

She led Rose back to the chair. 'I'm back in the gym tomorrow and the next day but then I'm at Paws Rescue for three days next week. I'll report back to you if she comes in, I promise.'

Rose wiped her eyes with the backs of her hands. 'I just can't believe it. I feel like I'm in a nightmare.'

Poppy took her hands. 'I know, babe. Look, I'll find out and then we'll see what we're dealing with. And I've got your back, I promise.'

Chapter Four

R ose had arrived at the wine bar early and was already
half way through her glass of wine by the time Poppy
arrived, two empty crisp packets on the table in front of
her. Too late, she tried to push them away, hoping to give
the impression that they'd been left there by someone else.
Dishevelled and breathless, Poppy grabbed the glass Rose had
already ordered and took a generous swig before taking off
her coat and shaking out her long curly hair. She eyed the
empty crisp packets but said nothing.

'God, I needed that! Mikey wouldn't get into bed and
Bethan was crying her eyes out. I feel sorry for Mum but I'm
sure she'll cope. I need to go out more often so they get used
to it.'

Rose was uncharacteristically silent. Tonight she had no
emotional capacity to sympathise with Poppy's domestic issues. She only had one thing on her mind.

'Well?'

Poppy bowed her head and then looked up at Rose, taking
her hand.

'Oh God! What is it? Oh God!' The sense of foreboding
was overwhelming and Rose, deep down, knew the time of
pretending none of this was happening was over.

'Rose...'

She sat back and put her hands palms down on the table. 'Tell me.'

'He's spending a lot of time hanging around her. And if ever I saw a woman giving someone the come-on it's her. There's a lot of casual touching going on but I've not seen anything more. I'm so sorry, Rose, but I have to say, I don't think Em is making it up.'

Rose looked at her hands, focusing on the feel of the grain of the table – desperate to hang on to any shred of normality.

Poppy was watching her anxiously. 'I'm so sorry, babe, but I know you'd rather have the truth.'

'Would I? Really?' Rose swung round to face Poppy. 'Why couldn't you have just told me it was all made up? Why couldn't you have been *kinder*!'

Rose heard Poppy's gasp from far away as a whirlpool of emotions swept any flimsy sense of reality away. She put her head in her hands.

'But you said...' Poppy's voice broke. 'I would never...' She leaned towards Rose. 'Rose!'

Rose gradually became aware of Poppy's distress and was shocked to see tears in her eyes. In all the years they had known one another, she had only seen Poppy cry once – when her cat died in Year 6. Not even when her husband left. But, then, maybe she just hadn't cried in front of Rose.

Rose reached out. 'Oh Pops, I'm so sorry. I didn't mean it. I just...didn't want to hear it.'

When had she ever turned on anyone like that? What was happening to her?

'Come on, let's go.' Poppy picked up her coat and they headed out into the rain where they gave each other a fierce hug.

'I'm so sorry, Pops. I don't know why I said that.' Rose's voice was muffled in Poppy's Puffa jacket.

'I'm sorry too. So sorry, Rose. I wouldn't wish this on you – what happened to me – on anybody. I know how it can make you into someone you're not.'

'Pops, I never realised...understood what it was like...to have your heart broken.'

Poppy took her arm and they started walking. 'Okay, enough of the sorrys and gushy stuff. What are you going to do, Rose Sugden?'

After a pause, Rose squeezed Poppy's arm. 'I'm going to do a bit of investigation work and see for myself, is what I'm going to do.'

'Atta girl!' Poppy clapped her on the back. 'Channel your inner Gloria Gaynor'

They moved into the shelter of a bus stop. 'When do you think Em will be in the gym next?'

'Well, she was there today, so I'm guessing maybe Monday?'

Rose sighed. 'And you're not in until next Thursday.'

'She'll probably be in then. I think Thursday is one of her regular days.'

'I can't wait until then, Pops! I'll go mad. And anyway, according to Em, Olly's taking her on some kind of date next week. I need to know before then.

'Oh Rose... I wish I could do more.'

'No worries. I'll think of something. You've got enough on your plate.' Rose made herself sound stronger than she felt. Poppy didn't need her problems, she had enough of her own. 'Tomorrow's my day off and I'll go to Paws. I can't just sit at home so I'll go and make myself useful.'

'There are always jobs to do, and maybe it's a good place to be when your head's all over the place. It really got me through the worst of my troubles.'

Rose nodded. 'What is it about animals that's weirdly soothing when you're going through shitty times?'

Rose turned to face Poppy, the rain travelling in rivulets down her hood onto her shoulders. 'I'm going to find out where she lives or where she goes, somehow. I'll find a way.'

She saw Poppy's bus approaching. 'Here comes your lift.'

Poppy turned as the bus approached. 'Good for you!' She grinned. 'This is a different Rose than the one I'm used to.'

She spoke through clenched teeth. 'I'm going to fight. Fight to keep Olly with me, come what may, We belong together.'

'Really? After what he's done?'

'No one else will have him if I can't.' Rose gave Poppy a final hug. 'Get yourself home...and thanks, Pops.'

'Love you.' Poppy blew a kiss as the bus rolled away.

When she got home, Rose ordered a takeaway as Olly was out. She deserved a treat after the last few days.

Her hunger satisfied and comfy in her PJs, Rose picked up her phone.

Why hadn't she thought of it before? She could see what Em was up to right here, right now – on social media. Rose wasn't a great fan of social media, and mostly only went on the Sugden family group chat or apps where she bought and sold used items every so often.

She remembered Em mentioning Instagram and searched for her there. She tried Em – Totton, Emily – Totton with no success. Rose sighed in frustration. She thought about Em – what would she call herself? Something a bit different – like lots of stars and celebrities who made up names for themselves – like Cher, or Dua Lipa. It would have to be something different but obvious. Rose muttered the name to herself, 'Em...Em.' And then it came to her. It was obvious really. 'Em...M' she said aloud.

Typing in 'M' Totton, she struck gold. There she was, pouting at the camera with her large lips, blonde extensions, and fake boobs. Rose had a sudden intake of breath when she saw the fifteen thousand followers that M already had.

Ready for a night out with my new man. Followed by various emojis.

Rose looked at the date – last night. But Olly had been here last night...hadn't he? Rose frowned at the screen. Of course it could all be fake news to keep her followers interested – but would she spend all that time getting ready for a non-existent night out? There was only one answer. Yes, of course she would! Even though she knew she was grasping at any glimmer of hope, Rose wondered once again whether Em was making it all up. But she knew Poppy wouldn't have told her what she'd seen if it wasn't true.

Rose scrolled further down. Lots of going-out pictures, complete with make-up hints. Then she saw something that made her lean into the screen, eyes wide.

New hair cut today – love my hairdresser Emmanuel. Followed with lots of heart emojis.

Rose clenched her fingers in her hair and stared, re-reading the caption over and over again until the phone beeped with a message, making her jump.

Sorry Babe. Held up. There's a bit of flooding at the gym. Won't be long. Have already eaten. Smiley face and red heart.

Rose stared at the message for a second or two before returning to Em's post. She needed to keep herself occupied – time to explore some video platforms. She set up a Tik-Tok account and found 'M' in no time. The videos were all about make-up and hints for de-tox diets – Rose was impressed at how confident and professional Em sounded and looked. She came across a video encouraging the use of seaweed drinks and her breath catching in her throat, she recalled Olly buying these very drinks online a few weeks ago. She had teased him at the time and thought nothing further of it.

Eventually, having exhausted her online search, Rose took herself off to bed, even though it was only 9 o'clock. She couldn't face Olly tonight – especially if he'd been lying about the flood and had been with *her* all along.

When he came in some time after, she pretended to be asleep.

Rose could sense him hovering by the bed, knowing he would be torn between waking her up and letting her know he was home, or letting her sleep – maybe so he didn't have to explain again where he'd been.

In the end he let her sleep.

Chapter Five

Rose couldn't settle the following morning, even though the little Westie she was cuddling soothed her racing heart for a few minutes. As she put him down, he whined giving her needy looks, his head on one side. Smiling, in spite of her anxiety, Rose took him into the field for a bit of exercise, and while he meticulously sniffed the entire hedgerow she checked her phone to see what Em was up to. Even though she would have heard any notifications – the irrational part of her still needed to look. She jumped as the phone sprang into life in her hand.

A shot of Em, immaculately made up, gym bag in hand was followed by:

Off for a session with my 'trainer' #profit #jayiscute

Heart emojis followed.

After an hour or so, Rose had cleaned out several cages and shown a couple around the feline area, but she still needed to do something with all the nervous energy simmering inside her. How long would Em be at the gym? Poppy had said it was usually a few hours. Putting her head around Cath's door, she said, 'Do you mind if I get off now? My next-door neighbour's had a fall, so...'

What was she doing? She didn't need to lie. As a volunteer Rose could come and go as she pleased.

Cath, the centre manager, looked up, glasses perched on the end of her nose. 'Of course. You go. It was good of you to come in. Thank you.'

Rose headed for the car, ashamed of her lie and of the fact that she was using Paws as some kind of coping mechanism, although she knew that Cath understood it was the reason many of the helpers were there. It was win-win. No. It was the lie that was bothering Rose. It had tripped off her tongue so easily, without a thought. It was if her mouth had taken on a life of its own. Her first instinct had always been to tell the truth – as Poppy said, she'd always been a crap liar – until now.

She waited impatiently in the car – constantly checking the time. Tapping the steering wheel, she thought back to what she had been doing this time last week. She had visited her sister-in-law, Becca, and they had both taken the children to the zoo. How had everything changed within a few days? She hadn't even thought about her nephew and niece today. Was she changing into a different person? Maybe. But when all this was over, she could go back to being the old Rose again and she and Olly could get on with their lives as normal.

Her phone pinged.

Oh my! Loving the shorts! Just time for a quick swim to cool down. Laughing face emojis.

An image appeared of Olly, leaning nonchalantly against the reception counter. The smouldering gaze in his eyes stopped Rose's breath in her throat. Was this the same Olly she had kissed goodbye this morning? Had he ever looked at her with that intensity?

Rose started the car, even though the gym was only five minutes away. She had to be moving.

It was a long fifteen minutes before Em emerged, gym bag over her arm, keys in her hand. Rose noticed that her hair was still damp – her real hair always curled before it was straightened. She smiled. This meant that Em would be going home to do her hair. She would never go anywhere else looking like that.

Rose had no idea where Em lived. Did she live in a flat? Shared house? Did she even have her own house? Rose doubted it. Any spare money Em had from her job at the supermarket - she would be spending on her appearance and her influencer career. Rose had seen her several times at the check-out in the superstore in Nottingham, where she had looked out of place with her carefully manicured nails and flawless make-up. She'd looked stunning even in the supermarket uniform.

She followed Em's small Kia (she would much rather have been driving a MINI Cooper – Rose was sure of that) to the large estate on the edge of Weldon. Rose stayed well back and when Em parked outside a small block of flats. She stopped the car, engine idling, as Em gathered her things and let herself in. Rose drove nearer and parked across the road, taking a picture of Em's car with the number plate showing. Looking up, she caught a glimpse of her closing a window on the first floor before she disappeared. Would she have gone out and left a window open? Maybe it didn't matter on the first floor. Rose was pretty sure Em lived on her own...in a tatty old council flat. Rose couldn't help feeling a little smug that she had a much nicer house – and life – than Em. She and Olly only had a rented house but it was a house, and they both had skilled jobs. After all, Em only worked in a supermarket – and lived in a fictional cloud cuckoo land.

After staring at the first floor windows for some time, Rose was about to leave, when Em suddenly appeared on the pavement. She ducked down.

When she dared to lift her head, Rose took a sudden breath. Em was helping someone into the passenger seat of her car. Someone who was using a Zimmer frame. Rose couldn't see whether it was a man or a woman. She noted that Em had dried her hair and had changed into a different outfit – so this was definitely where she lived. Having settled her passenger, Em put the Zimmer frame on the back seat, manoeuvring it with some difficulty into the small 3-door car.

Could this be a neighbour?

Rose started the car as Em drove off towards the end of the road. As they idled at the junction waiting for the lights to turn, Rose sank down in the seat as much as she dared, wishing she had allowed another car to come between them before pulling off. But then she might have missed Em at the lights. What did it matter if Em did see her? She had every right to be travelling along this road. Even though she reasoned with herself, Rose still heaved a sigh of relief when the lights changed.

Allowing other traffic to come between them, she followed at a distance until Em indicated for the turning to the hospital. Rose followed behind, but as Em turned into the car park, she had no choice but to drive on.

Rose drove to the burger place just down the road, and, munching on a burger, speculated about this new development in her picture of who Em was. She had taken care, making sure her passenger was settled before closing the door. This was somebody Em cared about. Perhaps a family member? In Rose's mind, Em was a single entity with no surrounding circle other than her followers. Someone who only thought about herself and her own needs. Rose thought about it. Em had never spoken about anyone else – so she had assumed there wasn't anyone. But she'd obviously been wrong.

How could she find out? She could casually ask Em at her next appointment but that wasn't for several weeks and she needed to know before then.

She would have to follow her again. At least now she knew where her prey lived.

As she pulled onto the drive, Walter appeared in his doorway, holding the casserole dish. Rose had forgotten all about Walter over the last day or two. She got out of the car and smiled.

'Thank goodness that rain has stopped,' said Walter walking across his tiny lawn towards her. 'Did you hear about the flooding down at the gym where your Olly works?'

Yes, he rang and said last night. He was there late, mopping up.' She looked up at the sky. 'It's certainly good to see some sun, though.' Rose's spirits lifted. Olly had been telling the truth, after all. About last night, anyway. She stepped over to the fence. 'How was Mum's casserole?'

'I dined like a king!' Walter made a regal gesture with his hand. 'Thank your mother very much. I hope the dish is clean enough. I know she was always very particular at school.'

'I'm sure it is, and thank you.' Rose didn't have the heart to tell him that her mother simply put everything in the dishwasher these days.

Walter turned to go back indoors. 'I'll be out sunbathing tomorrow,' he called over his shoulder.

Chapter Six

'So? Did you follow her? Where does she live?' Poppy leaned forward, eyes shining.

'Yes, I did. I followed her home to a tatty flat on the Ellerton estate.'

'And?'

Rose relayed what she had seen.

'I'm going to stake out the flat. I might get some ideas about when she's going out from her socials, although who knows how much of that is true? I can't do too much otherwise she'll recognise my car and get suspicious. Even Em isn't that stupid! But there's something else – take a look at this. I did a bit of online research.' Rose slipped her phone across the table for Poppy to see.

Poppy looked up at Rose, eyebrows raised. 'Jaz? You made an online profile? Isn't that called stalking?'

Rose snatched the phone and scrolled down. She thrust it back at Poppy. 'Look what she says about her hairdresser, *Emanuelle*.' Rose made quote marks in the air.

'Oh my God! What a nerve!!' Poppy's cheeks flushed in anger. 'But she's talking about your work! Isn't there some kind of hairdresser's copyright or something?' Poppy took a large mouthful of wine.

'I know! But scroll down.'

Poppy obeyed and her eyes widened. 'What the...'

Rose smiled, enjoying Poppy's reaction.

If your hairdresser is that great, you would think he would have replaced those tatty extensions by now!

You...Jaz said that? Wow. Bitchy!' Poppy said narrowing her eyes. She turned to Rose. 'I'm beginning to see a whole new side to you, Rose Sugden. Who knew that you had it in you? This' – she pointed to the screen– 'Is more the kind of thing I'd have written.'

'I know. I can't quite believe it myself. But when I saw what she'd said, I just couldn't help myself. I was so angry.'

'So did writing that make you feel any better?'

Rose thought as she sipped her drink. 'Yes, at first, it felt so good. But now I feel a bit bad about it.'

Poppy stirred her Mojito. 'It's odd isn't it? She seems to have two completely separate lives – M's perfect life online, and her real life which is...let's just say, much less glamorous.'

'Hmm. It's a bit weird.' Rose gazed over at the bar where a couple of girls – obviously underage were flirting with the bar tender, trying to order drinks.

She turned back to Poppy. 'What did you do, when Vic... What did you do about Cas?'

Poppy rolled her eyes.

'Nothing. Once I realised I was the only one who didn't know what a shit he was –' she gave Rose a sharp look '– I couldn't get rid of him fast enough.'

Rose felt a flush on her face.' I'm sorry, Pops. I should have said something. I realise that now.'

'I know there's still a part of you that would rather not have known about Olly, but I had to tell you, even though it was hard to be the one to cause you pain. I wish *I'd* known sooner. That someone had told me.' Poppy brushed her hair back from her face. 'But that's behind us. It's different for you. You love Olly and for some mad reason you want him back.'

'I know he's still the Olly I've always known, deep down. I just need to get him away from her or make him see her for the shallow liar she is.' She sighed and stood. 'Time for a refill. Same again? You need to make the most of your second night out in a week!'

When Rose returned with fresh Mojitos, Poppy, after a hurried sip, waved her hand to and fro across her face as if she couldn't swallow quickly enough, before hissing, 'I've got an idea.'

'About what?'

'Em!' She swallowed again. 'So, you work in a hair salon.'

'Yees!' Rose gave an exaggerated sigh. She knew how Poppy like to spin things out when she had an exciting idea to impart.

'Well, think about it. You have access to Em's hair. Presumably she has a drink while she's there, so you have a mug or whatever that she's drunk out of...' Poppy looked at Rose, eyebrows raised. When Rose didn't respond, she sighed impatiently and said, 'Think about it, Rose. You have samples of her DNA.' She sat back, arms folded and a smirk on her face.

At last understanding began to dawn in Rose's mind and she felt a shiver of excitement. 'So I could...what? Frame her for a crime or something?'

'Exactly!' Poppy slapped the table with her hand.

'Oh God!' Rose stared at the bar as she relished her new-found power over Em for a few moments before reality kicked in. 'No, I couldn't do that, Pops. It's not me. It's not who I am.'

'Then who are you, Rose? Jaz wouldn't hesitate, I'm sure of that. Are you going to let that bitch walk all over you and steal your husband? You're really going to just let that happen?'

'But it wouldn't be right.'

Poppy slapped her forehead with the flat of her hand in frustration.

Rose made a placatory sound and paused, thinking. Maybe just pretending wouldn't do any harm. 'Okay...okay. Let's just say, supposing...only supposing. What would we do?' She felt pleasantly excited at the thought of planning Em's downfall as the effects of two cocktails frayed the edges of reality.

Poppy answered immediately. 'How about you pretend you've had a break-in at the salon?'

'That wouldn't work. The police would expect to find her DNA there.'

'Hmm. Well what about an attempted burglary at your place. They wouldn't be expecting to find any evidence of Em there.'

'I guess she would have motive if I told the police about the affair.' The idea was taking hold in Rose's mind and even as it took shape, she knew it would be hard to erase it.

'But I don't think police do much about burglaries and I could hardly say, 'What about testing this mug for my husband's girlfriend's DNA? She would hardly stop for a coffee, would she?'

Rose thought as she swirled the drink around in her mouth. 'What about... what about the gym?'

Poppy leaned forward. 'Now that's an idea.'

Rose chimed in, 'What about if there was a spate of thefts from lockers. You've got a master key, yes?'

Poppy nodded, eyes shining. 'So I could...take a few things, like watches, jewellery, that sort of thing...'

'And plant a strand of Em's hair.'

'That could work.'

They stared at each other, thrilled with the audacity of the plan. 'Just supposing, of course,' Poppy said. 'My round.'

'Just supposing, of course.' Rose dissolved into a fit of giggles as Poppy returned. Now, on their third cocktail, she was enjoying herself, all inhibitions about the morality of their plans disappearing as she drank.

'Hi Babe.' Olly was watching the football when she got in. It occurred to Rose that Olly had always hated sport. She tried to order her fuzzy thoughts to remember when he had started getting interested in football, to no avail.

She made her way unsteadily over to the settee and plumped down beside him.

'Wow. Someone's had a bit to drink,' he teased gently. 'You'll be regretting that in the morning.'

Without responding, she snuggled up to him, enjoying the closeness. Everything would be okay, nothing could break their bond. Maybe Olly had changed in some ways but that was okay, wasn't it? When her head was less fuzzy tomorrow she'd be able to think more clearly.

'So what have you and Poppy been nattering about all this time?'

The question took Rose by surprise and she tried to rouse herself from the doze she'd fallen into.

'Oh, nothing much, really. Just this and that...you know.' Rose sounded unconvincing even to herself.

'Just...it's not like you to get...like this.'

A spark of anger flared in the midst of Rose's muddled thoughts. 'What's that supposed to mean?'

'Nothing. Okay, nothing.'

She felt the weight of his body shift away from her. Rose sat up. 'No, come on. Since when have I had to answer to you about what I do or how much I drink?'

Something in Rose forced the angry words out. How dare he question her after what he was doing? She knew she was over-reacting but somehow couldn't stop herself, her fear and hurt spilling over.

Olly didn't respond for several minutes. 'I'm not having this conversation when you're like this,' he muttered eventually.

'Oh, so it's my problem now? I can't believe you've got the nerve to...' Rose managed to stop herself from saying what she really wanted to say. It was too soon.

'I'm going to bed.' She stood and gave him a cold peck on the cheek.

In the kitchen she drank a glass of water, willing herself to sober up and sort her head out.

Once she was in bed, dozing on and off, she was aware it was a long time before Olly slipped in beside her. Once more, she pretended to be asleep.

Chapter Seven

'Twice in one weekend, we are honoured,' Cath looked up from a pile of paperwork.

'Where do you want me?' Rose ignored the comment.

'Litter tray duties?' Cath wrinkled her nose. 'Sorry but Pammy isn't here today.'

'No worries. I can do that.' Rose turned to go.

'Everything okay, Rose?'

'Yeah. All good.'

'It's just that, in my experience, when volunteers turn up for several days in a row it's nearly always because they don't want to be at home.'

That hit the mark. Olly had suggested a day out at one of their favourite spots and a pub lunch by the river as Rose fought her hangover with a strong, black coffee. She knew she should have said yes if they were to patch up their quarrel. It was an olive branch. But she found she couldn't face the thought of spending a day with him and had made an excuse saying she was needed at Paws. The look on his face would be etched in her memory for a long time. Although she desperately wanted to regain what they'd both had, somehow she couldn't make herself take the necessary steps.

Rose turned back to Cath. 'Olly and I had a bit of a row last night, that's all. I think we both need a bit of space today.'

Cath seemed happy with the half-truth and turned back to her work. 'Have fun,' she called as Rose left the room.

Emptying litter trays was one of the least favourite chores but Rose didn't mind this morning as she worked through the cages. It meant that she could spend time with each resident enjoying their foibles and varying characters without having to interact with any humans until her head stopped pounding.

When she got to Harold, a grizzled old warrior and veteran of many back-yard turf wars, he was sitting, inscrutable as ever, not moving towards her as she entered his space, simply watching her through narrowed eyes.

'I know you're a big softy, Harold. That haughty act doesn't wash with me.' Rose chuckled as she replenished the litter tray. As she worked, he lowered himself into a crouching position and began to purr.

Harold was a long-time resident of the sanctuary. No one wanted an old cat – especially one as battered as Harold, and those who had shown an interest hadn't been suitable, having small children or other pets. Harold was ready for a quiet life of sleeping and eating with the occasional foray outside.

'I think you're a bit lonely, old timer, although you'd never admit it of course.'

Harold continued to purr as she spoke to him. She thought of Walter and smiled as Harold reminded her of him – they were both proud in their own ways.

'I think I might know somebody who would be a perfect match for you, Harold.'

He continued to stare at her through half-closed eyes and a small sound came from his mouth.

Why hadn't she thought of it before? Harold would be a perfect companion for Walter. They could easily fit a cat flap and Harold would be pretty low maintenance. The only problem was broaching the subject with Walter. He hated cats digging in his garden and had been known to throw water over them. She would have to put some thought into this.

Buoyed by the idea, by the end of the morning, Rose was feeling much better, the bad taste of last night's row with Olly fading. She would go home and apologise to him, say she'd been too drunk to know what she was saying.

The only problem was that when she got home, Olly wasn't there. He'd left a scribbled note:

Gone to the gym. Back later.

The curt tone was unmistakeable and there was no kiss.

Rose's immediate reaction was to check Em's socials. There was no mention of the gym – today's post was all about making hand cream using shea butter, lavender and cedarwood oil.

No gym photos. She breathed a sigh of relief.

No matter, Rose would go to the shops and cook them both a Sunday roast to have when he got back.

On her way out, she met Walter standing by his gate. Now was the time to grasp the nettle.

'Hi Walter.'

'Good morning, Rose. What a lovely day.'

'Can I ask you something?'

'Oh course. Fire away.' Walter shot her a quizzical glance.

'Have you ever thought of having a pet, say a cat, Walter?'

His brows drew together in an ominous frown that took Rose straight back to primary school. 'Why would I do that? Dratted things. Always digging and making a disgusting mess.'

Rose ploughed on. 'It's just that there's one at the animal rescue place I volunteer at. No one seems to want him because he's quite old...and a bit grouchy.'

'Like me, you mean?'

'Oh no. I didn't mean...'

Walter laughed, his good humour recovered. 'It's alright Rose. I know you're trying to do a bit of matchmaking with that romantic heart of yours. You always did want to make everyone happy.' He swayed a little and held on to the gate to balance himself. 'But I'm happy as I am. Looking after an animal would be too much responsibility. I've got enough job looking after myself.'

'Well maybe think about it. Harold won't be going anywhere.'

'Harold?'

'That's the name of the cat.'

'Harold,' Walter murmured to himself as Rose waved and got into the car.

Rose made her way to the supermarket where she knew Em worked. And as she made her way around the aisles she kept a covert eye on the tills. There was no sign of her until she was in the queue to pay and Em appeared as the woman went on her break. Rose hesitated and almost went to join another queue but, something drew her like a magnet to Em. Initial relief that she wasn't with Olly turned to something else when Rose's turn came.

Em's eyes widened when she saw her. 'Hi Rose.'

'Hi.' Rose busied herself packing items in her bag.

'Looks like you're cooking a roast. Your husband is a lucky guy.' Rose's hands stilled and her head jerked up to look at Em but Em continued to look at her with wide, innocent eyes.

She didn't know who Olly was. Rose was sure.

'Yes, he is.' Rose wanted to say something else but couldn't form the words and continued packing in silence.

As she was turning to leave, Em said, 'Oh by the way, I've ordered some new extensions, they should be here this week. I'll ring the salon to see when you can fit me in.'

'Great.' Rose forced a smile. 'See you soon, then.'

Once she was driving home, she thought of many things she could have said – but it was too late.

Comforting herself with the knowledge that Em wasn't with Olly, Rose hummed as she prepared the veg and seasoned the meat. Her mother had been a good teacher and Rose could cook a good roast, complete with crispy roast potatoes. Her mouth watered at the thought as she worked.

Monday was often a slow day at the salon and they used the time to clean and replenish the products.

'Good weekend?' Chrissie asked as they dusted the shelves.

'Yeah, not bad. You?' Rose kept her tone casual. She didn't want to talk about how Olly hadn't come back until ten in spite of her messages about the meal. How the plated roast she'd left for him was still in the fridge, untouched, this morning. How she'd spent much of the weekend, talking, thinking about, and following the woman her husband might be having an affair with. How she was scared that her old life was slipping away and she was terrified of what the future might look like.

'...so anyway, in the end, we compromised and decided on the patterned ones.'

Rose had only tuned in to the final part of Chrissie's reply. 'Great. I always hate anything to do with curtains, they're such a pain to hang.'

'Rose!' Chrissie waved her hand in front of Rose's face. 'I'm talking about cushions! You obviously haven't listened to a word I've said.'

Rose put the duster down. 'Oh God! Sorry Chrissie. I was miles away.'

Great. Now I'll have to tell the whole story again!'

'No, please don't, Chrissie.' Shona blocked her ears. 'It was complicated enough the first time.'

'Okay, I'll spare you. Suffice it to say, I'll tolerate them for a few weeks and then there will be changes.'

'Everything okay, Rose?' Shona came over.

Rose nodded. 'Me and Olly had a row.' She could feel tears burning at the back of her eyes.

'Oh babe. You and Olly are solid. You'll patch things up,' Adele comforted her.

'Goes with the territory, I'm afraid,' added Shona, shaking her head. 'You haven't been married long enough to find that out yet.'

'We've been together for ten years and we've never rowed like this.' Rose could hear her voice cracking.

Shona led her to a chair. 'Honey, for a good chunk of those ten years, you were both children. Now you have to learn to navigate an adult relationship.'

Rose hadn't thought of it like that. 'I guess.'

'Time for cakes and coffee!' declared Adele. 'Get the kettle on while I nip over the road and get us some donuts. We need sugar and caffeine.'

Shona took Rose's hand. 'How many clients have you got today?'

'Only Wendy and...' Rose scanned the appointments, 'A new customer, Carol.'

'Well I think you should get yourself home after that and sort things out with Olly. Yes?'

Rose nodded, the half-truth that she'd told about their row weighing heavily on her mind.

Wendy was an easy client who mostly sat in silence as Rose trimmed her iron grey hair into a severe bob.

'It's two years ago today.'

Rose had been thinking about how she would make things right with Olly and took a few second to register that Wendy had spoken.

'Sorry, Wendy. I was miles away. What did you say?'

'I said...' her tone was curt. 'It is two years ago today.'

'What is, Wendy?'

'Since Agnes died.' Rose felt her cheeks redden. She should have remembered.

'I'm so sorry, Wendy. That must be so hard for you.'

Wendy grabbed a tissue from her sleeve and dabbed her eyes. 'Silly getting emotional, I know.' She sniffed. 'I can see Agnes shaking her head and saying, "For God's sake, Wendy. Pull yourself together!"' She gave a wan smile. 'I'm getting sentimental in my old age, but I do miss her – every day.'

Rose squeezed Wendy's shoulder. 'It's understandable, you had been together for so long.'

'Forty years. Of course, things were so much different when we met, and we couldn't live together openly for many years. I'm glad it's different for your generation.'

Rose thought about her and Olly. They'd been together ten years already. The years ahead stretched away into a time Rose couldn't even contemplate, but she could never imagine a life without him. Her heart went out to Wendy.

'I'm sure you have lots of tales to tell about what it was like when you first met Agnes.'

Wendy sighed. 'We did get into quite a few scrapes when we were younger. One or other of us was always being hauled into Matron's office.'

'You must tell me next time. I'd love to hear.' Rose took Wendy's cape, shaking the hairs from it.

'Thank you, Rose.' They walked to the reception. 'Thank you for listening.'

Rose watched, cape in hand, as Wendy left the salon and turned left, marching determinedly along the pavement, back straight. It was the most Wendy had ever spoken in the four or five years she had cut her hair. Apart from when Agnes had died, when she had informed Rose in an unemotional, manner, almost as if she'd been talking about the weather.

Her new client, Carol, was the complete opposite, and by the time Rose had discussed what she wanted and had cut her hair, she knew just about all of Carol's life history.

Once home, Rose went straight to Em's socials.

Hi gang! Big news! Jay's just invited me out on our first date – tomorrow night. Eeek! So all you doubters out there can stop tapping away. Soo much to do!!

Rose, her hand over her mouth read through the long list of things Em needed to get done before then, including having her hair cut. She hurriedly opened the salon appointment app, and sure enough, Em was booked in for 11 a.m. the following morning. One of the others must have taken the booking and forgotten to tell her. She was relieved to see that it was only for a shampoo and trim. Rose didn't think she could face extensions in her present frame of mind.

Olly came home and Rose suggested a takeaway. Once they'd ordered, Rose put her arms around Olly's neck saying, 'I'm so sorry about last night, babe. I was a bit out of it, and I'm sorry about the way I was.'

Olly removed her arms and stepped away. 'I don't think a takeaway is going to cut it, Rose.' He went into the lounge and turned on the TV. 'What's going on? You've never gone out and got drunk before, not without me. Surely those days are long gone. So what's going on?'

For a moment, Rose was close to telling him, but something stopped her. She didn't want to say the words, not until she was sure. It wasn't a conversation they had ever had before, and it would be pretty earth-shattering to have it now if it turned out to be something and nothing. Instead, she just shook her head and sighed in annoyance.

'So what? You're saying that just because you've given up alcohol, I can't go out and have a good time?'

Olly shook his head, focusing on the TV.

The evening passed, neither mentioning the ill-fated roast of the day before. They watched the screen side by side in near silence, the tension crackling menacingly around the room until Rose could stand it no longer.

'I'm feeling a bit rough. So I think I'll go on up. I'll sleep in the spare room – I don't want to keep you awake in the night if I'm ill.'

Olly made a grunting sound, acknowledging he'd heard, but didn't look up.

Chapter Eight

Rose was watching Em's going-out preparations online, listening through her ear buds. So far this had taken an hour and a half and she had only just got around to doing her hair. Rose watched with keen interest as she curled the long extensions with hot curling tongs. Knowing they were almost at the end of their shelf life, she wondered if they would maintain their body and shape. She had done her best, earlier to trim them and tidy them up, even though she'd had to work with gritted teeth. Em had talked of nothing but the date but the crucial piece of information as far as Rose was concerned was missing. Em didn't know where they were going – apparently Jay was going to surprise her.

Through her buds she heard Em's steady stream of excited chatter as she worked, much of which Rose had already heard earlier, at the salon. A covert glance at Olly slouched in front of the TV made her wonder if, after all, this was a figment of Em's imagination. But then she spotted a tale-tale movement – his leg jiggling ever so slightly – and knew that his mind wasn't on the football.

Turning back to Em, Rose saw she was now moving on to make-up. 'Less is more,' she informed her followers. 'If you really know what you're doing you can create a stunning effect without looking as if you've got much on.'

She applied foundation to her face, speaking from the side of her mouth as she smoothed it on. 'A friend of mine who works in make-up at Strictly gave me some tips.'

Picking up a brush and some powder, she looked straight into the camera. 'You wouldn't believe the stuff she's told me about what goes on behind the scenes.'

Rose reminded herself once again, that Em had a very loose relationship with the truth.

Just as they were getting into the technicalities of mascara, Olly stood and stretched with studied nonchalance.

Here it came.

Rose took the buds out, letting them dangle on her chest. 'Did I tell you that I'm meeting some of the gym lads for a drink?' Her heart stopped. It was really happening. And was that the best he could come up with?

Rose replaced the buds. 'No, but...whatever.' Then she had a thought and turned to face him. 'I'll give you a lift and pick you up, after. You won't be able to drive.'

She waited. How would he deal with that one?

'I've ordered a taxi – so don't worry.' He really did have it all planned out.

Olly came over and went to peer over her shoulder. Rose managed to snap the laptop shut just in time. Huffing, she took the buds out again. 'What?'

'Just wondering what's got you so engrossed. Not like you to be secretive, Rosie.'

'I thought you were getting ready to go out.' She couldn't keep the edge out of her voice.

'Not having some secret online romance are you?'

When Rose didn't reply, he laughed, and she could hear the nerves.

When he reappeared, twenty minutes later, Em had only just got onto lip gloss. Looking up, Rose saw he was wearing a shirt she hadn't seen before.

'That's new.' Olly hardly ever bought new clothes, happy to keep wearing the same old familiar T-shirts and jeans until Rose frog-marched him to the shops or just bought him items online. She couldn't remember him ever buying himself an item of clothing without her knowledge. It was a small thing, but it spoke volumes.

'Let me see.' Going over, she gasped at the designer label.

She saw the flush rise up Olly's face.

She caught his gaze but said nothing. What was there to say?

After an awkward silence, Olly shuffled his feet. 'Right. I'll be off then. Don't wait up.'

And with that he was gone.

Rose grabbed the car keys and while Olly waited outside, she glanced at her phone. Em was putting finishing touches to the work of art that was herself. Rose had to admit she looked stunning.

She saw a taxi come to a stop outside the house. As it drove away, she hurried to the front door and into the car. She was just in time to see it turn left at the end of the road.

She hadn't expected them to eat at one of the places in town but when it became apparent they were heading into Nottingham she looked anxiously at the fuel gauge. Her imagination had them meeting at a Brewer's Fayre somewhere anonymous. But she should have realised that Em wouldn't have settled for that. She had her followers to think of.

Her eyed widened as the taxi eventually deposited Olly outside *Shan*, a new expensive Japanese restaurant that had been all over the news. The chef/patron had been last year's Masterchef winner and everyone had been talking about the fact that he'd chosen to open his restaurant here rather than in London or Cornwall.

'Nottingham deserves to have culinary excellence as much as anywhere else,' he had cooed on Breakfast TV.

'More like big fish in a little pond,' Shona had huffed. 'Not so much competition.'

She'd stopped further along the road, but once Olly had disappeared inside, she pulled closer and parked, killing the lights.

She was sorely tempted to get out and look through the window to see if Em was there, but common sense told her to wait. Em would want to make an entrance – she would be late.

She picked at a piece of skin on the side of her thumbnail as she waited.

Eventually another taxi arrived. And there was Em, looking like a film star. All long legs, boobs and blonde extensions. Rose noted, mouth open, that the taxi driver even got out and opened the door for her. Em didn't miss the opportunity to film herself outside the restaurant, thanking the driver as if he were her chauffer.

When it was safe, Rose got out of the car, walked along the pavement and idly glanced at the menu in its glass case. She strained to see inside. The interior was surprisingly well-lit with the kitchen in open view to the diners. Then she saw them. They were in another dining space, behind the kitchen at the rear of the restaurant.

Rose clenched her hands in her pockets as she saw them clink glasses together, laughing and gazing into each other's eyes – for all the world like a golden celebrity couple. She felt sick and leant against the wall with her eyes closed for a few seconds.

Once the wave of nausea had passed, she turned back to the window and gazed at Olly. This was an Olly she didn't know. He appeared confident and quite at ease with his stunning companion.

'Can I help you, madam?'

The waiter stood in the open doorway.

'Uh no. Sorry, I was just looking.'

Her humiliation complete, Rose returned to the car. She was the ragged, shabby outcast looking in on a glamorous world that could never be hers. If she and Olly had been there, they would have been giggling at the prices and the names of the dishes, and side-eyeing all the pretentious customers. He had moved into a different world and left her behind.

Rose returned to her phone, tears burning her eyes. There were already images of the food as the phone pinged with a photo of Em planting a kiss on Olly's cheek, pointing to the dimple with a sly wink for the camera. Rose noticed that the rest of Olly's face was out of the shot.

Cute or what?

Rose dropped the phone into the footwell, swallowing the bile rising in her throat. She gripped the steering wheel and focused on the traffic lights at the end of the road watching as they changed colours. She counted the seconds between each change until she had the strength to think. This could not be happening. Surely she would wake up soon. This wasn't her Olly. Where had he learnt to be like this? How come she hadn't noticed the change in him?

When she got home, Rose studied herself in the hall mirror taking in the hastily clipped-up hair and slouchy shapeless clothes. Her unmade-up skin blotchy and pale. Her eyes swollen and red. Her head was full of tears and this time they overflowed. She could never compete with Em.

She looked back at their wedding photos and studied her twenty one-year-old self. A thinner, radiant Rose looked back at her. Her hair was piled up in ringlets crowned with a tiara, and the professionally applied make-up transformed her skin. Just three years ago, she could have given Em a run for her money. She returned to the mirror – it seemed that she had aged twenty years.

Pulling her hair away from her face, she studied the faintest of lines already forming on her forehead and at the corners of her eyes, her face puffy from crying. It seemed to Rose that she could go one of two ways: either sink into a self-pitying heap and take to her bed – she would never give Em that pleasure – or do something positive about the way she looked and fight to get Olly back. She'd always assumed that the person she was, along with their shared memories, was what Olly loved about her, not thinking about the way she looked. She'd been happy with her appearance...until now.

Chapter Nine

A reel of Olly and Em together played over and over on a loop in Rose's head as she'd had lain awake in their bed, back in the empty house. Em was casting a spell over Olly – luring him in. The nightmare was becoming manageable if she thought of it like that. That Olly was under a spell.

She had heard him come in, and sneaking a look at her phone, had seen it was 11.30. She felt a small relief that at least he had come home and not stayed the night with Em as she'd feared might happen in her darker moments. But she couldn't stop herself shrinking to the far side of the bed before he got in, once more pretending to be asleep.

Rose went through endless scenarios during a sleepless night, each more outlandish than the last. Her need to take revenge on Em filled her mind, leaving no room for any other thought.

She considered luring her somewhere by sending a message from Olly's phone – say a hotel room and then trashing it after she'd left. But she would text Olly to ask where he was and Rose couldn't risk using his phone anyway. Her thoughts always returned to the idea of staging a burglary at her home – smashing things – Rose could suggest to the police that Em would have had motive. They would have to question her, surely? But what about Olly? She would have to reveal to him that she knew about Em. But would that be so bad? Surely he would be appalled that she could do something so violent – invading the safety of their home. He would break it off...

Another thing, maybe she couldn't compete with Em in looks, but she had to do something – make an effort with her appearance. The reflection in the mirror had shocked her earlier. Why would Olly come back to her when someone as stunning as Em was throwing herself at him? She'd get Adele or Shona to sort her hair and put in some highlights. Rose of all people knew the impact of a new haircut. She'd get her nails done, maybe work harder at losing a bit of weight, and sort out a skin regime.

But most of all, she needed to know more about Olly and Em's movements before she could formulate a foolproof plan. Em was easy enough, especially now she knew where she lived. But she had to find a way to see what Olly was up to.

All these thoughts and possibilities raced around following each other in an endless night-time circle, going nowhere.

When Rose awoke the following morning, she was exhausted. Before leaving for work, she tried to hide the bags under her eyes with an old stick of concealer she found in the bottom of her make-up bag but ended up rubbing the lumpy mess off and doing her best with foundation.

Before last week, Rose had loved going to work and never found it a chore to get up and get going, but today she had to will herself to go out the door. The thought of having to face anyone, least of all her clients, was almost too much and she didn't know if she had the energy. But the alternative was to sit at home and obsess over Em's socials and Rose knew that going down that road would come to no good. She had to be proactive and find a way to get Em away from Olly...or was it to rescue Olly from Em? She shook her head in frustration. Either way she had to do something.

Somehow, she found herself at the salon where it was just another day.

'Busy day?' she asked as they got ready to open.

'Wall to wall,' replied Adele, sighing. 'But at least the time will fly by. Can't wait for tonight, we're having a girls' night out for Toni's birthday.'

'I finish at one,' said Shona. 'And it's Wednesday so I can escape for my afternoon off! Yay!'

'Could you do a trim for me? If you can, I'd owe you one. I could jiggle appointments around to be free then.'

Shona raised her eyebrows. 'Things still not sorted at home?'

Rose sighed. 'I want to make an effort...and I think a new hair cut will make me feel better.' Rose ran her fingers through her hair. 'It's about time,' she added ruefully.

Through the morning, Rose worked on autopilot, smiling mechanically in the appropriate places, her mind busy with possibilities. In the reality of daytime, she ruled out the more outlandish ideas she'd had during the night, and her thoughts coalesced around one purposeful next step, in addition to improving her appearance.

While she waited for Shona to finish with her last client, Rose messaged Finn.

Can you meet me here after work? I need to ask you about something.

Sounds weird. Everything okay?

Rose paused for a moment and then ignored the question.

About 5.30?

A thumbs-up emoji came in reply.

'So what would you like?'

Rose groaned. 'I don't know. Something better than this.' She held up a chunk of hair, letting it fall to her shoulders.

Shona studied her hair in the mirror. 'How about I tidy it up, cut it a bit shorter and add in a bit of layering?'

'I don't want anything that's going to be high maintenance.'

'That's what I was guessing. This way you'll still be able to clip it up at work, but it'll look good when it's down as well.' She ran her comb through Rose's hair. 'I'd just die for thick, chestnut hair like yours. It's such a gorgeous colour.'

Rose was taken aback. She'd never really thought anything about the colour of her hair, but now, looking at it with a stylist's eye, she could see that Shona had a point.

'When we've got a bit more time, maybe add a few highlights?'

'You read my thoughts.' Shona grinned. 'Right. Let's get this show on the road.'

Rose was still admiring her new haircut when Diana arrived. Shona had cut it in a way that accentuated the contours of her face, softening the wall of hair that generally hung like curtains on either side when she had it down. She could see how the colour brought out the hazel in her eyes.

'Wow, Rose. You look amazing!' Diana shrugged off her coat and gave it to Abby.

'Well it's all thanks to Shona, here.'

Shona breathed on her knuckles and rubbed them on her chest. 'I'm saying nothing. Never one to brag.'

She picked up her enormous bag. 'The shops are calling,' she sang as she let the door bang behind her.

'You need to show that haircut off on a cruise,' Diana said as she settled herself into the chair. 'Did I tell you, Jim and I are off to the Caribbean next week?'

It wasn't often that time dragged at work, but the afternoon seemed to stretch into infinity. Her 2 o'clock for colours and highlights had cancelled which left Rose with two unoccupied hours. Hours she would spend looking at her phone and driving herself mad.

She could be doing something useful.

'Adele, I'm popping out for a bit, but I'll be back for my 4 o'clock.'

'Okay, babe.' Adele turned off the hairdryer. 'Everything alright?'

'Yup. I've got time to pop out to the supermarket. Save doing it later.' She summoned up what she hoped was a convincing smile.

As soon as she started the car, Rose knew exactly where she was going, and ten minutes later was parked along the road from Em's flat. The first floor curtains were drawn. Rose pondered what that could mean. Either she was having an extra-long lie-in, or maybe she was ill. Serve her right. Or maybe she wasn't even in. Unlikely, as her car was there. Or maybe the room belonged to the mystery passenger from the other day.

A few other residents came and went, an older couple and a young woman with a couple of toddlers, one of whom was mid melt-down. Rose was admiring a beautiful chocolate lab out for a walk with its owner – a slim woman with matching chocolate-brown hair, when Em appeared.

As ever, she was immaculately turned-out. Phone in hand, she seemed to be making some kind of recording. Rose noticed the camera was angled away from the flats towards the park opposite.

Em got into the car and Rose got ready to follow her. As she moved off, glancing up, she noticed the curtains were still drawn in the first-floor window.

It turned out that Em was headed for the gym. Rose ground her teeth in frustration as she imagined her with Olly so soon after last night.

There was nothing to be done. It was still only 2.45. She had an hour and three-quarters to kill. Time to carry out the next item on her list.

Rose sat and luxuriated in the pampering. She'd only had her nails professionally done once before and that had been for her wedding and now she made a vow to get them done more often. She sat back and closed her eyes listening to the nail bar sounds around her, enjoying the fact that there was nothing to be done and nowhere to be for this space of time. The technician had suggested a deep coral colour which was mesmerising – Rose couldn't drag her eyes away from the transformation of her hands.

All the way back to Cutting It Fine, she splayed her fingers on the steering wheel admiring how the colour glowed in the sunlight.

Beryl noticed immediately.

'You've had your nails done, darling. Don't they look fabulous?' Beryl studied her own nails – a pearly pink. 'What made you decide to do that?'

Rose sighed inwardly at the personal question but outwardly gave a professional smile.

'Oh, you know. Maybe time to make a bit more effort. Who doesn't get their nails done these days?' She gave a hands in the air gesture and laughed.

'Girls, what do you think of Rose's nails?'

Abby and Adele crowded round as Rose held her hands out for inspection, 'Wonders will never cease,' Adele said. 'We'll make a glamour girl of you yet.'

Rose shuddered. 'I wouldn't go that far.'

Once all the others had gone, Rose idly flicked through the appointment diary, looking at the clock, her nerves frayed. The lift in her spirits from earlier had evaporated. Eventually at 5.45 Finn appeared.

She sighed in annoyance. 'Where've you been?'

Finn took a step back. 'Whoah! What's eating you?'

'Sorry, it's just. I'm just...'

Flicking his hair away from his face, Finn looked at Rose.

'Hey, sis, you look different' He looked at her, his head on one side.

'I've just had my hair cut a bit differently, that's all,' she snapped.

'What's up? Something's wrong, I can tell,' he said.

The concern on his face did something to Rose's insides and she fought to hold back the tears prickling in her eyes. She was not going to cry in front of her little brother. She took a deep breath.

'I'm going to tell you something, and I want you to promise not to tell Mum and Dad...or anybody.

'Oka-ay.' He took a step towards Rose. 'Hey what is it? You in some sort of trouble?'

'You promise?'

'Yes, I promise.'

'I think Olly is having an affair and I need to put a tracking thing on his phone.' The words tumbled out in a rush.

'*What? Olly?*' Finn drew his fingers through his long hair again. 'Oh, come on, Rose. Olly would never—'

'I need to know. Can you help me or not?' She didn't want to hear this from Finn. Poppy was right. Olly was a man – now an attractive man – and she had to be realistic.

'Well...I guess.' He paused and sat in one of the chairs and stared at Rose in the mirror. 'I don't feel good about doing this to Olly, though. What makes you think he's having an affair?'

'One of my clients told me.'

'*Told you?*'

'Yup. Although she doesn't know that Olly is my husband, She described his dimple, and...' Rose swallowed. 'She goes to the gym where Olly works. I've seen them out together.' As she said the words, they sounded ridiculous to Rose, but at the same time it made everything seem so much more real.

Finn let out a slow breath. 'Wow!'

'So what do you need me to do? It'll be hard for me to get his phone to you...' Rose thought. 'I know, why don't you come round? Remember he's been wanting to play that new game with you. Come round, and I'll distract him for a bit and you can download it then.'

'I suppose it's worth a try. Okay. It seems weird to be doing it though... to Olly.' He was silent for a few seconds. 'Let me know when.' Finn stood and gave Rose a hug. 'I'm going to feel weird being around him though, knowing all this.'

'I know. But do it for me. I have to know what's happening. I have to know more about what's going on before I do anything.'

'Do anything?'

'Finn, will you stop repeating everything I say!'

'Sorry, sis. Right I'll get off now – meeting the band at Micky's for a couple of hour's practise seeing as Mum and Dad are away. It seems odd not having Family Date Night.'

'I hope Dad's enjoying the cruise as much as Mum will be.' As she spoke it occurred to Rose that she could have invited her brothers around to hers before hastily dismissing the thought.

Finn stood. 'Let me know when you want me to come round and see Olly.' He turned to go but paused in the door-way, 'It'll be alright, you know. Hang on in there. I'm sure it'll turn out to be something and nothing.'

He was gone before Rose could reply. She watched him loping down the road in long strides and sighed. Had she made a mistake involving him in this? She hoped not. Finn and his band had their first gig coming up and she couldn't wait to cheer and whistle them on. She knew how much it meant to him in spite of his apparently casual attitude.

Chapter Ten

'**R**ose, Maya's here,' Abby called from the front desk.

Taking a quick sip of coffee, Rose hurried through.

'Hi Maya,'

'Hi yourself.' Maya smiled. 'Please make me presentable again. Since I've been in hospital my hair seems to have taken on a life of its own!' She pushed her fingers through her thick, wavy hair trying to shake out the thick growth. 'I feel like a yeti.'

'How're you doing? Did everything go well with the op?' Rose led Maya to a chair and drew her own fingers through the thick, blonde waves.

'Oh, you know. As well as any hysterectomy goes, I guess. I can't tell you what a relief it is to be able to drive and get out and about again!'

'Hopefully you'll soon feel well enough to be glad you had it done.'

Maya smiled. 'Let's hope so, but I don't think I'm quite there yet, honey.'

'Well in the meantime, let's tackle something we can make you feel better about. How about I thin your hair out a bit at the top and reshape? Are you happy with how you had it before?'

'Anything. Whatever you think, Rose. You have a desperate woman in your chair.'

Rose chuckled. 'Leave it to me.'

For most of the day, Rose was occupied with work. But every so often grim reality poked its head into her thoughts and it all came flooding back. She wondered how to organise Finn's visit. She knew that Olly wasn't working that night and so maybe it was best to grasp the nettle and get on with it. Maybe Finn could get hold of Olly's phone more easily if she wasn't there. In any case, she didn't want to have an evening alone with him at home. If they were playing a game, he'd have to get up and make a drink and get some snacks – that could be Finn's opportunity. She could stay at Poppy's until the coast was clear. The idea was clear in her mind when she messaged Olly at lunchtime:

Hi babe, Finn is wondering if tonight would be a good time to have a go at that new game.

The message came back almost immediately:

I dunno. I might be late tonight. Maybe some other time?

Rose pressed her lips into a thin line.

I think he's feeling a bit low. This was my suggestion really, he doesn't know I've asked you. He could use some brother-in-law quality time. It would mean a lot, please...

Rose took a shaky breath. This felt like new territory. She had never manipulated Olly like this before but something was propelling her forwards. Something unrelenting.

Five minutes went past and Rose had almost finished her lunch before her phone pinged.

Okay. Tell him I'll be home by half five.

Rose smiled and felt a tenuous sense of warmth. Whatever he was doing, at heart, Olly was still the kind person she'd always known.

I'll hang out at Poppy's. Give you two some time. Thanks babe xxx

Time to chat later? She fired off a quick message to Poppy.

Can you come by Paws? I'm there till 7 then we can get something to eat. The kids are at Vic's. You need to fill me in on what's been happening!

They hadn't had chance to catch up since Olly and Em's date, and Rose felt ready to talk about it now. She sent a quick message to Finn explaining why he would have to act a bit stressed and down.

I think I can do that without too much trouble. It's going to be a bit stressful anyway. I'll message when it's done and I'm leaving.

Rose only had time for a quick response.

She couldn't believe that the afternoon panned out just like any other afternoon considering she was doing something so momentous. Who planted tracking software on their partner's phone without their permission? Weird, controlling types. That's what she would have thought before...all this. But she was doing it to save their marriage – to save Olly from that blonde bimbo. Em would never be able to make Olly happy the way she did. No one knew him like she did. And she would do whatever it took to get him back.

Rose spent some time with the cats while she waited for Poppy to finish up at Paws. She lost herself in playing with a couple of kittens, watching them chase around after a cotton reel, enjoying the feel of their tiny furry bodies in her hands when she picked them up. They felt so fragile in spite of their sturdy beating hearts.

'I know. They're mad aren't they?' She grinned at Harold, sitting on his haunches, eyes half closed, his tail neatly wrapped around his toes, tolerating the shenanigans of the youngsters from his next-door cage.

He blinked at her, unmoving.

'I think I've found just the place for you, old-timer. I think you and my next-door neighbour, Walter, would be good for each other.'

Harold didn't move, but Rose detected a faint purr as he screwed up his eyes.

'You and Walter both need someone to chat to.'

'Ready?' Poppy put her head around the door. Her eyebrows raised. 'Nice haircut, Rose Sugden. Good for you.' She nodded approvingly.

Rose got up and brushed herself down. 'Bye you monsters. Bye, Harold.'

Harold blinked and turned his head away.

As they walked to their cars, Rose told Poppy about her plan to persuade Walter to adopt Harold. 'Now I've mentioned it to Harold, I feel like I'd be letting him down if it didn't come off – raising his hopes.

'Stop right there, Rose. He's a cat! Honestly, sometimes you are such a softy.'

Rose felt the sadness which came over her from time to time that she couldn't have pets in her own house. She would have adopted Harold in an instant. But, then, it had been a small sacrifice to be with Olly.

'Smatters?' Poppy suggested a wine bar on the High Street.

'Yep. See you there.'

Once they were settled with drinks, Poppy dived straight in. 'Right. So tell me everything.'

Rose told her what had happened. 'I feel so dowdy next to her, Pops. Honestly, she looked stunning. How can I compete with that?' she flung her hand in the air, conscious of the whiny tone in her voice.

'Hold on, what's this?' Poppy took her hand and examined the nails. 'Since when have you been having your nails done? And more to the point – without me? And your hair!'

'It was a spur-of-the moment thing. I had a cancellation yesterday and had them done.'

'They look great.'

'Thanks, Pops.' Rose took a chip from the bowl as their food arrived. 'I've let myself go. I need to make more effort if I'm going to get Olly back.'

'Maybe...' Poppy wrinkled her brow. But don't forget it's you he fell in love with, Rose Sugden. Don't underestimate the bond between you and the history you share. He has none of that with her. It's like...all cream and no sponge.'

Rose almost choked on her third chip. 'So what? Are you comparing me to sponge now?'

'You know what I mean. You can't survive on a diet of cream. It needs some kind of foundation to set it off.' Poppy shook her head. 'I think I'm digging myself a bigger hole here.'

Rose chuckled. 'I'm saying nothing.'

Once they had finished their food and pushed the plates to one side. Poppy leaned forward on her elbows.

'So what are you going to do?'

'I've asked Finn to put a tracker on Olly's phone so I can see where he's going and get an idea of where they're meeting. Because I'm sure there will be other times, if what I saw on her socials is anything to go by.'

'Wow! What did Finn think about that?'

'He wasn't sure at first but once I told him what I knew, he agreed to do it. He's round there now, playing some game with Olly. He's going to message me when it's done.'

Poppy blew out a breath.

After a few sips of wine, she turned to Rose. 'You know that stuff we talked about the other night. I can't remember much of it – we were pretty smashed – you're not thinking of actually doing anything like that, are you?'

When Rose didn't reply, Poppy shook her arm. 'Are you?'

'It's all I can think about, Pops – making her suffer for how she made me feel – standing there out on the pavement while they were in there...' she clenched her teeth. 'Enjoying themselves. I was like some kind of sad outsider.'

'I get it. But, come on, Rose. We were just messing around. Don't do anything rash. You need to have it out with him, now. Let him know you know.'

'I know...you're right. But I just can't. Not until I know more. I can't have that conversation with him yet.' Rose looked at her phone. 'Finn should have messaged by now. What can they be doing?' She turned to Poppy, eyes wide. 'You don't think Olly caught him at it, do you?'

'If that had happened I think you'd know about it. Look I'd better get going, babe, I've got the early swimming class tomorrow.'

Poppy put her coat on and Rose followed suit. 'Are you going to be alright?' she looked at Rose anxiously.

'I'll be fine.' She gave Poppy a tight hug. 'Get yourself off and I'll let you know what's happening.'

Once in her car, and having scrolled through Em's socials, Rose could feel the burger and chips she had enjoyed so much doing somersaults in her stomach. She kept looking at her phone as the time crept on. 9...9.15...9.30... what on earth was Finn doing? She couldn't go home until the she knew the coast was clear. *Had* Olly caught him in the act? Rose's stomach lurched even more at the thought. Unable to stand the tension any longer, she started the car. She would go home and find out for herself. She had to know what was happening.

Just as she was moving off, the phone pinged.

All done sis.

Rose let out a huge sigh and rested her head on her hands, still clutching the steering wheel.

Is everything okay? What took you so long?

Yeah – just playing the game. We forgot the time.

She pressed her lips together. Sometimes Finn could be so annoying! But she owed him after this.

The thought of going home and having to continue her façade with Olly made Rose feel exhausted. How much longer could she keep this up? Maybe Poppy was right. She should have it out with him and clear the air. But then she thought about the other night. How she'd felt.

You never forget how someone makes you feel.

She was sure she'd read that on a fridge magnet somewhere.

When she dropped her keys in the bowl, Rose called out her usual greeting. 'I'm home.' There was no response. She went into the lounge, full of dread, to find Olly still playing the game. She folded her arms across her chest and held them tight.

'So how did it go with Finn? Thanks for doing that.'

Olly replied without turning. 'S'okay. We had a good evening actually. This game is pretty cool. Hang on just a sec.'

Rose waited still holding herself in a tight grip. She sat on the edge of the settee.

'Yesss!' Olly fist-pumped the air. 'Done!'

He turned and came to sit beside Rose. 'He seemed a bit tense at first – you were right. But once we got into the game he was fine. Medal for best brother-in-law coming my way.' He rubbed his knuckles up and down on his chest.

'Good time with Poppy?'

'Yeah. I went to Paws and met her there and then we had something to eat.'

The conversation was stilted and Rose felt stifled by it. Olly hadn't noticed the haircut or her nails the previous evening. Or if he had he'd chosen not to mention it.

'By the way, I'm thinking about looking into male modelling.' Olly looked at the frozen screen.

'What?'

Several of the guys at work think I should give it a go. I've got the physique for it.' He turned and flexed his muscles.

Rose felt sick.

'Who's idea was that?'

There was a brief silence.

'There's this girl at the gym, Em. She's one of these influencers with thousands of followers. She reckons she has the contacts to get me a photo shoot. She really appreciates the work I've put into looking like this.'

The implied criticism hung heavy between them as Rose swallowed the bile rising in her throat.

'Well, if this *Em* thinks it's a good idea, then I guess you should go for it.'

Rose ignored the burning in her eyes. She would not cry in front of him. 'But remember, she doesn't know you like I do.'

'Maybe that's for the good.' There was bitterness in the barb.

Rose had reached breaking point. 'I'm off to bed.'

She got up and made herself walk out of the room and up the stairs.

Chapter Eleven

R ose found that looking at her phone was becoming increasingly compulsive. She was constantly either checking where Olly was or following Em online. She'd set up notifications for her fake profile. Even when she was working her eyes would stray to her phone, her fingers itching to pick it up. So far Olly had been to work and nowhere else. Rose knew that he would be there until the end of his shift at 5 pm, but she still had to keep checking. Em had been posting more about her mysterious man, promising to reveal more about him soon. Rose noticed that several fans were wondering if he even existed:

Maybe he's too good to be true?

Is that who you were with the other night?

Why so shy??

So far, Jaz hadn't posted anything, as Rose had been content to watch, but the idea of joining in and stirring things up a bit was becoming more and more attractive. She imagined comments she might make.

*Maybe you paid that guy to go out with you the other night.
He looked like a male escort to me. I think this Jay thing is a
wind-up.* Angry face emoji.

Rose studied the comment, part of her disbelieving that she
could have actually typed such a thing. But it wasn't her, was
it? It was Jaz, and this was the sort of thing Jaz would say. She
pressed Post.

'Everything alright, Rose?' Rose brought herself back to the
moment and to Marjorie's enquiring face.

'Yep. Sorry, Marjorie. I was miles away.'

'You don't seem yourself, dear. Something on your mind?'

Marjorie's green eyes drilled into Rose's as if she could see
inside her head and read all her thoughts. In the mirror, Rose
saw a faint blush appear on her cheeks and turned away to
blow her nose.

'Sorry. Just a bit under the weather, I think. And the boiler's
gone wrong so I'm waiting for a call to say when they're
coming.'

When had lying become so easy?

'How's that gorgeous husband of yours?'

Rose felt the question as an almost physical punch in her
stomach.

'Good, thanks, Marjorie. How's your Henry? Won any more
golf tournaments lately?'

'He's had to step back a bit until he gets his hip done
– he's so frustrated and driving me mad at home.' Marjorie
scrutinised Rose's hands in the mirror. 'You've had your nails
done! What a pretty colour. And I have to say that haircut
really frames your face beautifully.'

Marjorie looked at her own nails, resplendent in crimson
red, setting off her green outfit. As always, she had dressed
with care, her make-up immaculate.

'New suit, Marjorie?'

'A little pick-me-up.' Marjorie drew the flat of her hand across her skirt. 'There's nothing like a new outfit for bucking up the spirits.'

'It's lovely. That green really suits you,' Rose replied. Marjorie had found it hard when her term as mayor had ended and had never lost the habit of dressing as if every day was an occasion.

'We girls need to feel good about ourselves and there's nothing like having your nails done.'

Rose nodded. 'I know. I enjoyed it. I think I'll make it a regular thing.'

As she ushered Marjorie to the till, Rose heard one of the other clients hiss, 'Mutton dressed as lamb, that one with her airs and graces. Ridiculous.'

Rose wondered whether Marjorie had heard. If she had it didn't show as she sailed towards the reception. She'd probably heard it all before, after all, she imagined you didn't get to be mayor without having a thick skin. Although Marjorie's sense of occasion bordered on the ridiculous sometimes, Rose admired her for it, wishing she was strong enough not to care what people thought of her. She knew she herself was something of a people-pleaser but that was just the way she was, and Rose felt, deep down that she was a nicer person because of it.

She beckoned, Dan, her next client over, sneaking a quick look at her phone while he was getting settled. There were a couple of likes on her comment.

'The usual?'

'Yes please. Us policemen aren't known for our fancy haircuts.' He grinned.

Rose concentrated on the task in hand. Her male clients tended not to be as chatty as the women. Most men seemed happy to sit in silence for the ten or fifteen minutes it took to cut their hair which was often a relief after a day of talking and listening.

Dan had been to the salon several times and Rose knew how he liked his hair cut, Number 4 around the back and sides longer on the top, so it was easy to let her mind wander.

'Are you working today?' she asked in an attempt to keep her thoughts off Olly and Em.

'Yup. Working a late shift.'

'So what time do you start?'

'It's eight 'til eight. A bit of a long slog around here if it's a quiet night. Mind you, tonight's Friday so there'll probably be a bit of action.' He gave a wry smile.

Rose had known all too well about Friday nights in Weldon when she and Olly used to go out in their younger days. A few drinks at the Red Lion and then on to Wetherspoons before ending up at Sparky's – the nearest thing Weldon had to a club. It was mostly a kind of drunken school reunion as most of their co-drinkers were friends they knew from school. Nowadays, though, she and Olly preferred to stay in with a film and a takeaway.

'It's a bit different from when I worked in the Met.' Dan's comment drew Rose back to the present.

'You worked in London?'

'Yeah, that was real policing!' Dan sounded regretful that there wasn't more crime in Weldon.

'So what made you move here, then?'

'Ohhh.' Dan sighed. 'I guess I was ready for a bit of a quieter life. London's no place to bring up a family.'

Rose asked the obvious question. 'How many children do you have?'

'Oh.' He laughed, waving a hand across his face. 'None yet. No wife either. I'm just thinking ahead.'

In the silence that followed, Rose's mind started whirring into frenzied action – here was a police officer, the perfect person to answer some of her questions.

'What department do you work in?' Rose asked, her hands still busy with the scissors.

'I'm a detective – CID. But before you ask – it's all pretty boring. I spend most of my time at a desk making phone calls or looking at a screen.'

Rose smiled. 'I'll bet you get to know all about some pretty weird cases, though. Are they as far-fetched as those on the telly? I can't imagine some of those things happening in real life.'

'I don't know about that. Don't you remember that woman last year who murdered her husband and his girlfriend?' Shona chimed in.

'Oh yeah, she invited them round to dinner and poisoned them – the girlfriend was one of her best friends,' Adele added.

'Tried to pretend it was accidental food poisoning, my ass! Your lot got her in the end though.' Shona glanced towards Dan.

'Yes, there are always crimes of passion. Love and jealousy and betrayal are powerful motives, but in my experience, money is at the root of most crime.'

'Hold still while I do around your ears.' Rose was silent as she concentrated, wondering how to get the conversation around to her problem without being too obvious.

'Actually, I've got a friend who's writing a murder mystery.' She did her best to sound casual.

'Oh yeah, who's that then?' asked Shona.

Rose concentrated on Dan's neckline. 'Oh you don't know her. I do have friends that don't live in Weldon, you know.' She looked back at Dan. 'I bet she would love to pick your brains.'

'She'd have to join the queue. I need ideas on what to do about my Brian first.' Shona chuckled as others around the salon echoed, 'Me too!'

In the mirror, Dan gave Rose a look she couldn't read. 'If she needs my advice, unofficially, of course, I'd be more than happy to help.'

'Really?' Rose felt a hot flush running through her body. What was going on here? Why hadn't she kept her mouth shut?

There was something about Dan's gaze that drew Rose in. If anybody could help her, Dan could. She cleared her throat. 'I could message her and see what she says.'

What was she doing? This time there was no mistaking the flush on Rose's face, obvious in the mirror.

'I could always meet you...and your friend for coffee to discuss anything she needs to know if she doesn't live too far away.'

'Oh...no. She's only in Balton.'

Rose swallowed her panic. She hadn't been expecting this. Fleetingly she wondered how he would have the time to help some writer that no one had ever heard of, never mind actually being the one to suggest it. Her heart persuaded her brain to put the red flag down. He was just a nice guy being helpful. Maybe he even fancied her.

His face was questioning in the mirror. He was expecting an answer.

'That would be great. Thanks Dan. I'll message her.' The words came out of her mouth, unbidden.

'How about Sunday morning? I'm usually around then,'

Rose felt herself being pulled out of her depth by some invisible current that she couldn't control. This man could give her valuable information. As long as she pretended the whole thing was about someone else, she would be fine.

'Okay, sounds like a plan.' Rose gave a bright smile. She would work out how to explain the absent friend later.

Dan held out his hand. 'Let me put my number in your phone. Then you can let me know.'

Rose hesitated. She would never normally give her personal number to a client. But what could be the harm in giving Dan her number? He was a policeman, after all.

As soon as he was gone, Shona was at Rose's side. 'Are you sure you know what you're doing, Rose? Giving a client your number? You don't know anything about him.'

Rose huffed. 'I'm just meeting him for a coffee that's all. It's not a crime!' She flinched at her own joke and joined in with Shona's laughter. 'Okay, babe. Just being a caring manager.' Rose flapped her hand, signalling for Shona to move away. 'I'm sure caring managers have more...caring things to be doing.'

As soon as Shona was out of earshot, Rose snatched up her phone, hurriedly unlocking the screen. Olly was still at the gym. Rose wished she could track Em's phone as well. She needed to know if she was at ProFit too. Even though Em documented her whole life and everything she did on her social accounts, Rose knew by now there was a side to Em's life that never made it into the public eye.

Her latest post took Rose's breath away.

Hi gang. Wouldn't you love this hunk to be your personal trainer? How lucky am I? And this is Jay for those of you bitches who are suggesting I'm sad enough to make this up.

This poisoned arrow was accompanied by a selfie of Em pouting at the screen draped around Olly who looked... She couldn't find the words.

Rose studied her husband. The confident assurance that she knew everything about Olly had worn thin, but even so, she didn't recognise this expression. His chin was up and he was staring straight into the camera. Dark and moody. That was it. That was what he was communicating. She had never seen Olly like this. A chill went down her spine. She didn't know this Olly. Where had he come from and how come she hadn't noticed?

He seemed to be relishing having his photo taken. Posing – knowing how attractive he was. She remembered what he'd said about getting into male modelling and had to admit he certainly had the looks, and a good coach in Em.

As Rose was looking, comments began to appear on the screen:

Wow! Is this your new man?

I can see why you've been keeping him under wraps!

Why so secretive?

By the time Rose's next client arrived there were many more comments but Em hadn't replied to any of them. Was that because she and Olly were together, at this very moment? She was definitely at the gym.

'I won't be a minute,' she called over her shoulder. Rushing into the staffroom she messaged Poppy.

Pops can you see where Olly is...and Em? I know they're both at the gym.

Rose tapped the counter, rubbing her other hand over her forehead. She had to know.

Abby popped her head around the door. 'Mrs Moss is getting a bit antsy. Are you going to be much longer?'

'I'll be there in a minute, okay?' The words slipped out, sharp as knives.

Abby took a step back. 'What's wrong?'

'Sorry. Sorry. It's nothing. I just—' Her phone pinged with a message.

Yup they are both here and I can see them. And before you ask. They're just chatting.

Just chatting? Show me!

A photo arrived and Rose held her breath. There were Olly and Em – they seemed to be laughing about something.

Okay, Rose? I need to go. We'll speak later. Hugs xx

'Rose.' Shona popped her head around the door. 'Are you okay?' She came into the room. 'You look terrible.'

Rose gave a shaky sigh. 'No, I'm alright, just a bit of a dizzy turn. I'm fine now.'

'Well, if you're sure. Mrs M isn't happy. Why don't I tell her you're ill?'

'No.' The word raced off Rose's tongue. 'No, I'm going out to her now.' If she didn't deal with Mrs Moss now, she would never hear the end of it the next time she came. It would be like the Spanish Inquisition. As it was, Mrs M was one of her nosiest clients always asking probing questions about her personal life. Most clients were more than happy to talk about themselves – not Mrs M though.

Rose splashed her face with some water. Dried it carefully and went back into the salon.

'Are you ill, dear?'

'The usual today, Mrs M?' Rose ignored the question.

'You look a bit peaky.' Rose's stomach sank as she noticed a familiar gleam in her client's eyes. No. No. not this again. Not now!

'You're not...you know...' Mrs M eyed Rose's stomach.

'No.' Normally this would have led to some banter about Mrs M being the first to know. But today, Rose couldn't face it.

'Abby, could you wash Mrs M's hair?'

'But you always wash my hair.' There was a childish whine to Mrs M's voice.

'I've got a lot on today, but you'll have my full attention next time. I promise.'

Abby led a reluctant Mrs M over to the sinks. 'There's something up with Rose, you know. She's not herself. That can only mean one thing in my book.' The muttered words didn't escape Rose and she stifled an exasperated sigh before retreating back into the staff room.

Mrs M was right about one thing. This business with Olly and Em was making her snappy and impatient. She wasn't herself. Rose felt tears prickle in her eyes. She was never short with customers. The others always said she had the patience of a saint. But Olly had changed, she was changing and it felt as if her safe, ordered, life was slipping out of control.

Chapter Twelve

'**Y**ou've what?'

'I know. I know it's mad. But think about it, Pops. Dan could give us ideas for a much better plan to deal with Em.'

'But he's police. Don't you think he would find out and put two and two together?' Poppy stood up and paced around the kitchen. 'A writer friend? Really? No way!'

'It would just be for an hour or so. You always said you wanted to write a book.'

'No way. I'm not getting involved in this. It's mad. You need to have it out with Olly. You need to sort things out with him. It's about you and him – not her. This obsession – it's not healthy, Rose.'

Rose sniffed back tears. 'But it is about her! If she wasn't around, I could get Olly back and we would be just like before. She's got her claws into him, putting all these ideas about modelling into his head. I can't believe he actually came out and mentioned her name...'

Poppy rinsed plates in the sink, the tap running too fast. 'I know we've talked about some mad stuff – but we were drunk. Things are getting out of hand. None of this was ever meant to be serious.' She turned and her tone softened. 'Come on, Rose.'

Rose gave into the sobs that had threatened ever since she arrived.

Poppy turned off the tap and sat down beside Rose, putting an arm around her shoulder. 'Be honest. You're never going to feel the same, or trust him in the same way again, are you?'

'I don't know. It doesn't feel like it now.' Rose sniffed and wiped her nose on a tissue. 'But surely all the years we've had together must count for something. There must be some...foundation we can get back to. To re-set and start again.'

'Take it from me. It won't ever happen.'

Something snapped inside Rose's head. She was sick of Poppy constantly comparing her and Vic's relationship with Rose's and Olly's. They were worlds apart.

'Just because you couldn't keep Vic. Doesn't mean I'm not going to fight for Olly! Maybe you just didn't love him enough.'

A thin layer of ice settled over the room as Poppy recoiled, hand over her mouth.

Rose stood and picked up her bag. 'So it looks like I'm doing this on my own.'

Still quivering with rage once she was in the car, Rose looked at her phone. Olly had left the gym and seemed to be heading out of town. She looked at the time. 2.30. Where would he be going at this time? Surely his shift didn't finish until 5 o'clock.

Shoving the car into gear, Rose took off.

It didn't take her long to catch up with him on the ring-road, but Rose had to be careful and hung well back. He would recognise her car in an instant.

She followed him into Nottingham where he parked in a multi-storey car park. Rose had to be careful not to be spotted and parked a floor above him, risking driving past him as he was parking. Turning into the nearest space, she flung herself out of the car and, not waiting for the lift, hurtled down the steps.

Once at the bottom, she rushed out onto the street, heart racing and out of breath, hoping she hadn't lost him. She looked left and then right – just catching a glimpse of a so-familiar form disappearing around the corner.

Rose followed as he strode purposefully down an unfamiliar side street and disappeared from sight. She hurried to the spot – there was only one entrance he could have gone through. She peered at the sign outside the door. Promise Photography Studios. Appointment only.

She leant against the wall gasping in great breaths, trying to control her breathing and fend off the panic attack that was threatening. She'd never had one before but imagined this was what it was like. It seemed an eternity before she managed to get her body under control.

Olly was a stranger to her now. She didn't know this new David Beckham-like Olly. She could never have imagined this. This was what Em had done to her – lured her man away with promises of fame, glamour and money.

She sagged against the wall.

In the nearest coffee shop, Rose ordered a slice of cake and a hot chocolate. She couldn't go home yet. Sugar was what she needed to regain her equilibrium.

After a second slice of cake and another drink, Rose felt drained. Once the swift pleasure of savouring the sweetness of the cake and chocolate – she knew she'd eaten it too fast in her desperation to fill the void inside – was over, she was left with nothing but a heavy feeling in her stomach and an uncomfortable sadness about what she'd said to Poppy.

It was as if, more and more often lately, some malevolent force was taking over and making her say and do terrible things. She felt shame and fear in equal measures. What was happening to her? Who could she turn to for help? The person she had always turned to had become her tormentor because of Em, and now she had pushed her away. Poppy who had always been there for her.

She stared idly out of the window, remembering the day she and Poppy had become friends in Year 5. Rose had come across her in tears in the playground at lunchtime and had sat beside her until, eventually, Poppy had admitted she hated Weldon and Appledale Primary. She wished she was back home in Sheffield with all her old friends. Once the novelty of her being the 'new girl' when everyone wanted to be her friend had worn off, she had been abandoned. Rose's heart went out to her and she felt bad that she hadn't noticed. From then on, she made sure that Poppy was included in everything and their friendship was cemented. By the time they were all at high school, Poppy was one of the most popular girls in the year, but she was always loyal to Rose and no one was ever allowed to encroach on her BFF status.

All through the history of their relationship, this morning's falling out would have been unthinkable, even a few days ago. But she still felt, deep down, that Poppy had been insensitive, but Rose knew she had said cruel words and hated herself for it. She would have to find a way to put things right.

It was almost dark when Rose eventually made her way home, although Olly's car wasn't outside. The app had informed her that he had returned to the gym at around four o'clock. Knowing he wasn't there, she hadn't been able to face the thought of sitting at home, her head full of him at the photo shoot. She was tired after several hours of mindlessly trudging around the shops and a strange kind of numbness had come over her, as if she were moving through a fog, her thoughts about Olly and Em, distant and unclear.

'Hello, Rose.'

Her heart sank at the sound of Walter's voice.

'Hi Walter.'

She moved purposefully towards the front door.

'Everything okay?'

'Yes, just busy with work, you know. I'm pretty tired actually. I think I might be going down with something. How about I pop round next week sometime?'

'That would be lovely. I'll look forward to it. See you then, Rose. I hope you feel better.'

Rose's heart clenched as he shuffled towards his own front door.

As she let herself in, Rose pictured him as the headmaster she had known at primary school. Back then he had seemed so tall – taller than her parents. He'd exuded a particular kind of power – her mother still called him Mr Powell and spoke of him in deferential tones. From her twenty-four-year-old perspective, Rose could see that he'd been kind but fair, even though no one wanted to be the target of his anger.

How was he reduced to this shell of his former self? There was a vulnerability about him that Rose found disquieting. This was the destiny for all of us – the downward spiral of old age? Suddenly, she had a sense of the inconsequential nature of her current crisis in the inevitable march of time. Something that was all-consuming now – what would it all mean in fifty years' time when she would be seventy-four? Some distant memory eclipsed by other life-changing events, maybe?

She slipped into a daydream of herself as a wise old woman giving youngsters the benefit of her vast experience in life, as they hung on to her every word: 'When I was your age, I thought my life was over. Looking back on it now, even though it was overwhelming at the time, it seems far away compared to all the things that have happened since. The things that happen when you're young help you to learn how to face the future.' Maybe she would even include the words 'character building.'

She shrugged off her clothes. Who was she kidding? She'd probably end up like Miss Havisham – old and bitter. Her brain understood the logic of the argument, but her emotions couldn't make the leap back to see the bigger picture.

Getting into a hot shower, Rose made a determined effort to rid herself of morbid thoughts. What about Beryl, Diana and Marjorie, who were growing old gracefully and still enjoying life to the full. She wished Walter could have the same – he spent so much time on his own these days. She made a mental note to talk to him about Harold and find out exactly how much of a struggle getting around had become when she saw him next.

She tipped her head back and enjoyed the hot water pummelling her body, imagining it washing all her cares away.

Chapter Thirteen

R ose stirred her cappuccino, still going over phrases in her mind. Dan had messaged her last night and suggested a time and place to meet. She'd almost forgotten about him in the maelstrom of yesterday's events but when she re-read it this morning, she'd replied with a thumbs-up. Her mission to get Em out of Olly's life had grown in urgency as she replayed the reel of him striding along the road to the photograph studio. Em had even made him walk differently.

But now she was here, nerves had kicked in and she had to explain the absence of the non-existent author.

'Sorry Kate couldn't make it, but she's given me some questions all the same.' Or 'Sorry to waste your time – Kate doesn't exist. I just made up an excuse to see you again.' (Where did that thought come from?) If it were true, that would make her as bad as Olly. But maybe, if he were to find out, it wouldn't be such a bad thing. It would give him a taste of how she was feeling and then they would both realise what they had to lose.

'Hi. Sorry I'm a bit late.' Dan looked pointedly at the empty space beside Rose. 'No friend?'

'No, something came up at the last minute and she couldn't make it.' So that was the version that her brain chose to produce? Right. Rose shifted on the chair, pushing it away from the table slightly.

'Ri-ight.' The way he drew the word out made Rose's skin prickle with shame and a tinge of fear. It was as if he could see right through her.

She watched as Dan ordered coffee noticing he was surprisingly short for a policeman. She doubted he was six feet. Wasn't there some height requirement to join the police force? He held his back very straight – in a military kind of stance – feet planted firmly apart.

'So, tell me about this story.' Dan settled in his seat and took a sip of coffee. Black espresso, Rose noted. She felt the power of his presence.

'So...' Her mouth was dry and the words wouldn't form. She took a sip of coffee. 'It's about this woman who finds out her husband is having an affair.'

'So far, so normal.' He grinned.

Normal? How could he think this was normal? Rose reminded herself that this was supposed to be a story, not real life. She needed to act the part and not give her true feelings away. She cleared her throat.

'She finds out and wants to punish the woman he's seeing but she doesn't know how to go about it. She's thinking of framing the other woman for a crime of some kind. That's as much as I know, really.'

Dan eyes widened with interest and he leaned forward, resting his elbows on the table. 'Right. Let's call the man Colin, his wife Ang, and the woman Lucy for now. What kind of person is Lucy? What kind of crime could your writer friend imagine her committing? Shoplifting, maybe? Some kind of damage to Ang's car?' He furrowed his brow.

In spite of her misgivings, Rose was still drawn to her and Poppy's original idea. 'The thing is. What if Ang had access to Lucy's DNA. Couldn't it be planted somewhere – at a crime scene?'

'Dan narrowed his eyes. 'You mean...like hair?'

Rose could feel herself getting hot. She shrugged off her coat.

Dan smiled. 'I think there are better ways to incriminate Lucy. If DNA comes into play, there has to be a valid reason to suggest a crime. It would have to be somewhere that Lucy wouldn't be expected to be. And a reason for her hair to be there. A single hair just lying on the floor might not be convincing and could lead to suspicion falling back on Ang. We police are not stupid, you know. We can spot a fit-up when we see one.'

Keep acting a part. Keep acting a part. Rose repeated the mantra in her head.

Fortunately, Dan couldn't see Rose's hands clenched under the table, her nails digging into her palms. Part of her was horrified at how seriously Dan was taking this, but the other part was fascinated by the possibilities.

'What about Colin? Wouldn't Ang want to punish him, too?' he asked, head tilted.

'Oh no! No. Ang loves Colin and wants him to come back to her. She just wants to punish Lucy and get her away from Colin. She wants Colin to see the error of his ways.'

Rose sat back in her chair, her heart thumping. There was no way she could carry on pretending this was just about her friend's book after that outburst.

After a sip of coffee, Dan tilted his head to one side. 'Although, thinking about it. DNA used in the right way could work. What would Ang have access to?' His slate-grey eyes bored into her. Maybe she hadn't given herself away, after all.

'Well, hair and maybe a mug she had used.'

'How would she have access to these things?'

Rose clenched her hands and looked at the table as silence hung between them for a few seconds. 'Umm—'

'Sounds very much as if Ang might be a hairdresser.' Dan cut across her hesitation.

'Well, I don't—'

Dan smiled and cut in again. 'I get it. And I agree with Ang. Lucy *is* the one who should be punished.'

The realisation that at last someone saw things from her point of view washed over Rose like an intoxicating wave of relief. She felt a treacherous tear run down her cheek and brushed it away with her finger tips, hoping he hadn't noticed.

Dan leant forwards once more, clasping his hands, elbows on the table. 'I understand. I get it... *Ang*. Let's nail that bitch, Lucy.' He emphasised the word Ang. 'People like her should be punished. I'm sure I can think of something that Ang could do.'

'But you're a policeman.'

'Who better to come up with a plot for the perfect crime?' He stirred his coffee. 'Plenty of ex police officers have written crime novels. Let me have a think about the plot and we'll meet again.' It was a statement, not a suggestion. 'Maybe your...friend will be able to come next time.'

Rose reminded herself how Em had made her feel when they were in the restaurant. She pictured Olly going into the photography studio, an Olly she didn't know – who had been stolen from her. Summoning up those feelings – the humiliation and crushing betrayal gave her the spur she needed to keep talking.

'You can get a sense of what Lucy is like here.' Rose took out her phone and opened the social media app at Em's page and handed it to Dan. 'She's just like this. Her whole life is here for everyone to see...well the part she wants the world to see. It's all made up. I know that the reality isn't quite so glamorous. She lives in a crappy council flat and works in a supermarket.'

Dan took out his phone and snapped a picture. 'Okay so she's living a lie. There seem to be a lot of pretend stories going on around here. Hard to know what's real and what's fiction.' His eyes pinned her down once more, and Rose felt the colour rise up her neck and on to her cheeks.

He drained his cup, pushing it way from him in a sudden movement 'Right, I'm off. I'm due back at work.'

Rose stood with him, taken by surprise at the abrupt end to their conversation. 'Thanks for coming,' she managed, unsure about where they stood.

As if he could read her mind, he said, 'Oh, and if you're wondering, I understand perfectly. We're on the same page here, Rose.' He gave her a nod and a searching look. Rose dropped her gaze to the floor. She didn't need to say anything.

'I'll be in touch,' he said as he turned to go.

Rose left the coffee shop, her head buzzing with ideas and conflicting emotions. The main thing was that Dan had understood. He had taken her seriously – not telling her that Ang should snap out of her rose-tinted bubble. She would focus on that positive thought. But even so, she had an uncomfortable flashback to how she had left things with Poppy.

Rose had secretly felt for a while that Poppy had overreacted to Vic leaving – she seemed to think that all men were now like him – feckless and untrustworthy. The pressure cooker of her own distress, sadness and anger had released the thought and Rose had said it out loud. And now she couldn't take it back. Whether she liked it or not – Poppy was probably right – she could never be the same old Rose again after this.

Already the pain of not having Poppy's friendship was becoming a dull ache in the very core of her being. Rose knew she had to put things right.

Poppy, I'm so sorry about last night. I guess I'm just not myself at the moment.

The screen remained uncommunicative after she pressed Send. Rose sighed and headed off to her car. She would try again later.

Right now, she had to gather more info about Em.

Rose wasn't as lucky this time when she parked outside Em's flat. Her car wasn't there. She worried the skin on the side of her thumb. There was no point in staying. She would go to one of Em's other haunts.

As she was starting the car, the chocolate labrador she had seen before came out of the door with its owner and before she could second-guess herself, Rose opened the car door and stepped onto the pavement.

'Hi.' The woman turned. She was about Rose's age.

'Sorry to bother you, but...' the dog approached Rose, who put out her hand. She gave an exploratory sniff.

'Oh you are gorgeous, and don't you know it?' Rose looked back up at the woman.

'What's she called?'

'Doris. She's a bit of a diva, I'm afraid.'

'She's lovely.' Rose felt a twinge of envy. How she would love a dog like this.

'Sorry, I was looking for Em. Emily Totton?' Rose cast around in her mind for a suitable reason, but came up with nothing that wouldn't involve more lies. As it was, she needn't have worried – the woman was more than happy to talk.

'Yeah, I know Em. Talking of divas.' The woman scanned the road. 'Doesn't look as if she's here though, her car's gone. Maybe she's taking her sister to the hospital.'

'Hospital?' Rose echoed. Em had a sister?

'Yeah, she's got MS or something. I know Em is a bit of a pain, but she's good to her sister. They've only got each other – the mother died a while back and they moved here when Jen was diagnosed.'

'Do you know them well?'

'Just in passing, you know. Jen's got a sweet spot for Doris.'

'Why did you say you were looking for her?' The belated question caught Rose off-guard and she felt the colour rise in her face.

'Oh she made an enquiry about home improvements. I was in the area and thought I would call on the off chance. No worries. I'll come back another time then. Thanks for your help.'

'You could put a message through her door.' She moved to open the main entrance door.

'No!' The woman glanced back at Rose's exclamation before she took a breath and added, 'But thanks anyway. I'll ring her and make a proper appointment.'

Rose bent down and scratched Doris behind the ears. 'Bye Doris.'

Back in the car, she processed this new piece of the jig-saw of Em's life. Em had a sister. That explained the open window on her first visit and the trip to the hospital. In many ways it was an unwelcome piece of information. It would be much easier if Em had remained the selfish influencer who lived on her own – the persona that Rose had created for her. But now she had to factor in that Em had a caring side, that she actually had someone to look after, someone who was dependent on her. It didn't fit the rest of the picture at all. Rose sighed and gripped the steering wheel. Whatever happened, she didn't want to feel sorry for Em, or even like her. She had to keep those emotions contained in a firmly sealed box.

Chapter Fourteen

P oppy's silence communicated more anger than any reply could have done. Several messages and voicemails had gone unanswered over the last few days and Rose knew she had to go and apologise face to face. But first she needed to keep her promise to Walter.

He was already standing in the doorway by the time Rose had walked up the path. She wondered how many hours he spent looking out the window and when he had stopped his daily walk to the paper shop.

'Rose. Lovely to see you.' His watery eyes shone.

'Hi Walter. Is now a good time?'

'Any time is good for me these days, my dear.' He gave a rueful smile as he turned, walking with some difficulty towards the kitchen. Rose noticed how he used his hand on the wall to steady himself.

'You don't mind sitting in the kitchen, do you?' he said over his shoulder. 'I'm not as steady on my pins, and I rather think a tray might be beyond me at the moment.'

'Of course not, Walter. I'll be happy anywhere as long as there's a cup of coffee available.' She hoped he'd take the hint and remember that she didn't drink tea.

'Here you go. Take a pew.' He pulled out a chair for her, and Rose sat on the cushion secured with ties to the back of the wooden chair.

'Yes, I know it's coffee for you.' He started preparations for the drinks, and Rose noticed how his hand shook as he filled the kettle under the tap.

She jumped to her feet. 'Let me do that, Walter.' She stretched out her hand.

'You'll do no such thing, Rose Sugden.' His eyebrows were drawn together in an ominous frown, and suddenly she was back at school in Mr Powell's office. Rose hadn't been a frequent visitor, as on the whole she had been well-behaved always wanting to please the teachers, but the few occasions she had faced Mr Powell's disapproval were firmly etched in her mind. The most serious offence had been when she'd got into a fight with another girl. She and her friends had been taunting Olly about his slight frame and constant wheeze. Without a second thought, Rose had marched over and planted herself firmly, nose-to-nose with Olly's tormentor. 'Take that back!'

'Or what?' Rose could still hear the sneer, even after all these years.

The red mark caused by Rose's slap had started to appear almost immediately, as Fran Watts screamed and called a teacher over.

'Miss! Rose Sugden just slapped me.'

Mr Powell had judged the offence to be serious enough to call Rose's parents in, but Rose had remained defiant, and the obligatory apology had been forced through clenched teeth.

At home her father had taken her to one side. 'That isn't the way to deal with bullies, Rose. They will always come out on top of any confrontation. You should have told one of the teachers or Mr Powell instead of taking things into your own hands.'

Rose had stared at the floor, knowing that although her father was right, she didn't regret her actions for a moment.

'And did you stop to think how Olly would feel? How humiliating it was for him?'

This had struck home and Rose had been truly upset at the thought she might have made things worse for Olly.

She'd apologised to him the following day, and she still remembered his reply. 'It's alright Rose. You were just doing what you thought was best. Don't worry about it.'

Rose thought about how different Olly was now. But even though he could fight his own battles, was she fighting Em this time instead of Fran Watts? Was she making the same mistake again? She considered the possibility and came to a rapid conclusion. No, this was different – she was fighting for their marriage. They weren't at primary school any more.

As if to emphasise the point, Rose heard Walter's voice. 'There we go.' Two cups of coffee had appeared on the table. She was relieved that Mr Powell had only made a fleeting visit and that Walter was back. 'Oh, and I've even got some biscuits, I believe.'

Once the biscuits were laid out on a plate, Walter sat down with a grunt.

'How've you been, Walter? I'm so sorry—'

Walter cut her off. 'No apologies. I know how busy you young people are. You don't need to be worrying about an old fogie like me.'

Rose sipped her weak coffee.

Walter sighed. 'You young people have it so much harder than we did at your age. Back then, for us, further education was free and if you worked hard you were more or less guaranteed a job for life, especially in a profession like teaching. Nowadays so many teachers are burnt out by the time they're forty. And the experience of older teachers is worth nothing.'

Walter took a biscuit. 'Right, sermon over. Sorry, Rose, but it makes me so mad!'

Rose smiled. 'We do okay. There are a lot worse off than we are.'

Walter stirred his coffee and laid the spoon carefully in the saucer. 'Changing the subject, I've been thinking about Harold. Since he's had a name, he seems real. I was wondering whether I could come to the rescue place with you and take a look at him, meet him.'

'Of course! We can do that any time.'

'I'm not making any commitments, mind,' he added quickly.

'No. Of course. I'll arrange a visit.' Rose felt a warm glow – she could still make some good things happen in the world.

'Is everything alright with you and Olly?'

The question seemed to come from nowhere. 'Of course. Why?' Rose bristled at the question and knew her answer sounded defensive. She also knew that Walter was the master of spotting liars.

'I noticed you hardly seem to be at home together, and...' he looked at Rose. 'I couldn't help hearing raised voices the other night.'

Rose felt the flush travel up her face. 'We're okay, Walter. Just a bit of a hiccup.' *Just a bit of a hiccup?* Had she really just said that? 'We'll get over it. Sorry if we disturbed you.'

'Oh I'm a light sleeper these days. Probably should cut out the daytime nap.' He took a bite of his biscuit.

'I don't think I've slept a whole night through since Annie went.' There was an uncharacteristic tremor in his voice. 'Somehow it's not the same without her beside me.' Walter looked down into his empty cup and sighed.

'It must be so hard to get used to.' As Rose spoke, Walter jerked his head up, almost as if he had forgotten she was there.

'Hark at me, moaning on.' He stood and collected the cups and saucers, placing them in the sink. Rose resisted the urge to offer assistance.

When he returned to his seat, Rose said, 'Talking of changing routines, I notice you don't go to the paper shop anymore.'

Walter waved a hand in front of his face in dismissal. 'Just a bit stiff, that's all.'

Rose ploughed on, she wasn't going to give up now. 'Are you struggling with walking that far?'

This time it was Walter's turn to be defensive. 'It's just a bit tricky at the moment. I'll soon get back to it though.'

'Would a walking stick help?'

Rose sensed the frown threatening to reappear and hastily added, 'Surely it would be worth it so you could get out and about again?'

Walter appeared to be fighting an internal battle.

'You must miss reading the paper.' Rose tried another tactic.

'I think you might be right, Rose. I need to swallow a bit of pride I think. And yes, I do miss the paper and getting out and about. I don't see anybody stuck in here all day, except you and Olly, of course.'

'I could order you one online.' Rose got out her phone and flicked through several pages. 'Here we are. Fancy any of these?' She slid the phone across the table.

Walter picked it up gingerly and scrolled up and down. 'I think this one might do the trick.' He passed the phone back. 'It's got a good sturdy rubber on the bottom to keep me steady.'

'It says that if I order, it'll be here tomorrow. Shall I get it?'

Walter nodded. 'If you don't mind, Rose. Hang on, I'll give you the money.' He reached into his jacket pocket and took out a wallet. He counted out a few notes and passed them to Rose.

'But it's not that much,' Rose protested.

'I know, but you keep it. Call it a thank you for sorting me out.' He put a hand over hers pressing the money into her palm.

'There. All ordered. I'll pop it round when it comes.'

'Already? It's amazing what you can do with a click of a button these days.'

Once she was home, Rose tried ringing Poppy once more, but the call went to voicemail.

'Poppy, it's me. I'm sorry. What else can I say? Come on. Let's not let this get between us. Call me?'

She swallowed back a sob as she ended the call.

'You look great, Mum. Cruising obviously agrees with you.' Rose hugged her mother tight as Jack and Jill danced around, barking excitedly.

'It was wonderful. I loved every minute of it. But it's good to be home, even if these two are driving me mad.' She picked the two dogs up, kissing each one on the head as they squealed and squirmed in delight.

'I guess the hardship of being looked after by Finn has made them appreciate their luxurious lifestyle after all,' she chuckled as she stooped to put them down.

'Rosy Posy! Come here and give your old dad a hug.' Her father put down the chopping knife and held out his arms as she went into the kitchen.

Rose relished the moment in her father's arms. He'd always seemed so big and strong to her, but now she sensed that some of that was missing. It wasn't that he was frail – just getting older, she thought. Or maybe she just wasn't a child anymore.

He went back to chopping the vegetables. 'It's good to get back to home cooking again – although the cruise was wonderful,' he added quickly, winking at Rose.

'So what's on the menu tonight?'

Before Rose's mother could answer Pete and Becca arrived with Fern and Harry, and suddenly the kitchen was crowded.

'Shoo! Off with you until this is ready.' Rose's mother made a shooing motion with her hands. 'Uncle Finn, take your nephew and niece and entertain them.'

Fin made a mock grimace. 'Oh no! Not the monsters!'

Five-year-old Harry shrieked, 'Yes. Yes. Uncle Finn. Can we play G'raffs and Ladders?'

Sighing and holding his hands up in surrender, Finn headed for the lounge. 'Come on then.'

Following a nursery visit to the zoo, Harry had developed a phobia of snakes, and the reptilian version of the game had made him hysterical. Finn found a Harry friendly version for children with reptilian phobias – of whom there were a surprising number – called Giraffes and Ladders, and it had become part of the Wednesday night tradition.

Rose followed, and once the game was underway, she said to Finn, 'Everything okay?'

'Yeah. Have you found anything out?'

'Still working on it.'

Finn nodded. 'Are you going to say anything to Mum and Dad?'

'Not yet. I need to know more first.'

'It's just... It's weird not telling them. The whole thing is weird. Why don't you have it out with him? Why all the secrecy?'

'Uncle Finn. It's your go! Come on!'

Finn turned away from her and picked up the dice. He shook it with an exaggerated motion and held his hands over the board.

'Drum roll.'

Harry and Fern obediently provided the sound effect and he let the dice fall.

'Oh no! I've been swallowed by the biggest giraffe. Arrrgh.' He clutched his throat and fell to the floor. 'Here I go down his long neck,' he yelled, as his nephew and niece screamed with delight.

Rose watched with a smile, but inside she was already regretting having involved her little brother in her problems. She felt uneasy about dragging him into the deception, but it couldn't be undone now.

Chapter Fifteen

E m breezed into the salon, casually passing her jacket to Rose and heading for her usual chair with a cursory, 'Hi.'

Rose had never felt more like the hired help as she arranged the jacket on a hanger and, with gritted teeth, crossed the salon. She had considered asking Adele to do the extensions as she didn't know whether she'd be able to endure several hours in Em's company without letting everything spill out in a torrent of anger. But Rose had steeled herself to not waste this opportunity to find out more about Em and pump her for information she might be able to use against her.

Rose hadn't heard from Dan since they'd met on Sunday and was beginning to think his keen interest had been a passing fad and that he'd forgotten all about her. Part of her hoped so.

As Em had dropped the extensions off the day before, Rose had prepared them and had them laid out ready, but first she had to remove the old ones, a fiddly and lengthy job.

'How are you doing, Em?' She forced a smile. 'Ready for the marathon?'

'You know me,' Em tittered, 'I'm happy to put in the effort to make sure I look my best.'

Scissors in hand, Rose took up the first weft.

Em studied her in the mirror, tilting her head to one side just as Rose was about to cut the first thread. She stifled an exasperated sigh.

'You've had your hair done, Rose! Oh my, maybe you are taking a leaf out of my book, after all.' She turned and took one of Rose's hands. 'And your nails!'

Rose snatched her hand away in a reflexive movement, still holding the scissors in her right hand.

'No need to be shy, Rose.' She sniggered. 'I always did love the ugly duckling story., it could have been written for you.'

Em was making it easy for Rose to hate her again and any feelings of sympathy towards her disappeared in an instant.

'I'll need you to hold still, Em, if we're ever going to get this done.' She kept her tone calm and businesslike.

Em made a slapping of her wrist motion and turned the corners of her mouth down. 'Okay, I promise to be good now.'

Rose was determined not to be provoked by the mock-childish tone and was glad of several minutes silence as she made steady progress removing the old extensions.

Em couldn't stay quiet for long, however. 'Did I tell you I went out on a date with Jay, last week?' Her eyes shone. 'He took me to *Shan* that posh new restaurant in Nottingham. I don't expect you've heard of it. That guy who won *Masterchef* opened it. My followers are loving the pics I posted.'

Em paused, seemingly expecting some comment from Rose.

'Try and keep still for me if you can, Em.'

The silence lasted another few minutes.

'Anyway, the number of my followers has gone bonkers since I've gone public with Jay. It's mad! Honestly, Rose, you wouldn't believe the difference a good-looking man at your side makes to how people see you.'

'Hmm.' Rose replied absently, remaining focused on her work.

Once the last of the extensions had been removed, Rose straightened her aching back.

'Time for a coffee. Want one, Em?'

Em wrinkled her sculpted nose. 'I suppose it's instant?'

When Rose didn't respond, she sighed and said, 'Okay but could you make it decaf?'

'Will do.' Rose escaped to the staff room where Shona was engrossed in her phone.

'You look like you could do with something stronger than coffee.' She grinned.

'Too right.' Rose flopped into a chair, waiting for the kettle to boil.

'Good job not all of our clients are as high maintenance as her, otherwise we'd only get through about two a day. You really do have the patience of a saint, Rose.'

Rose opened her own phone and went straight to Em's socials.

Off to the gorgeous Emmanuel this morning for a pretty intense session. Remember, guys, it takes time and effort to make the most of yourself. Followed by various emojis of scissors, hearts and locks of blonde hair.

Jaz: *About time! Those extensions were looking pretty scraggy. They are extensions, aren't they? I'm assuming you're not a natural blonde. I guess your hair is fake like everything else about you.*

Rose glanced over at Shona as she pressed Post, wondering what she would say about Rose's trolling, alter ego, Jaz.

When she returned with Em's coffee, her client was looking perturbed.

'Everything alright?'

'Yup. All good.' Em turned her phone over in her lap. 'Everyone's dying to see what I look like.' She smiled a radiant smile and took a sip of coffee, closing her eyes as she swallowed, as if she was drinking some vile-tasting medicine.

As Rose embarked on the task of weaving in the new extensions, Em said, 'You should go to ProFit, the gym I go to. You would lose those extra pounds in no time. There are some great people there who would give you lots of encouragement.'

'Isn't that where your Olly works?' Adele chimed in.

Rose's hands froze mid-weave. It was if there was a belt tightening across her chest.

'Oh? Who's Olly?' Em's eyes widened in interest. 'You haven't mentioned you know anyone there.'

'He's Rose's husband,' Adele answered helpfully. Rose glared at her, but Adele only shrugged in a questioning motion.

Rose looked down at Em's head, and willed herself to move, to say something.'

'Oh, didn't I mention? He only works part-time, though. Mostly in the pool area.'

She held her breath.

'It's weird that, because sometimes people at ProFit call Jay, Olly.' She studied Rose through narrowed eyes.

'Well, it's a pretty common name. There were three Ollys in his class at school.' Rose gripped the extension hard, her nails digging in to the palm of her hand. Why did she always talk too much when she was nervous...or lying?

'You've known him since you were at school? Oh that's so sweet,' Em simpered.

'Anyway my Jay isn't *your* Olly obvs, cause you've seen a photo of him. And what kind of woman wouldn't say anything? Your Olly doesn't sound like the type who would take a girl to *Shan*.' She tittered and waved a hand in front of her face. 'No offence!'

Had Em ever thought about the wisdom of slagging off her hairdresser, especially when she had a pair of sharp scissors to hand and could ruin her look in seconds? Rose thought not.

'So where did you move here from? You're obviously not from Weldon.' Rose was determined to change the subject and find out more about Em before she let her go.

'Oh we moved here and there. My father was in the RAF so we lived all over the world.'

From the corner of her eye, Rose could just make out a sceptical raised eyebrow from Shona. She resisted the urge to smile back.

'So do you have any family?' Rose made the question sound as casual as she could.

Em sighed, her eyes suddenly brimming with tears. She waved both hands in front of her face. 'Sorry. It's just...'

'Oh I'm sorry, Em, I didn't mean...'

'It's okay. It's okay.' Em swallowed. 'You weren't to know.' She sniffed and shook her head. 'My family were all killed in a car crash about five years ago. So it's just little old me now.'

'How awful for you.' Rose struggled to make her sympathy sound sincere, especially as she knew it was one big fat lie. She finished inserting Em's extensions in almost unbroken silence after that, Em occasionally sniffling into the tissue.

As the door closed behind her, Rose leant her back against it and closed her eyes.

'Wow! That was all pretty heavy,' Adele said through an exhale. 'God!'

'Hmm. I'm not sure. I've heard of sob-stories, but that one takes the biscuit.'

'Shona!' Adele gasped. 'That poor girl lost her whole family. You can't say something like that!'

'Well, babe, I just did.' Shona pressed her lips into a firm line as Rose tidied up.

Rose held the walking stick up in front of her, waving it in the air as she approached Walter's door.

'Here it is.' She handed it to him. 'What do you think?'

Walter pressed the rubber tip into the ground and leant on it. 'It'll need lengthening,' he muttered.

'Easily done.' Rose took the stick, and using her jacket to protect her fingertip, pressed in the button and slid the stick to the next notch. 'There. That's added another inch or so.'

Walter tried again. 'Do you know, I think this might work.'

'What do you say to a visit to meet Harold? You could give the stick a go while we're there.'

'What now? Oh, I don't know... Maybe another day.' Walter's voice tailed off and Rose sensed his vulnerability.

'Harold will be expecting you.'

Walter sighed and gave a hint of a smile. 'Well, in that case it would be rude not to come. Let me get my jacket.' Ever the gentleman, Walter would never be seen dead on the street without a jacket and tie.

He reappeared minus the pullover and complete with jacket.

'Okay let's go.'

Rose hovered at Walter's side as he took a few tentative steps. 'I feel like a right ninny with this,' he grumbled under his breath. But as they reached Rose's car, he was already moving more confidently.

Once they were on their way, Walter asked, 'How are things with you and Olly?'

Rose didn't reply. What could she say? That she was tracking her husband's movements because she didn't trust him?

'Still not patched up?' Walter was not going to take silence as an answer.

'He's having an affair.' From the corner of her eye Rose saw Walter turn and look at her. She kept her attention firmly fixed on the road ahead.

'What? Your Olly? Are you sure?'

Rose nodded, feeling the prickle of tears at the back of her eyes.

'Oh Rose. I'm so sorry.'

He put a hand on her arm. 'How do you know?'

She sighed. It's a long story, but I've seen them together, and the woman has been talking about him on social media. Pictures of him and her.

Walter made a tutting, hissing sound. 'This social media stuff has a lot to answer for. I'm glad it wasn't around in my day.' He was silent for a few minutes as they drove.

'What did he say about it? I'm guessing that's what the raised voices were about.'

Rose mumbled, 'I haven't spoken to him about it yet.'

Walter put his hand on the dashboard and turned to face Rose again. 'You haven't? Why not? It's not good to let these things fester on.'

Rose was thankful they had reached the turning for Paws. 'Right. Here we go, Walter. Sit tight and I'll come round and open the door.'

Once Walter had extricated himself from the car with the help of the walking stick to lever himself up, he straightened his jacket and brushed a hand over his hair.

Rose smiled to herself as she thought of *First Dates*. Maybe there should be a programme like that for people and prospective pets. After the day she'd had, it was a tonic to be around something positive.

'Right. Lead on, Rose.'

Having collected the key from Reception, Rose led Walter to Harold's area. As ever, he was sitting tall, surveying the world around him through half-closed eyes.

'Well. I've heard a lot about you, Harold. It's nice to meet you at last.'

Harold shifted his gaze to Walter but remained silent.

Rose unlocked the door and laid a few treats in Walter's hand.

'Just put them on the floor for him.'

Walter did so, grunting as he straightened himself. After several seconds of studiously ignoring them, Harold stood and stretched, arching his body, and ambled towards the treats, eating them as a loud purr signalled his pleasure.

'Harold. This is Walter. He's come to see you.'

Rose knelt and held out her hand, Harold came towards them, his gaze on Walter. He allowed her to smooth his back a few times before jumping up onto a raised area.

'Can I?'

'Of course. He's inviting you over,' Rose said. 'I've never seen him react like this before. He usually ignores everyone.'

'I think you and I have quite a bit in common, old timer.' Walter held out his hand as Walter sniffed and pushed his head into Walter's hand, prompting him to smooth his back.

Rose stifled a gasp. Harold was acting quite out of character.

112

'What would you think about coming to live with me? I can't promise much – it would be a fairly quiet life for the two of us.'

Harold purred loudly and rubbed himself against Walter's sleeve.

'I think you should take that as a yes.' Rose chuckled.

On the way home, Walter was animated as they discussed the things Harold would need once he moved in. Rose was sure her father would come and fit a cat flap, and she and Walter planned a shopping trip to get everything else.

Once Walter was at his door, he seemed taller and less frail. 'Thank you so much, Rose. I think Harold and I are going to be great house mates! Oh, and thank you for this.' He waved the stick in the air before disappearing indoors.

Chapter Sixteen

Rose's stomach fluttered with dread and excitement in equal measures to know what Dan had come up with. The message had simply said:

I've got some ideas. Same place tomorrow morning. 10 a.m.?

In spite of her reservations, she'd been pleased to hear from him and wanted to hear what he had to say. Since her session with Em at the salon, Rose couldn't get enough of fantasising about humiliating her. After all, it was all in theory. It wasn't as if any of it would actually happen.

Once they were settled with coffees, Rose could wait no longer. 'Well?'

Dan smiled. 'You're really up for this, aren't you?'

Rose drew her chair closer to the table and picked up her cup.

'You seem way more invested in your friend's book than I would expect. It's almost as if it's personal for you.'

Rose froze, the cup poised halfway to her mouth.

'Colin, Ang and Lucy aren't characters in a book. Lucy is Em, isn't she? You even showed me her social media page.'

He smiled and tilted his head, eyebrows raised, waiting for an answer.

'I...' Rose's brain refused to supply any words as his grey gaze immobilised her.

Then her mind burst into life with a terrible thought. It occurred to her that Dan might arrest her. She had more or less admitted that she wanted to plan a crime to entrap Em - to a police officer, of all people. Her throat closed and she gripped the sides of her chair as she waited, almost expecting him to produce a set of handcuffs then and then.

'It's okay.' Dan soothed. 'I get it.'

'What?' Rose stared at him.

'I get it. I'm with you on this, Rose. Lucy...Em, needs to be punished.'

Rose closed her mouth. 'But you're a police officer...' she couldn't finish the sentence

Dan finished it for her. '...whose job is to catch the bad guys, right?'

'Yes, but...'

'Let's say I'm prepared to go rogue sometimes, to catch the bad guys when the system can't. And Colin and Lucy have treated you badly. Colin has betrayed your trust and broken the promise he made to you when you got married. Em has lured him away and he has let her. They should both be punished.' Dan held up a hand as Rose went to interrupt. 'I know what you're going to say... That they haven't broken any laws. But the system would let them get away with it and that's not right.'

'But—'

Dan continued, ignoring Rose, almost as if she wasn't there. 'The main objective is to punish Em.' His eyes shone with excitement, and with a chill, Rose realised that he was enjoying this.

'Right...but—'

'But maybe give Colin a slap on the wrist at the same time? I think we should kidnap Colin.' Dan looked at Rose, as if suddenly remembering she was there.

Rose gasped. 'No!'

'I can't keep calling him Colin. What's his real name?' He shook his head impatiently.

'Olly, but—'

'Hear me out.' Dan held up his hand, palm towards her. He took a breath. 'I'll take Olly somewhere – just for a day or two. Don't worry, I'll look after him...or you can.'

He held up a commanding hand once more as Rose went to interrupt again. 'Now, here's the good bit – how we frame Em. You tell the police about their affair and tell them that Olly was going to finish it – but you believe she couldn't lose face in front of all her followers so she keeps him imprisoned somewhere. We could leave some useful DNA around. What do you think? Oh, and when Olly comes home, you tell him he's got to corroborate the story or else...'

'Or else what?'

'Or else you'll leave him. I could add another little incentive if it would help.'

Dan leant back in the chair, a satisfied smile on his face.

Rose felt as if she had slipped into some kind of parallel universe where arranging to have your husband kidnapped was a normal occurrence. She struggled to get her head around what Dan was proposing.

'So let me get this right. Your plan is that we...you, actually kidnap Olly and say that the kidnapper is Em?'

'That's it in a nutshell. What do you think?' Dan raised his eyebrows.

'I think you're mad! For a start, Olly is not just going to allow himself to be "kidnapped" and he's not going to incriminate Em just because you or I tell him to. You don't know him like

I do – he's obviously not perfect, but he's still a kind, honest man.'

'I wouldn't say that having an affair was particularly honest, would you?'

Rose ignored the question and stared at the table, resting her head in her hands. Why was she even discussing this with him?

'Come on, Rose. Think about it. Em will fall straight into the trap. Her weak spot is that she needs to impress her followers with this new man at all costs. What better way to hang on to him than to keep him prisoner?'

'It all just sounds...ridiculous.' She glanced around the coffee shop at the other patrons enjoying a relaxed morning coffee. Did they know what was going on right in front of them? Rose felt as if she was living in two worlds at once.

'I get that the plan is a bit rough around the edges at the moment. Give me some time to work out the details before you say no. There's no harm in looking into it a bit more. We won't be doing anything until you're happy with it.' He smiled. 'Just let me explore the idea, at least?'

An appealing vision of Em being led off in handcuffs with no make-up and her hair in a mess appeared in Rose's mind, and she wavered. Dan was right – she did want Em to suffer. Surely there was no harm in just 'exploring' the idea, as Dan said.

Rose stood to go. 'I'll think about it.'

Dan's smile broadened. 'Let's meet again next week and pool our ideas.' He paused. 'I don't think we should meet here, though. Let's meet at my place. We don't want to run into people either of us might know.'

Rose felt a twinge of unease. 'No I'm not happy about doing that.' She paused. 'I'm happy to take the risk and meet here again.'

'You might be, but I'm not.' He smiled through the chill in his voice.

Rose felt cornered. What could she say? She should walk away from all this right now, but something was stopping her.

'Think how good you'll feel when she's in handcuffs, humiliated like she made you feel. Then she would be the one on the outside.'

How could he know about that feeling? Rose thrust the thought to one side. She had got quite good at resurrecting that date-night-photography-studio-salon feeling now and could almost raise it at will. She waited for it to wash over her now and enjoyed it when it came.

Chapter Seventeen

‘**P**oppy, wait!’

Rose pushed against the door as Poppy went to close it.

‘Please. I’m sorry. Please hear me out.’

Rose felt the pressure ease on the door and stood back. ‘Come on. Please let me in.’

Poppy stood aside, her mouth set into a thin line.

‘You know, I never realised how little you understood of what I’ve been through these last few years. All the times I thought you had my back...’ her breath caught in a sob ‘...and you were secretly blaming me.’

‘No, Pops. Of course I wasn’t! What Vic did was cruel and terrible, and maybe I’m only just learning what that hurt feels like, and I...I don’t know...but I want Olly back.’ Rose couldn’t hold the tears back. ‘I’m so sorry. I don’t know what’s happening to me. It’s like I’m in a nightmare.’ She clung on to the banister and sobbed.

‘Oh Rose.’ Poppy threw her arms around Rose and held her tight.

‘And I’m sorry for being so prickly. But I think you’re beginning to understand that feeling now.’

Rose nodded her head against Poppy’s shoulder.

'Come on. We need something stronger than coffee. The kids are at Vic's tonight so we can get lathered.'

Rose wiped her eyes with the backs of her hands and tried to control the sobbing breaths.

Poppy put an arm around her shoulders and led her into the kitchen where she took a bottle of wine out of the fridge and poured two glasses. She passed one to Rose as they sat at the table, Poppy pushing a pile of washed laundry to one side.

'Poppy and Rose, forever!' Poppy held up her glass and clinked it against Rose's.

'I've missed you so much, Pops.' Tears threatened again but Rose swallowed them back.

'Me too. Every time you messaged or rang, I wanted to reply, but... I don't know... I suppose I was angry at you and ...

Rose reached across the table and took Poppy's hand. 'You were right. You needed to let me know how much I'd hurt you. I'm so sorry, Pops.'

Poppy took a large mouthful of wine, swallowed it, and sighed in appreciation. 'No more mushy stuff. I'm just glad we're okay.' She put the glass on the table. 'So come on. What's been happening? Have you been doing any more online stalking?'

'I'm beginning to become a bit obsessive,' Rose admitted with a chuckle. There's this one picture...'

'Oooh show me!'

Rose scooted her chair around the table, glass of wine in one hand.

'O.M.G. she's actually posted a selfie with Olly!'

Poppy turned to Rose. 'Ohh Rosy.'

'Look at what Jaz commented though. It was the other day when I had to endure two hours of putting in her new extensions.' Rose opened her phone and indicated the post she'd written while Em was in the salon.

Poppy gasped. 'I can't believe you, of all people, did that! While she was actually in the salon!' She made a bowing movement towards Rose. 'Welcome to the bad-ass womens' club.'

As Poppy refilled their glasses, she exclaimed, 'But why didn't you get someone else to do it? I wouldn't have been safe with those sharp scissors if it had been me!'

'Well, talking about Em not being safe, you know what we said about DNA and framing Em for a crime?'

'Oh Rose. Not that again!'

Rose moved the base of her glass in a circle on the table. 'Remember Dan?'

'Oh God! You didn't actually go and meet him, did you?'

Rose turned to Poppy. 'I had to know what he thought. I just can't get the idea of making Em pay out of my head and it's wasn't doing any harm to pretend it was research for a book.'

'That the author of hadn't turned up.'

Rose bit her lip.

'Oh Rose, he would have seen through you in a second. You're hopeless at pretending – I should know. Whenever we got into trouble it was always you who let the cat out of the bag.'

'He knows the truth. But he understands and thinks like I do that Em should be punished. He's come up with a plan.' The words tumbled out before Poppy could object.

'What? He knows? God, Rose! How many times have you seen him? Why haven't you said anything?'

'I couldn't exactly tell you as you haven't been returning my calls.'

Poppy was silent for a few moments. 'I don't know what's going on with you any more, Rose. Why can't you have it out with Olly? You said you needed to know for sure before you did anything and now you do, so why haven't you confronted him about it?'

'I can't. I just can't bear the thought of that conversation because it will shatter everything. Things will be said that can't be unsaid. If I can just break the spell Em has over him and get Olly back – we'll never have to have that conversation and can get back to being us.' Rose was conscious of her voice growing louder as she became more agitated. She shifted on her chair. 'And before you say it, I know Olly has changed. I know it won't be the same. But with her out of the picture, at least we have a chance.'

Rose looked out of the kitchen window and studied Jasper, Poppy's cat, sitting on the window sill. He stared back at her through the glass. She couldn't bear the thought that Poppy didn't understand her, that she was judging her, that her best friend didn't have her back.

As if reading her thoughts, Poppy sighed and said, 'Okay, so tell me about this plan.'

'Well – it's not anything really at the moment – just the idea to use Em's DNA to frame her for something.'

'Oh God! Not this again.' She stopped abruptly and Rose could see that Poppy was making great efforts to be patient and listen.

'He knows all the procedures.'

'Exactly! He's in the police force, Rose!' Poppy studied her. 'Why would a serving police officer even begin to get into a conversation like that? To encourage you?'

Rose felt a prickle of panic curl in her stomach.

'What if he's luring you into a trap? Secretly recording your conversations or something?'

'I need to do something, Poppy! You've got to understand. And at the moment, he's the only one who *does* understand.'

Sensing that she was on thin ice, Rose took Poppy's hand. 'I'm not getting at you, babe. I know you've got my back. You're just looking out for me.'

Poppy drew her into a hug. 'Just be careful. And yes, I am looking out for you. Just tell me you won't see him again. Promise.'

Rose had no answer.

Rose put all her effort into relaxing – trying to focus on the whole body relaxation exercise she had learnt on her de-stress app. But her mind wouldn't obey and kept jumping here there and everywhere, always returning to the same dilemma – what to do about Dan and his plan. She envied Olly, sleeping peacefully next to her, with a spark of anger. How unfair was it was that he, who had caused all this, wasn't suffering like she was? Much as she tried, it was getting harder to conceal her anger while she was around him.

Things had gone from bad to worse when she'd got home, earlier.

Olly had been sitting at the kitchen table, her lap-top open in front of him. Normally this wouldn't have bothered Rose. Although they'd always respected each other's privacy, they'd never had anything to hide before.

'What're you doing?'

Olly shut the lap-top abruptly. 'Why? You got something to hide?'

Rose felt the tell-tale flush in her cheeks.

'So who's the guy then?' He crossed his arms, staring at her.

'What guy? I don't...'

'Oh come on, Rose. Take a look.'

Olly passed her his phone and Rose's breath caught in her throat at the image of her and Dan, deep in conversation at the coffee shop.

'What, so you're spying on me now?'

'Euan saw you both and thought it was strange, so he took the photo. He was being a good mate,' he added defensively.

She played for time and sat down at the table, forcing herself to face him. 'You know Poppy's always had this idea to write a book. She's planned it out but is a bit stuck with police stuff. He's a police officer who happens to be a client of mine so I put them in touch. But when it came to it, she didn't turn up – I felt like a right dick.' She managed a thin laugh.

'How come you never said?'

There was that flicker of anger again. 'Since when I do I have to tell you everything I do?'

Rose got up and ran a glass of water at the sink. 'I don't ask you about everyone you meet.' She paused. 'I trust you.'

She side-eyed him and saw the brief tightening of his jaw. A sure giveaway that the arrow had hit its mark.

He stood abruptly. 'This is ridiculous. I'm going to bed.'

Rose had sat for a long time, listening to Olly moving around upstairs. The tension was unbearable and everything in her was pushing her to run upstairs, apologise, and make everything alright. But anger kept her rooted in place. Why should she?

The obsession with Em seemed to be infiltrating every part of her life – even causing her to fall out with Poppy. The frightening thing was she didn't seem to be able to control it – it had a life force all of its own that was taking her over and making her into a different person.

When eventually she had crept upstairs, undressing in the dark, Olly had been asleep.

Before Em, Olly would have laughed Euan's photo off – knowing there would be a good reason for it. But would there? Before Em, Rose couldn't imagine a reason why she would have even been meeting someone like Dan outside of work.

Rose abandoned the relaxation attempt and turned on her side. She needed to get Em away from Olly, away from all of them. Then things could get back to normal. She knew now that things would never be like they were. Poppy was right. She and Olly had outgrown the childlike, naïve, trust their relationship had been built on and they would have to reinvent it into something more realistic. Olly had changed – she couldn't do anything about that – and in some ways she was glad for him. She was changing too, but what she might change into was the scary thing. She didn't know. But first she had to deal with Em.

She would meet Dan and in the meantime think about how their plan might work without causing any upset for Olly. At least she would be doing something positive and constructive to sort this mess out. There was no way she would agree to his whacky idea though – it would have to be something less dangerous. Less criminal.

Chapter Eighteen

H arold crouched down in the cat carrier emitting an occasional throaty cry, voicing his disapproval of such an undignified mode of travel.

Walter patted the carrier with his hand. 'I know you don't like it, Harold, but we're nearly there now and then we can get you out of this thing.'

Rose glanced across and smiled, glad that she had managed to do something good. She had high hopes for Harold and Walter.

Once they arrived at Walter's house, Rose took the carrier and held it as Walter levered himself out of the car. As they walked up the path, Harold began to scratch at the carrier and make mewing sound that became more frantic as they went into the house.

'It's almost as if he knows he's home, and can't wait to get out,' Walter said as Rose lifted the carrier onto the kitchen table. With trembling fingers he released the catch and a ginger blur sped past them and scrambled up the shelves causing cups and saucers to rock and rattle. From the top shelf, Harold crouched and glared at them with his green eyes, growling under his breath.

A solitary plate fell to the floor with a crash but Harold didn't flinch.

'He's mad at me. But then I'd be mad if someone bundled me into a cage and took me off somewhere without my permission. I think I might break a plate or two in protest, too.' Walter sat heavily and looked at his new houseguest. 'I'm sorry Harold.'

'How about we put down some food for him and then leave him to get his bearings?' Rose suggested. 'I don't think he's going to move while we sit here staring at him.'

'You're probably right, Rose.'

The sound of hammering echoed through the kitchen and Harold seemed to shrink into himself, trying to make himself smaller by squeezing back against the wall.

'Let's leave him for now. I'll get the stuff out of the car and put a litter tray down for him. Maybe you could go and see how Dad's getting on with the cat-flap.'

'Good thinking, batman. The least I can do is offer your father a cup of tea for all his hard work.'

As Walter got to his feet, Rose said, 'We just need to make sure we keep all the doors shut until Harold feels more settled.'

Walter gave a mock salute as he headed for the back door.

As Rose was unlocking the car, Olly drew up.

'Just getting Harold settled with Walter,' Rose called.

'Right.' Olly went into the house without looking at her. Rose sighed. It was going to be a long evening.

It took several trips to ferry all Harold's accoutrements into the house. Walter had splurged at the pet store and they had come away laden with various soft toys laced with catnip, a scratching post, comfy bed in the shape of a little house – 'He'll need his own space,' Walter had said – a litter tray with two bags of litter, and various tins of expensive cat food and some treats.

She smiled at the pile in the hallway before extracting the litter tray and some cat food. Opening the kitchen door gingerly, she crept in and set up the litter tray and put a few treats in a saucer on the floor. Harold stared at her, unblinking, from his vantage point on the top shelf.

Out on the back step, her father was deep in conversation with Walter about the best time to plant out begonias.

'How's Harold doing?' her father asked as she sat on the step watching him clear away his tools.

'Still protesting. But he'll come round once he realises he's on to a good thing.'

'I'll go in and put the kettle on and just carry on as if he's not there.' Walter chuckled. 'Tea okay for you, Bob, and coffee for you, Rose?'

'Lovely, thanks, Walter. I've worked up quite a thirst,' her father replied with a mock gasping sound. As Walter carefully opened the kitchen door, closing it quickly behind him, he came and sat beside her on the step. 'That was a brainwave, matching Walter with Harold.'

Rose nodded. 'D'you know, I think I can see a change in Walter already. He seems to have a new lease of life. More energy.'

'He's become a lot more frail since I last saw him, though. I'll ask Mum to cook him a few meals that he can put in the freezer. I assume he does have a freezer?'

'Yes, I think there's one in the larder. That would be great, because I'm not sure how much he's cooking for himself. I've a feeling he might be eating mostly sandwiches with the occasional boiled egg, especially now he's not getting to the shop. Although Olly and I drop in some groceries when we do a big shop.'

'Talking of Olly. What's wrong, Rose?'

She looked at him. 'What do you mean?'

'Something's not right. You're not yourself. What is it?'

Rose looked down, moving her foot to and fro on the ground.

'You know, you used to do that when you were small and didn't want to tell us something.' Her father nudged her arm with his.

'Come on, Rosy Posy. What is it?'

Rose stood. 'I'm not a little girl anymore, Dad. Stop calling me that.'

'Rose?' There was alarm in his tone now as he looked up at her.

Rose felt that she would explode and shatter into tiny pieces if anyone else asked what was wrong. Deep down, she knew that it was because they cared but she couldn't find a way to acknowledge that. Couldn't bring herself to talk about how she felt in a way that any of them would understand.

'I can sort out my own problems. Can you stop prying!'

She strode into the kitchen where Harold was now gobbling treats from the plate. 'I think we've established a rapport,' Walter said, smiling. 'I've made the drinks.'

Bob inched through the door, a bag of tools over his shoulder. 'Sorry, Walter, but I've got to be going, I forgot I promised Jane I'd be back in time to collect Fern and Harry from school.'

'I'll have to have that tea another time.'

'Oh, I understand. Thank you so much for doing this today, Bob.' Walter tried to hide his surprise.

'See you tomorrow evening, Rose?'

Rose said nothing as her father hesitated before giving her a brief peck on the cheek.

Once the front door had closed Walter and Rose sat in uneasy silence as Harold munched his way through the treats.

'Is everything alright between you and your father?' Walter put his cup down carefully.

'Yes fine. He was in a rush. He'd forgotten the time,' Rose lied.

When she left Walter's after helping him to set things up for Harold, Rose saw that Olly's car had gone. Relief was all too quickly followed by suspicious dread.

She hurried indoors and opened the app on her phone. He was at ProFit. Quickly moving to Em's socials, she could see posts showing off her new extensions.

Emanuelle is a magician with my hair!

Rose, used to these posts by now, scrolled on down.

Getting ready for a night out with my man.

This was accompanied by a video showing Em trying on various skimpy outfits, pouting and batting her eyes to the camera.

Rose clutched her phone as her whole body tensed and tightened.

Jaz: *Looking just like the cheap whore you are. Everything about you is fake – your hair, boobs, lips, and anything else you can think of. What kind of man would lower himself to your level?*

Rose pressed Send before she thought better of it.

She stared at the message and then at the photos on the walls around her. Who was she becoming? The old world was disintegrating around her and she didn't know what to do about it. Her fragile belief that Em was lying about the whole thing had faded days ago. There was no doubt about it now. They were planning to meet tonight.

The silent house seemed to have absorbed the tension of the last few weeks. It didn't feel like her and Olly's special place now. Rose drew up her knees and leant her head on folded arms. With her eyes closed, she was lost in a dark maze, clutching at straws and taking random turnings. There was no good ending to this, just an endless, circular torment. Maybe Poppy and Walter were right, she should talk this out with Olly instead of going down rabbit holes trying to get him to break up with Em and making her pay. And Jaz? How could she have turned into someone like that? Rose burned with shame. And she would have nothing more to do with Dan and his mad schemes. Hopefully she wouldn't hear from him again.

Feeling more positive, Rose picked up her phone. Olly was on the move. Grabbing her keys she rushed out to the car, set on catching him up, ignoring the part of her that reasoned she should leave it. Her good intentions of a few minutes ago evaporated and disappeared in an instant. She had to know. It was like an addiction where there was never enough knowing.

By now, Olly was on the ring road and heading towards Nottingham. Rose fumed as every traffic light turned red as she approached. A heavy feeling of dread settled in her stomach as she eventually turned into the budget hotel car park and spotted Olly's car and, beside it, Em's Kia.

Rose sat, imagining the scenario unfolding in the hotel room, tormenting herself with every detail. She knew she should drive away, but her body wouldn't respond, refusing to start the car. Staring at the rows of identical windows, she tried to guess which room they were in. There were at least ten with lights on. Would they have kept the lights on? She clutched her hair with both hands and squeezed her eyes shut, tears making their way down her cheeks, until everything ached and her legs were numb.

Eventually Rose had to move, not knowing or caring how long she had been sitting there, letting her body hold the tension. Opening the car door, she got out and walked a few steps, holding onto the side of the car as the blood started to flow and feeling returned to her legs. She kept her back to the windows.

Hearing her phone signal a message, she leant back into the car and retrieved it from the passenger seat.

Hi Ang/Rose Lots of ideas to run by you. Here's my address. Come after work tomorrow? Dan. Smiling emoji.

Looking up at the clear sky, Rose tried to make out some of the constellations. She'd had a Ladybird book of the night sky when she was little and had known how to identify quite a few. But now, she couldn't make sense of the bright pinpricks of light.

She turned back to the hotel and felt a visceral hatred deep inside, banging the roof of the car with a clenched fist. How dare Em do to this to her again, steal Olly and flaunt it in front of her very eyes, humiliating her!

Re-reading his message, Rose knew she would go and see Dan. Maybe he might have come up with a workable plan, although in that moment, Rose would go to any lengths to make Em pay, legal or not. After all, he was the only one who really understood how she felt and that must count for something. What she would give to see Em humiliated, to be the one on the outside with nothing, looking in on her and Olly, safe, together in their own world.

Chapter Nineteen

R ose turned into the sprawling development on the edge
of town which had sprung up over the last year or so.
The developer's signs referred to it as The Belford Quarter.

'Anybody'd think we were in San Francisco,' Shona had
scoffed when the development had been announced. 'Why
not just call it what it is, the Belford estate?'

'Because if they stick the word "Quarter" on it, they can
bump the prices up,' Chrissie had said. 'We looked at some of
those houses, gardens like handkerchiefs – such a rip-off.'

As she drew up outside the house, Rose noticed two cars
parked nose-to-tail on the small drive. It hadn't occurred to
her that Dan might live with someone. For some reason she'd
assumed he lived on his own – just like she had with Em. She
felt reassured by the presence of a second car, though.

Dan opened the door as soon as she rang the bell – almost
as if he'd been standing right there, waiting.

'Come in.'

A tall, willowy woman appeared behind him and held out
her hand. 'Hi, I'm Sal.'

Rose's initial relief at the presence of another woman was
tempered by uncertainty. Since when did women shake hands
with one another when they met? This felt more like a business transaction.

Rose pushed the feeling away. 'Hi, I'm—'

'Rose. Yes, Dan's already told me. Shall we?' She indicated a room off the hall.

There was no offer of a drink.

Dan spoke for the first time. 'I've filled Sal in on the plan so far.'

'You didn't tell me you were married.' Rose said as she took a seat on the low settee.

'Oh,' He chuckled. 'Sal's not my wife. She's more...let's say, a business partner.'

This didn't feel right at all. Suddenly Rose didn't want to hear Dan's plan or have anything to do with him and this...Sal, whoever she was. Now she was here, in his presence, her need for revenge on Em took a back seat as a different emotion took over.

Fear.

A claustrophobic fear of being trapped. She should never have agreed to come here.

'Actually, you know what? I've changed my mind.' She stood up in an ungainly motion from the low seat. 'I don't think this is for me, after all. Thanks for all your ideas and everything, but—'

'Whoa! Hang on! Do you think you can walk away from this now?' Sal's tone was hard as steel.

'Just watch me.' Rose hurried to the front door only to find it wouldn't budge. A vague recollection of hearing a key turn in a lock as she'd entered the hall a few minutes earlier trickled into her mind.

She turned to find Dan standing a few feet away.

'Open this door. Now!' A flush of panic flooded her body.

'Come and sit down. You're not going anywhere until we've sorted this out.' Dan smiled and softened his tone. 'Come on, Rose. No need for the melodrama.'

Grabbing her arm he steered her back into the lounge and pushed her down onto the settee. Rose instinctively moved forward and perched on the edge of the seat, poised for flight.

'You see, the thing is, Rose. We can't let you just walk away. Not now – you know too much.'

'But you said—' she glanced at Dan '—that no one would believe me anyway.' When neither Sal nor Dan replied, she added, 'I won't say anything to anybody, I promise. Let's just forget all about it.'

'Ah but it's not that easy, Rose.' Sal sighed and clasped her hands. 'You see we've already started making preparations and certain commitments have been made.'

'But I never agreed to anything!' Rose protested.

'If I remember rightly, you came to me, no?' Dan tipped his head to one side.

'But—'

Sal seemed suddenly impatient. 'Let's stop messing about here. You are going to be part of this.' She turned to Dan. 'Did I tell you I saw Rose's sister-in-law, Becca at the school the other day with those two cute little children? Fern and Harry, isn't it?'

'What—'

Rose couldn't complete the sentence before Sal continued, her voice now silky smooth. 'I think she gets the message now, don't you?' Sal turned to Dan.

'Yup! I think she does.' He crossed his legs and leant back into the armchair, smiling.

Rose's only coherent thought was that she had to get out of there, and if she had to go along with them until they were happy to let her go, she'd do it. There was no way these two were going anywhere near her family.

She held up her hands in defeat. 'Okay. I get it.'

'Good. Now we can all relax.' Sal gave a satisfied, feline smile.

Rose felt her real life slipping away out of focus. Was it only less than a week ago she'd been playing Giraffes and Ladders, with Fern and Harry safe at home?

'Right.' Dan was suddenly businesslike. 'We all know the outline of the plan.'

Rose nodded. She would agree to anything to get out of there.

Dan continued. 'So the outline is that we make Olly disappear *somehow*.' He glanced at Rose. 'Tell the police he's been kidnapped and frame Em.'

'I'm not agreeing to Olly being kidnapped.' The words slipped out, unbidden, and Rose gripped the edge of the seat, annoyed with herself.

Dan sighed. 'But that's the point of the whole plan.'

'Olly can disappear another way.' Rose realised that if she was too compliant they would be suspicious, so maybe some resistance was a good thing, after all.

'How? In a way that's going to look convincing. Come on. What's your plan, then?'

'I don't know. I haven't decided yet,' Rose muttered.

Dan spoke. 'I've got a little holiday caravan on the coast – I could take him there. It would only be for a week at the most. It would almost be like he was having a holiday.'

Dan fixed her with a gaze before continuing. 'We can place a couple of strands of Em's hair around the place. You could get a mug that she's drunk out of from work – we could put that in the caravan too...'

'But Olly will know that it's not Em!'

'I'll wear a mask – disguise myself. We could say Em paid someone. We already have helpers lined up who are only too happy to earn a few bob, babysitting. Isn't that right, Sal?'

Sal smiled but remained silent.

'No! No! You're mad!'

Dan's silence caused a familiar tickle of fear in Rose's stomach but she had to stay strong. Act a good part, as if she was really on board with this madness. 'Even if we did that. Olly would still never say that it was Em. It wouldn't work. It's ridiculous.'

Dan leant forward resting his elbows on the arms of the chair. 'I obviously underestimated how much you want to punish Em – to get her out of your lives. You obviously don't have the guts to go through with it. So what will you do instead? Have it out with him? Become the nagging wife and push him into her arms? Divorce him? Start again?' His eyes bored into her.

Rose couldn't stop the tears forming in her eyes. She could no more imagine life without Olly than flying to the moon.

She brushed some strands of hair back into the clip. 'But Olly would never say that it was Em. He would tell the truth.'

Dan spoke slowly and deliberately, placing his fingertips together. 'If he was blindfolded and heard her voice, he wouldn't know that she wasn't actually there. It's easy enough to make Em say anything with AI. A hint of her perfume and hey presto!'

It all fell into place. Suddenly, Rose could see how the plan might work. It horrified her. But what if this was the only way to get Olly back? To make him see the mistake he was making. To turn him against Em. Maybe Dan was right about one thing – the more she confronted him, the more he'd run to her.

'So what would I need to do?' She swallowed.

'Nothing much. My helper will look after Olly and I know someone who can create an AI voice avatar copy of Em. There is so much footage of her talking that they'll be spoilt for choice – a regular gold mine of vocal sounds. You need to collect a few strands of Em's hair and a mug that she's drunk out of. Make sure it's just a run-of-the-mill mug – nothing identifiable as coming from Cutting It Fine.'

Rose couldn't think of anything to say – it all seemed to be falling into place too easily. She reminded herself that she was only going along with it so she could get out of the house. None of it would actually happen – she'd make sure of it.

'Oh and you'll need to report him missing, which won't be difficult, because he really will be missing.' Dan chuckled to himself. 'I think I'm going to enjoy this.'

Again, that curl of fear wormed its way through Rose's stomach and she felt a chill run through her entire body.

'You okay?' Dan's tone was not caring.

'Fine. But I need to get back now.' The urge to get out of the house was almost overwhelming.

'Just get things together your end, and I'll let you know when we're ready to go.'

Rose heard Dan speaking as if from far away. She couldn't get back to her car fast enough.

Chapter Twenty

R ose wished that she didn't have to go to the family date night, tonight of all nights. Her hands were still shaking as she clung on to the steering wheel. But if she didn't go there would be even more questions. As it was, she didn't know how she was going to face her dad after what she'd said at Walter's. It was becoming increasingly hard to hold things together. Her head was in a whirl and she needed to sit quietly at home and sort out how she felt. Things had been hectic at the salon as Abby had been off sick and she'd been functioning on autopilot for most of the day, and then there had been that nightmare visit to Dan. Now that Rose was alone in the car, exhaustion overwhelmed her. It was all too much. Em would have been impressed with the amount of make-up she'd had to wear today to hide the shadows under her eyes.

The initial relief of escaping Dan's house was wearing off and she was left with the reality of the situation. Dan and Sal appalled her. What was she doing? Poppy had been right, she had let things go way too far. And yet... And yet she couldn't deny the thrill and exhilaration of the thought of getting her own back on Em, but only if she pushed everything else out of her mind for a few moments – like the threat to her family. Maybe it was easier to play along for now, to keep Dan happy until she could think of something else. It was the best way to keep her family safe.

All too soon, she turned into her parents' road. She wasn't ready to face them yet so she pulled over and parked a little way up the road. She needed more time. What if she blocked Dan and ignored his messages? Maybe he would go away. But she had a feeling that he wouldn't, not now Sal was involved, and she might risk putting her family in danger. What had she done? Rose felt herself being sucked further into the dark maze her life had become.

She jumped at a sharp rap on the window.

'God, What the hell, Pete!' Her heart thumping, Rose couldn't hide her exasperation with her brother.

'Woah!' He stepped back, raising his hands. 'What're you doing parked here?' He leaned into the window. 'Are you okay, Rose? What's going on?'

'I'm fine!' Rose huffed and put the car into gear. 'Just needed a moment, that's all. It's been mad-busy today at the salon.'

There was the usual hub-bub of greetings, in jokes and teasing as Rose, Pete and Becca arrived. But the warm, cosy blanket feeling that Rose usually felt on Wednesday evenings had unravelled. She felt as if she was on the outside, looking in on her family, no longer part of it. She had never felt so lonely. Fern and Harry were having a sleepover with their other grandma, for which Rose was grateful. She didn't know how she could have faced them this evening.

As they sat to eat, Becca looked at Rose. 'Oh, I met your friend, Sal, earlier. She was outside the school. You've never mentioned her before. Apparently she's planning on sending her son there. She was looking around.'

All eyes turned to Rose. Her insides had turned to stone and she couldn't move, the fork motionless, half-way to her mouth.

'Rose? Everything alright?'

Her mother's worried tone brought Rose back to reality. She put the fork down and swallowed. 'Oh yeah. I know her from Paws. She comes and helps out sometimes.'

Finn gave her a worried, questioning glance that didn't escape their mother's eagle eyes.

'Right, you two. What's going on?'

Finn looked down at the table, a flush rising up his face. Rose came from a family of bad liars.

'Nothing. It's just...something I'm doing with Finn.' She took a breath. 'Nothing important.' She tried to keep the irritation from her tone.

'So what's the latest on your gig?' her father asked Finn, changing the subject.

Rose sent a silent thank you to him.

Finn didn't meet her gaze and seemed to be gripped by something outside the window. 'Er well we've got a running order organised – just need more practice now.'

Rose didn't miss the narrow-eyed look her mother gave him. Somehow normal service was resumed.

Once the others were clearing away, Pete cornered her in the hall. 'So come on, Rosy-Posy what's going on? You don't think I was taken in by Dad changing the subject, do you?' He shifted his feet and leant against the banister. 'What are you and Finn up to?'

'Stop calling me Rosy Posy! For God's sake!' Rose couldn't stop herself. She pushed past him, almost causing him to lose balance and ran up the stairs. In her old bedroom, she sat on the bed staring at the simple, uncomplicated life of her younger self.

All her Harry Potter books were still lined up on the small bookcase, and Taylor Swift and Adele were still adorning her walls, along with a montage of selfies and photos from the high school leaving prom. Fairy lights still framed the window. She turned them on and climbed onto the bed clutching a cushion to her stomach.

She remembered the excitement and joy she'd felt, sitting here the night before her wedding to Olly. Even though they'd been living together for a while, her mother had insisted on her leaving for the hotel from home. That kind of innocent happiness seemed a world away now. She closed her eyes and leant back on the bed, wishing she was still eighteen.

When she eventually summoned up the energy to go downstairs, Rose made an excuse about having a headache and tried to make a quick exit. But not before her mother caught up with her in the doorway. 'Come on, Rose, what's going on? You can tell me.'

Rose relaxed, just for a moment as she felt her mother's strong arms around her, but the sensation was fleeting and she pulled away.

'Are you pregnant?'

Rose gasped. Why did everyone think that the minute she was a bit different that she was pregnant?

'What? No!' She could feel the tears starting to form. 'Mum, I'm fine. It's just been a hell of a day and I need to get home.' She pulled away and got into the car and drove away without looking back. At the end of the road, glancing in the rear-view mirror she glimpsed her mother still standing on the step, watching her.

When she got home, the downstairs was in darkness. Putting on the lights and going into the lounge, she realised that Olly had already gone to bed. A feeling of despair crept over her. Em had poisoned their love. And she, Rose, had made things so much worse.

She crept up the stairs and, sure enough, Olly was in bed – snoring gently. She rubbed the skin on the side of her thumb. It was now raw and sore. The anger she felt somehow always loomed larger when she was in his presence – his casual indifference to her hurt made it difficult to be in the same room. And then there was the other evening when he had confronted her about her meeting with Dan – she clenched her teeth at the thought. And yet, the way his hair still curled into the nape of his neck and a hint of the dimple, evident even in sleep, could still make her heart swell with love.

She went back downstairs and turned the lights off. Sitting in the silent darkness was strangely soothing. She could just hear the faint hum of the Sky box whirring away in the corner. Vaguely she tried to remember what they were recording. It had been set in another life and seemed irrelevant now.

Rose went over her conversation with Dan and Sal for the hundredth time. She had to stop them, but how? She couldn't confide in anyone. If she went to the police she would incriminate herself, and would they even believe her? Especially as Dan was a police officer. She had to keep her family safe, whatever. As she sat, a plan began to form in her mind.

She needed to speak to Dan on his own.

We need to speak. Tomorrow at Holton Country park at 5? I can come after work.

She waited in the timeless darkness. Eventually the screen lit up.

Okay. Great. I've got more details. Smiley face emoji.

Rose sighed with relief that he hadn't insisted on meeting at the house again. This time things would be different. She would be safer...and in control.

Chapter Twenty-One

D an looked up, his lips forming a smile as Rose approached the picnic table.

'I was beginning to think you'd bailed on me. What would you like?' He indicated the mobile coffee van.

'Hot chocolate.' The last thing Rose wanted was a drink, but she needed a bit of space to get her head together – to summon her strength for what she was about to do. She hadn't planned on being late but Mrs Moss had been difficult to get rid of. Rose had already told Abby not to give her a late appointment again when there were no waiting customer to hurry things along and was annoyed at the oversight but hadn't been able to say anything as she was at college on Thursdays. In retrospect, Rose thought it was for the best, as she might have said things she would regret in her current jittery state. Taking the seat Dan had vacated, she ran her fingers through her hair, resting her head in her hands for a few moments and took several deep breaths, checking her phone was recording. As Dan waited for her drink she rehearsed for the hundredth time what she planned to say.

The spring sunshine filtering through the trees was warm on her back and strangely comforting. She made herself focus on it for a minute or two, as her wellbeing app suggested in times of stress. *Take yourself away from the situation and concentrate on something else – something calming if only for a minute.*

She felt Dan's presence as he returned, the picnic table shifting as he clambered to sit down.

'Thanks.'

Rose took a slow sip of her drink noticing that Dan was shading his eyes against the bright sunlight. She smiled inwardly – good move, Rose. Now it was time. She enjoyed the sweetness of the chocolate, savouring it. It would probably be the only sip she would have as she was not planning on staying long. Tucking a strand of hair behind her ear, she looked straight at Dan – it took every ounce of nerve she possessed.

'I'm not doing this, Dan. It's ridiculous. I'm not going to put Olly in danger. We're done, and I don't care what you or Sal threaten me with.'

Dan didn't respond, simply holding her gaze in a way that made the hairs on her arms stand up.

Rose knew she should get up and go, but she needed Dan to say something, to admit to his part in all this. She hadn't expected this oppressive silence. She had to get him to say more and willed herself to prompt him. 'I can't believe you're in the police force. If this is how the police behave, there is no law. You're just a glorified vigilante.'

As the silence continued, Rose's courage deserted her. She'd said what she needed to, and now she had to get out of there – away from him. She swung her legs around and stood beside the picnic table, reaching for her bag and the phone underneath it.

'Sit down!'

Rose felt a tremor pass through her body at the command. She couldn't do this. She had to go.

'No way! I'm out of here.' Rose began to walk away. She just wanted to get away from him. He couldn't physically stop her in a public place.

'As a police officer, I can have you arrested for perverting the course of justice.' Dan's voice was louder this time, his tone flat but at the same time menacing.

Rose stopped. The gaze of some of the occupants of neighbouring picnic tables turned in Dan's direction and then swiveled to her.

Could he arrest her? Rose couldn't take the chance.

An icy hand gripping her insides she returned to her seat, keeping her legs on the outside of the picnic-table bench.

'After all, I've witnessed you planning to frame an innocent person for a crime. All I have to do is take you down to the station and make a statement. And I have another witness in Sal.'

'But...but that was you. Not me. It should be me reporting you. And who the hell was Sal?'

'Ah, Sal' He spoke fondly. 'She's my go-to when I need someone to comply and keep on message. She can be very persuasive.' He licked his lips. 'Oh and maybe I should have mentioned that she is also a police officer.'

Rose knew she was cornered but was determined to put up something of a fight, even if only to get Dan to incriminate himself further.

'I'm going to the police. You can't do this!'

'Oh yeah? Who do you think the police would believe?' He took a sip of coffee. 'This is *my* plan. And this is what we're going to do.'

'No!' Rose hissed between clenched teeth. 'No way!'

'I don't think you have any choice now, Rose. You've passed the point of no return.'

This time it was Dan who stood, catching Rose off guard. 'I'll be in touch when I've got everything finalised, and let you know what you need to do.'

He turned back. 'Don't forget it's me doing all the hard work here – putting my neck on the line – you'll hardly have to do anything, except watch Em's life fall apart.'

Rose stayed, motionless, her mind unable to process what had just happened. She had a confession of sorts on her phone. Evidence that Dan was clearly threatening her. She should go to the police now, before things got any more out of hand. But then she thought – who would the police believe? Maybe recording someone without their permission didn't count. She needed more evidence. Why oh why had she been so stupid and naïve to confide in him with such a flimsy cover story? She should have listened to Poppy.

Rose stood, her legs feeling as if they might collapse. She clung on to the edge of the table.

'Is everything alright?' A passing dog walker stopped, concern in his voice.

'Yes. All good.' She forced a smile and walked steadily, putting one foot in front of the other, to the car where she gripped the steering wheel and stared across the carpark.

What had she unleashed in Dan? Whatever it was, she couldn't control it. Rose had never felt so alone – there was no one she could turn to, no one to help her. She couldn't even drag Poppy into this mess.

She had to get away from this place but couldn't go home. Not yet. She wouldn't be able to face Olly. She drove away from town to a fast-food outlet on the ring-road but instead of going in and ordering, she laid her head on the steering wheel and closed her eyes. Listening to the passing traffic, she tried to block everything out until she could think straight.

When Rose opened her eyes again, the road was quieter and the coffee-shop lights and been turned off. Looking at her phone she gasped as she saw the time. 12.30.

Had she actually fallen asleep? She got out of the car and took a few breaths as the full force of the nightmare returned, hitting her like a sledge hammer.

Returning to the car, she banged the door shut in frustration. Why had she wasted all this time? She needed to get to Olly and warn him – now! There was no knowing when Dan would put the plan into action.

Only as she was driving home did it occur to Rose to wonder why Olly hadn't messaged to see where she was. Even though things had been strained between them, he would still have been worried, surely?

Unless...

Rose felt bile rising into her throat. Unless she was too late.

Putting her foot down, Rose knew she had to get home – sod the speed limit.

Chapter Twenty-Two

R ose stifled a sob as she screeched to a halt outside their house. Olly's car wasn't there.

Leaving the car door open, she raced to the front door, fumbling with her keys before wrenching it open and rushing into the hall.

'Olly?'

She hurried through the downstairs rooms before taking the stairs two at a time, heading for their bedroom.

'Olly? Come on! Where are you?' Her voice ended in a desperate whine.

The house was strangely silent – the kind of silence that settles when no one is at home.

She rushed back downstairs and into the kitchen. This time, putting the light on, she saw Olly's phone. Snatching it up, she saw a note underneath it.

As you can see, I've not hung around. Now it's your turn, Rose. Tomorrow morning you go to the police and report Olly missing. Don't forget what that slut Em's done to you and how much you want her to pay. You can get Olly back and bring her down in one go. Not bad, eh? I need that DNA evidence – hair and the mug. Let me know when you've got it. Use the phone on the counter to contact me – do not use your own!

Rose saw a small phone on the counter beside Olly's. She couldn't bring herself to pick it up. She looked back at Dan's note.

BTW When you look at Olly's phone, you'll see that he invited Em to your house last night. Olly's phone was easy to hack into. Useful to have evidence of Em in your house. Olly was most helpful when I got here after she'd gone. It seems she was called away to her sister who was taken ill.

Rose screwed the note up and threw it across the room. The thought of Dan manhandling Olly was more than she could bear. Even though she knew Olly was strong enough to hold his own, Rose had a creeping fear that Dan wouldn't have come without backup – maybe Sal, or some other thug.

She took a breath and picked up the burner phone – she'd seen enough TV dramas to know what it was – and saw that there was only one number in the Contacts. She dialled the number. It rang once or twice and then the call was disconnected. Shaking the phone as if that would make the call connect, she tried again with the same result.

'*Damn you!*' she muttered through chattering teeth. Suddenly she was chilled to the bone, even though she hadn't taken her coat off. She grabbed a throw from the settee and wrapped it around her shoulders, pushing away the thought that Dan or one of his cronies might have touched it.

With shaking fingers she opened the doorbell cam app on her own phone and tried to scan back over the previous few hours, but was greeted with a *Data is not available* message. Of course, Dan was always one step ahead and wouldn't have left any evidence for her to find and use. She scrolled back further – the whole system had been wiped.

Remembering she had left the car door open, Rose hurried outside to close it. What should she do? Various possibilities flashed through her mind: Go to the police with the evidence she had? Too risky. She wasn't sure that she had enough – a recording on a phone could easily be discredited as being created using AI. Ring Poppy? No, she couldn't drag her into this, not at this time of night. Ring her parents? No, for the same reason. She had to deal with this alone.

Returning indoors and retrieving the crumpled note, she spread it out on the counter, regretting the creases her earlier reaction had caused. Opening the camera app on her phone she took several pictures before placing it carefully in a plastic bag. Maybe there would be DNA or fingerprints – a slim chance, but worth a try.

She re-read the whole message. She didn't have Em's DNA. She wouldn't have it until her next appointment, which was when...?

Her hands were shaking so much, it took Rose several minutes to log into the salon appointment diary.

She scrolled and bit her lip when she saw Em booked in for Saturday. Today was Thursday – she looked at the time – Friday morning. There was nothing she could do about it. It would look suspicious if she tried to bring it forward to today.

She struggled to type the message with shaking fingers.

I can't get the DNA until Saturday, when she next comes in!

The phone lit up with an instant reply.

Okay, well we'll just defer things a bit. Go to the police tomorrow and report Olly missing. Don't mention Em at this point – we need her to make the appointment on Saturday. Once she's been – go to the police and tell them you suspect her.

I'll collect the DNA from you at the Weldon motorway services car park. Then you can start messaging her – say you didn't want to say anything in the salon in front of the others, etc etc. Olly sends his love, by the way.

Where have you taken him?

Rose jabbed the message into the phone.

Best all round if you don't know.

Rose kept typing – if complying with what Dan wanted kept Olly safe, she would do whatever it took, and sod Em.

What do I say to the police?

Whatever you want. He's disappeared hasn't he? Tell everyone that, but don't mention the affair yet. Not until I have Em's DNA.

Without replying, Rose dropped the phone onto the counter. She opened a packet of crisps and poured herself a glass of wine. She kept eating and drinking until her hands stopped shaking.

She desperately wanted to phone Poppy but knew she couldn't.

How would she get through today?

Picking up Olly's phone, she remembered the now useless tracking app Finn had installed. Rose closed her eyes thinking about her little brother. She should never have involved him in this. She had been so swept along by her need to find out about Olly and Em, she hadn't thought about the implications for those around her. Looking through Olly's phone, she saw the earlier message, presumably written by Dan or one of his cronies.

Need to see you. Let's live dangerously and meet at mine!
Three red hearts

Rose gasped her hand over her mouth. She picked up her own phone and opened Em's socials. Rose was glad she was already sitting because here was her kitchen and lounge – Em and Olly together pouting at the camera. Em really had been in her house, only hours ago! Was there nothing she wouldn't stoop to? The anger she had felt a few weeks ago now returned in a flood of emotion – she hated Em with all her being, an emotion that would have been unknown to the Rose of a month or so ago.

She thought, biting her lip. However wrong and mad Dan was, he had a point. She did desperately want to get even with Em, even more so now. But how? How could she do this on her own? Now that he had Olly.

She replayed the recording of her earlier meeting with Dan. She could take this to the police now – this minute...but, apart from the evidence not being watertight, she couldn't bring herself to let Em off the hook that easily. The fact that she had responded to his request and had actually invaded her and Olly's home without a thought, using their place for her own ends, tipped the scales. She had crossed a line.

Rose closed the recording app. She would keep this as an insurance. Dan had promised that Olly would come to no harm, so maybe there was a way this could all play out as planned and she could get Olly back once he knew what Em was capable of.

She lay down on the settee covering herself with the throw and closed her eyes, not expecting to sleep.

Chapter Twenty-Three

B y the time early light filtered in through the curtains Rose was up and dressed, following a night full of dreams about Olly and Em together, laughing and tormenting her as she looked on through a glass partition. In the end it had been easier to get up and get ready. She'd already tried to contact Dan, her messages becoming increasingly desperate, asking whether Olly was alright, but he wasn't answering. She had no idea where he was keeping him other than the holiday chalet beside the sea he'd mentioned. That could be anywhere. She clung on to the fact that at least no harm would come to Olly, but even so, she would do anything to get him home. If he ever found out about her part in this, would he ever forgive her? That had been another nightmare – Olly finding out she had arranged his kidnap, and hating her, running to Em. Even now she was awake, it was all too real. Rose shook her head. She wouldn't go there...not now.

Several slices of toast generously spread with butter later, along with extra strong coffee, Rose watched the clock. She'd decided to wait until 9 o'clock to go to the police station – her stomach churned and she regretted the extra butter. Time crept at a snail's pace. She filled the minutes by scrolling through Em's socials. There was a flurry of comments on the photo of her posing in Rose's house.

Cool, M. Is that your house?

You both look stunning! Move over, Beckhams. They are so old-school!

Wow! Does Jay have a brother...or three?

Who is that in the photo on the wall behind you?

Rose examined the selfie again, zooming in. Behind them was a photo taken at her and Olly's engagement party. The two of them locked in an embrace.

Em was nothing if not thorough in editing her pictures and Rose was almost certain this was deliberate. Olly would have been oblivious, just thrilled to be in her presence, although... Rose looked at Olly again. She knew him so well, and yes, there was a hint of discomfort in his gaze. Not like the smouldering looks in the other image she'd seen.

Meanwhile, M had answered:

Thank you, guys. Your messages all mean so much. Several heart emojis followed this comment. *I've no idea who is in the pic on the wall – I didn't even notice. Maybe some old girlfriend of Jay's? Who knows. Yes, it's Jay's house, so now we're official.*

As she re-read the messages, more appearing all the time, Rose felt herself disappearing as if she was shrinking into a dot. She had become numb and couldn't feel anything, her emotions shrinking along with her sense of self. She would go and report Olly missing – at least she could do something to help get him back.

As Rose looked at the clock yet again, something on the shelf caught her eye. Olly's inhaler – he never went anywhere without it. How had she not noticed it last night? She tried to tamp down the panic rising in her chest by reassuring herself that he always kept a spare in the car.

Without hesitation, she grabbed the burner phone once more and punched in Dan's number. She had to tell him. Her fingers clutched the phone so tight that when she put it down with a sigh as it rang unanswered, they were difficult to straighten. A few minutes later she tried again, this time it rang for several minutes. He was messing with her like a cat toying with a mouse. She fired off a message.

Olly needs his asthma inhaler. There's one in the glove compartment of his car.

By ten to nine she could wait no longer and, grabbing her car keys, headed out. Walter was standing at the front gate. From the corner of her eye she saw Harold sitting on the doorstep. She had a fleeting sense that it was as if he had lived there for years.

'Notice your Olly isn't home... Rose. Is everything alright? Can I do anything?' He left the question hanging.

'No. no thanks, Walter.' Rose's brain refused to supply any further answer as she opened the car door.

'He was here last night though...when you were out.'

As she went to close the door, she caught the tail end of a sentence.

'... a blonde woman it was. She left in a rush.'

'Sorry Walter. I've got to go.' Rose's mind was laser-focused on getting to the police station.

Having parked in the first available space, she hurried to the desk – not needing to fake her panic and distress.

'I need to report a missing person. My husband is missing.'

The desk sergeant picked up a pen and without looking up asked, 'When did you last see him?'

'Yesterday before I went to work. But he didn't come home last night.' Rose fought to keep her voice steady.

The sergeant sighed and looked at her. 'I expect he'll be back today. Maybe just had a bit too much last night? You two had a row?'

Rose couldn't hide her annoyance at his casual tone. 'What? No! And he doesn't drink.'

'What's his name?' the sergeant spoke with a reluctant sigh.

'Oliver Walker. Everyone calls him Olly. And he doesn't have his asthma inhaler with him.'

Rose gave their address and details of ProFit as the sergeant entered everything into the system with slow 2-finger typing. Rose resisted the urge to lean across and type it in for him. He then recorded everything for a second time on a manual form.

'Right. If he hasn't turned up by tomorrow morning, let us know and we'll take things further.' The officer turned away to place the piece of paper in a tray behind him.

'Is Detective, Dan...' Rose faltered realising she didn't even know Dan's second name. She started again. 'Is a detective called Dan here?' The sergeant gave her a longsuffering look. 'I know him, that's all. Maybe he could help.'

'There's no one here called Dan, love.'

Without answering, Rose turned and left.

Sitting in the car watching the people of Weldon going about their everyday lives, Rose marvelled that life could carry on as normal for others while hers was falling apart. A few weeks ago, she'd been one of them – without a care in the world. Content with her life. But now...

She didn't know anything about Dan and had simply taken his word for it when he'd said he was a police officer. How stupid and naïve she had been! If he wasn't who he said he was, then who was he? Was Dan even his real name? Rose tried to remember how long he'd been coming to the salon – there had only been two or three appointments – six weeks, maybe?

And then a further thought followed hot on the heels of the previous one. She had no guarantee that Olly was safe. She didn't know where he was or who he was with. Panic and fear were now joined by a deep sense of shame. What had she done to her Olly?

Leaning her head back against the headrest, Rose closed her eyes. She would not cry, she didn't deserve to. She had to keep her head and find a way to get Olly back. She owed him that. It occurred to her that for the first time in her life, she was learning what it truly meant to have responsibilities and she had to learn fast.

Rose started the car before realising she was late for work and that she hadn't messaged Shona. Putting the handbrake back on, she took out her phone and groaned at two missed calls and several messages:

Everything ok, Rose? Your nine o'clock is here.

Followed twenty minutes later by:

Rose? Are you ill? Chrissie has done Mr Wills.

The last message had been about five minutes ago.

Rose took a deep breath and dialled the salon. Abby picked up the phone.

'Abby, it's Rose. Is Shona there?'

'Oh thank God, we were worried. Are you okay?'

'Something's come up. I need to speak to Shona.'

'Do you want me to reschedule your appointments?'

Rose struggled to keep her voice steady. 'No it's okay, I'm coming in now.'

'Rose? Where are you? Is everything okay?' Shona sounded breathless as she came on the phone, even though she had only stepped across the salon.

'Look, Shona. Olly's gone missing. He didn't come home last night.'

'Oh Rose. That doesn't sound like him! Have you been to the police?'

'That's where I've just been. Sorry I didn't let you know earlier, it's just that... I've been in a bit of a state...' Rose tailed off.

'Go home. We can manage, You—'

'No.' Rose cut her off. 'No. I'm on my way in.' And before Shona could object, Rose ended the call.

'Are you sure you should be here?' Shona passed Rose a mug of coffee as she hung up her coat ten minutes later.

'What else can I do? I'll go mad if I'm sitting at home staring at four walls.'

'Okay, but go easy and you can always change your mind, remember.' She gave Rose a one-armed hug. Abby's already washed Marjorie's hair so she's all yours.

Rose became aware that the salon was unusually quiet, everyone speaking in low voices, as if someone had died. Word travelled fast in a small workplace like Cutting It Fine. She decided to ignore it and strode over to Marjorie.

'Morning, Marjorie. Sorry I'm late.' Rose reclipped her hair, trying to sound business-like.

'I'm so sorry to hear about Olly, my dear.' Marjorie shook her head. 'So I'll let you off not washing my hair this time.' Rose sensed Marjorie might not be joking and didn't comment.

'So you've no idea where he is? How stressful, especially in your condition.' In the mirror, Marjorie looked meaningfully at Rose's stomach.

'I'm not—' Somehow Rose knew not to say the word. Even in denial, it would have been lighting a touch paper. Instead she changed the subject. 'Oh I'm sure it'll turn out to be something and nothing,' she said as she drew a comb through the wet hair. 'He's probably lost his phone or something and never thought to call. You know men,' she added with a grin.

'I do indeed.' Marjorie sighed. 'Still it's a worry until he turns up.'

As the morning went on, the tension seemed to dissipate from the salon, and by lunchtime things were more or less back to normal. They had taken their lead from Rose who had been herself as much as she could. She had endeavoured to keep everything on track by immersing herself in her clients. Fortunately she'd had a fully booked morning. It was the only way to cope – by pretending it wasn't happening. There was nothing else she could do.

At lunchtime she checked her phone and covertly looked at the burner phone. Both had been silent. She wondered if she should say something to her family. Word would soon spread and she didn't want them to hear from someone else. But she wasn't ready for that yet. She would ring them later, and if they heard something in the meantime, she'd play it down. Maybe even admit to a marital tiff as an explanation, although she remembered she'd already denied this to the police officer earlier.

The first of her afternoon clients appeared and Rose threw herself into work.

Chapter Twenty-Four

R ose dropped her bag in the hall as Poppy enveloped her in a hug. 'Oh my God! I can't believe it – this isn't like Olly.'

The tears Rose had been holding in all day fell freely as she sobbed into Poppy's shoulder.

When she'd got home after work, the house was still empty. Rose messaged Poppy knowing she couldn't stay in the empty house on her own, and Poppy had insisted that she come straight round. The children had been fed and were absorbed on various screens complete with headphones. 'I've given them an extra hour tonight,' she said, explaining the silence.

When Rose's tears were spent, she led her into the kitchen.

'You don't think... You don't think he's gone off with Em, do you?'

Rose stepped back and stared at Poppy.

'I mean... I know you don't think he would...' Poppy tailed off under the intensity of Rose's gaze.

How she wanted to tell Poppy everything, but if she was going to get Olly back and punish Em she had to play the game and, unwittingly, Poppy had just given her the perfect opening.

'I can't believe he would do that.' She sniffed. 'But I guess it's a possibility.'

'Have you looked on Em's socials?'

As Rose shook her head, Poppy strode over to the cupboards. 'I'm going to make us both a hot chocolate – cream, marshmallows, the works.' She tilted her head 'You know me, I always have these things ready – just in case of emergency, of course.'

'Of course,' Rose echoed, her mind already anticipating the intoxicating sweetness coming her way. How could she be thinking of enjoying something like a hot chocolate when Olly was missing?

'Okay, let's see what Em's been up to.' Poppy took a sip and placed her brimming mug on the table, wiping the cream moustache with a tissue.

Rose clasped her fingers around her own mug, savouring the warmth and comforting sweetness spreading across her tongue. She braced herself – she had to look surprised and horrified. She could do this! She could do anything to get Olly back.

'Oh My God!' Poppy leaned towards Rose, tilting her phone so Rose could see. She gasped and some marshmallow caught in her throat causing a coughing fit as she gasped for air. Poppy patted her on the back and urged Rose to take another sip.

As Rose peered at the photo she'd already seen, she didn't need to pretend to be upset. A wave of emotion rolled over her as if she was seeing it for the first time.

'Wait! Isn't that your house?'

Rose nodded, fresh tears rolling down her cheeks.

'And that's the photo from your engagement party on the wall behind them!'

'Yup.' Rose blew her nose into a tissue.

'What a bitch! This looks like it was taken last night!' She scrolled further down. 'Look at these comments!'

Poppy read further. 'I can't believe Olly actually invited her into your house! This doesn't seem like something he would ever do, Rose.'

'I think she's got him under some kind of spell.' It sounded lame to Rose, even as she uttered the words.

Suddenly Poppy turned to her. 'Where were you? Weren't you home last night?'

Rose studied the comments and answered without looking up. 'I had to go round to Pete and Becca's. We're planning something for Mum's birthday.'

'Hmm. He didn't waste much time, did he. Bastard!'

Rose's head jerked up at Poppy's comment but she bit her tongue. She couldn't say anything in Olly's defence, although everything in her was screaming for the truth to be told.

Poppy put an arm around her. 'I know it's hard, babe, but you can't pretend this is all her fault. Not now. And it can't be a coincidence that she was at your house the same evening he goes missing. She's got to have something to do with it. Have you been to the police?'

Rose nodded. 'They're not interested. If he's not back to-morrow, I've got to go back.'

Poppy huffed a frustrated sigh. 'For God's sake!' she muttered under her breath. After taking a sip, she place her mug on the table, turning suddenly to Rose. 'You need to take this social media post to the police!'

Rose nodded once more, saying, 'You're right. I will,' knowing that she wouldn't be doing anything until after Em's appointment in the morning.

As she sipped the hot chocolate realisation slowly dawned that Em was unknowingly incriminating herself with some of the comments she had made. Stupid, vain, Em.

He's all mine now, gang!

I'm never letting this one go.

Rose laid her head back against the cushion, suddenly spent.

Then Poppy asked the question she'd been dreading. 'Have you heard anything from that detective guy? Dan, something?'

'No.' the answer came almost too quickly.

'Come on, tell me. I know when you're lying, Rose Sugden.' Poppy fixed her with a stern look.

'I...I messaged him...just to say that I didn't want to see him again. That's all. Honest.'

Before Poppy could respond, Rose's phone rang.

'Rose! Oh my goodness. Why didn't you ring us last night?' Her mother sounded frantic. They'd been out when Rose had rung earlier, for which she'd been grateful. It meant she could leave a message without having to answer a barrage of questions.

She mouthed to Poppy that her mother was on the phone.

'I'm okay, Mum. Look, I'm just at Poppy's. I'm going home now and I'll ring you from there.'

'I need to get home. Mum's going mad.' Rose sighed as she put her coat on. 'Thanks for everything, Pops. I'm so lucky to have you.' She couldn't stop the tremor in her voice.

'Come here, you big softy.' Poppy gave her a hug and steered Rose towards the front door. 'I'm always here for you.'

Rose arrived outside her house to find her parents and Finn already there, waiting in their car. They jumped out as she arrived. 'Have you heard anything?' Her mother asked as Rose approached the front door, key in hand.

'No. I don't think the police are going to do anything until he's been missing at least 24 hours.'

She opened the door, giving her mother and father a quick peck on their cheeks as they came in. Finn wouldn't meet her eye.

'You needn't have come round, you know. There's nothing we can do.' Rose couldn't help the irritation in her voice. She didn't want to be around her family this evening. She just wanted to sit with her own thoughts which were running in increasingly frenetic circles.

'Can't you use the tracker Finn installed on his phone to find out where he is?'

Rose froze at the question from her father. She finished taking off her coat and hung it up without speaking. She turned and glared at Finn, feeling the inevitable flush on her cheeks.

'Sorry, Rosy,' Finn muttered, 'but when I knew Olly was missing I had to say something. It might be a way of finding him.'

She softened at his obvious discomfort. He was her little brother and she'd had no right to drag him into this mess. 'It's okay, Finn.' She gave him a smile.

As if reading her thoughts, her father said, 'I'm surprised at you, Rose, asking Finn to do such a thing. And he should have known better than to agree,' he added.

Rose felt herself shrivelling into something small under her father's disapproval. She stared at the floor. 'I know. I'm sorry, Finn. I don't know what I was thinking.'

Her mother broke in impatiently. 'The main thing is. Where is he?'

Rose led them into the kitchen, swiftly hiding the note and burner phone in a drawer. She pointed to Olly's phone. 'I can't track him if his phone is still here.'

Her mother gasped, her hand to her mouth. 'He wouldn't go anywhere without his phone!' She turned to Rose. 'What on earth is going on, Rose? Did you tell the police about his phone?'

Rose shook her head and found herself bursting into great sobs of despair. She had never felt more ashamed and worthless. Her father took her into his arms, his tone softer now. 'Come on, Rosy, we'll find him. He'll come back.'

His sympathy made Rose feel even worse – why couldn't she tell them the truth? Because she knew they would be horrified and shocked and there would be no coming back from that – she couldn't bear to be shut out from her own family.

She had to get Olly back, and the only way to do that was to follow Dan's instructions. It was the only way out of this mess.

Chapter Twenty-Five

Rose was at work early the next morning, thankful that Em was her first customer and that Shona had the day off. She didn't know how she would cope with Em and Shona, who missed nothing, in the same space. Wiping her palms on her leggings for the umpteenth time, she didn't know how she would react when she had to deal with Em face to face. Would she be able to keep up the act? To hide her anger?

After she had eventually persuaded her family to go home, the sleepless night which followed left Rose jumpy and irritable, and when oblivion had come it had brought dreams of Olly. Olly gasping for air, reaching for an inhaler that wasn't there. When she awoke, Rose tried to calm herself with the thought that Olly's inhaler would be in the car. Surely Dan or someone would have fetched it after her message. But deep down, she had real doubt about that. After all, who was Dan? Whoever he was, he certainly wasn't a police officer, so who knew what he was capable of?

Rose was desperate to get the DNA and get to Dan and get Olly back. Maybe he would bring Olly with him. After all, once he had the DNA, Olly would serve no further purpose.

Em was late and Rose was almost at breaking point when at long last the door opened and she appeared.

'Hi Em,' Rose called out – amazed at her own confidence. 'How's things?'

As she came forward with the gown she noticed the pallor on Em's face – something which even the magic of make-up couldn't hide.

'Everything alright?' Rose drew her fingers though the long extensions.

'Yeah, I guess...'

Rose ignored the implied opening for her to ask a question. 'A trim and tidy up today?'

'Yeah, sounds good. Why are you wearing gloves?' She looked at Rose in the mirror.

'Oh these?' Rose waggled her fingers in the blue protective gloves. 'Just a touch of eczema. Just being careful.'

'I didn't know you had eczema.'

Rose fought to keep cool. 'It's just something that flares up occasionally. It's no biggie.'

Em dropped her gaze without responding.

'I'll get you a coffee.' Without giving Em the option to say no, Rose bustled off to the kitchen and prepared a coffee in the bland white Ikea mug she had brought in earlier. While waiting for the kettle to boil, Rose felt a tickle of alarm. What was wrong with Em? She would never normally have let the subject of a skin complaint go without at least a recipe and several pieces of advice.

Then it occurred to her. It was obvious! Em would be worried about Olly, too. She wouldn't have heard from him. Maybe she thought he had dumped her or was ghosting her. Rose decided she was not going down that road – she would do Em's hair, collect the DNA and get her out of the salon as fast as possible. It didn't seem like she'd be in the mood for chatting, anyway.

She placed the coffee on the stand and Em held up the mug, turning it this way and that in her hand. 'This isn't one of your usual mugs.'

'We had a few breakages so we've just got some bog-standard ones until we can get a fresh batch of our usual ones.'

'Okay.' Em took a sip having already lost interest in the answer to her question.

Rose washed Em's hair and took great care combing it out.

'Ouch!' Em hunched down in the chair and put a hand to her head.

'Oh God, I'm so sorry, Em. There was just a little bit of a tangle.' Rose carefully laid the harvested strands of hair on her trolley.

The next half hour passed mostly in silence and Rose had to resist the urge to ask Em what was wrong. Normally she would have done that without hesitation – like many hairdressers she could turn her hand to a bit of therapy when necessary – but not today.

When Em had gone, she heaved a sigh of relief. In the kitchen, she placed the hair in an envelope and wrapped the mug in a freezer bag, making sure her back was to the door. Having placed the items in her bag – thank goodness for large handbags, she took off the gloves and, checking Abby and Adele were occupied in the salon, picked up the burner phone.

Got what you need. Usual place? I'll be there in 30 mins.

'Adele', there might be some news about Olly. I need to go. Can you manage?'

'Oh my God! Of course. You go.' Adele waved her hand towards the door.

Rose grabbed her coat and bag and fled.

But much as she wanted to get straight to Dan, there was something she needed to do first. Something crucial if the plan was to work. She headed to the police station and strode to the counter.

'My husband is still missing. The other sergeant I spoke to yesterday said to come back if he hadn't come home. He's been missing since Thursday. You have to do something now.' Everything was coming out in a gabble, as if she couldn't speak fast enough.

'Right.' The new sergeant typed into the computer. 'Name?'

'Oliver Walker. I came in yesterday.' Rose tapped her fingers on the counter as the officer took an age to search on the computer. He obviously had all day.

'Yup. Got him. Right, could you come through?'

Rose hesitated – what would happen if she was late for Dan? She'd assumed that, as they already had the details, her second visit would be a mere formality to get the ball rolling. That she would be on her way within ten minutes or so.

He stood holding the door open. 'Everything alright? You do want to report a missing person, yes?'

'Yes, of course I do, sorry. I'm all over the place.'

He smiled. 'Don't you worry, Mrs Walker. I'm sure this'll be sorted in no time. Come on. We just need to take some more details.'

He escorted her into a room, sparsely furnished with a desk and two chairs. A wilting plant on the window sill and a cheap print on the wall – small attempts to make the space more welcoming.

'If you wait here, someone will be along in a moment.'

Rose rushed off a message to Dan:

Stuck at the police station. They're opening a missing person's enquiry. Have you given Olly his inhaler?

The answer pinged through immediately.

No worries. That's good. Don't forget to mention your suspicions.

Before Rose had time to worry about the lack of answer to her question, the door opened and a uniformed officer came in, holding a file. She exuded an air of calm efficiency.

'I'm DC Emma Brown. Right then, Mrs Walker. Let's see if we can find out what's happened to your husband.'

Having noted all the main details, DC Brown carefully put down her pen and clasped her hands on the table. She fixed Rose with a searching gaze which made her want to squirm, but she willed herself to meet the gaze and remain motionless.

'Do you have any ideas about where he might be? Even a vague thought could be a useful start.'

Rose found she was unable to speak.

DC Brown tried another tack. 'Have you been together long?' Her voice was gentler now.

'We've been together since we were at school. We've always been together.'

'Good. So you must know if there are any places that he likes to visit – friends. Maybe someone from the gym?'

This was Rose's chance. She had to grasp it now.

She pulled her fingers through her hair and sighed. 'Well, there is something...but it's probably ridiculous.'

A gleam appeared in DC Brown's eyes and she picked up her pen.

'Go on, Rose – can I call you that? Anything might be important.'

'I've had a suspicion that Olly might have been...not having an affair exactly – he wouldn't do that, but something has been going on with one of the clients at the gym.'

'Who is it?' DC Brown's pen was poised.

'She's called Em – short for Emily I think – Em Totton.'

DC Brown noted something down before looking up again. 'What made you suspicious?'

'My friend works there and saw them together. And the night he went missing she posted this.' Rose handed her phone to DC Brown. 'That was taken in our house.'

DC Brown studied the image and scrolled through some of the comments.

Passing the phone back to Rose, she said, 'Did you mention this to the officer when you reported him missing?'

'No, I didn't see it until after. But I'm showing it to you now.' Rose knew her tone was defensive.

'Have you spoken to Olly about this relationship?'

'Yes,' Rose lied. 'He knows what he did was wrong.' She took a breath, clenching her hands together under the table. 'He's promised to finish it with her so we can get back together.'

'So you think he finished with her on Thursday night, after this was taken? After she was in your house?' DC Brown paused. 'Or do you think it's possible that he didn't finish it and has gone somewhere with her?'

Rose put her head in her hands to avoid DC Brown's gaze. If only that was how it really was. This was all too much. She couldn't do it. She should tell the truth.

To her surprise, DC Brown got up, walked around the table and crouched at her side. 'I know this must be awful for you, Rose. I do understand. But nine times out of ten missing people turn up perfectly well. I'm sure he'll make contact with you soon.' She patted Rose's shoulder and stood, smoothing her uniform. 'Maybe he needed some space to get his head together. It sounds like things have been quite intense between you both.'

Rose nodded, unable to speak.

'I need to go home. What if he's come back while I was here?' The urge to run out of the police station was almost overwhelming.

'I think that's a good idea. I'll send some officers round later to take a look and see if there are any clues as to where he might be.'

When Rose, standing, didn't respond, DC Brown said, 'Rose? Is that alright with you?'

Rose nodded and turned to the door. Just as she was about to step into the corridor, DC Brown said, 'Oh, by the way, I assume you've tried to ring Olly.'

Rose stopped and turned to face DC Brown. 'He doesn't have his phone with him. It's at home. That's why I'm so worried.'

The police officer raised her eyebrows in surprise. 'Did you not think to mention this when you came in yesterday?'

Rose felt the tell-tale blush creep across her face. Why hadn't she thought about that?

'I only found it this morning.' The lie spilled out easily. Rose continued, 'I'm sorry. I'm in such a state, I don't know what I'm doing.' She sobbed, sure that DC Brown knew she was lying.

'Don't worry. It's okay. My officers will collect it when they come later. Maybe it will shed some light on where he is.'

DC Brown came around the table. 'Let me see you out.'

Rose forced herself to put one foot in front of the other and walk behind DC Brown until they reached the foyer.

As they walked to the entrance, she said, 'Do you have someone who can be with you? A friend or family?'

Rose kept her eyes on the automatic doors. Only a few more steps and she could go and get Olly. 'Yes, my parents will come round.'

Chapter Twenty-Six

Rose drove as fast as she dared, her focus razor-sharp. Within the hour, she would have Olly back and they could head home. Although Rose knew that wouldn't be the end of it, at least they would be safe in their home and could start rebuilding their relationship. It was as if her emotional reserves had been used up and she didn't have the capacity to feel anything anymore apart from this driving need to bring this disaster to an end. She glanced at the bag on the seat beside her containing the key to unlocking the nightmare.

She thought back to how Em had seemed at the salon and felt a twinge of pity for her. She must genuinely care about Olly. Did she deserve what Rose was about to do to her? Probably not, now that Rose knew more about her, knew that she had a sister who was dependent on her. But she wouldn't go down that road – she knew Dan wouldn't be diverted from his plan to make Em pay and she had to get Olly back. Em shouldn't have been messing about with other's lives for her own gain.

By the time she drove into the motorway services car park, Rose had persuaded herself that what she was doing was justified. After all, Em had almost destroyed their marriage without a second thought.

As she entered the car park, Rose saw Dan's car facing away from the entrance in the far corner. There was no space next to him so she parked a few rows away and raced over, clutching the bag, desperate to see if Olly was in the passenger seat.

Dan got out of the car with slow, deliberate movements.

'Here it is – just like you asked.' She thrust the bag at Dan's stomach.

He took a step back at the unexpected impact.

'Where's Olly. Is he with you?' Rose glanced around almost as if she was expecting him to appear out of thin air. 'Where is he, you bastard!' she hissed.

She pushed past him and flung open the passenger door to see the seat was empty, as were the back seats. Rose turned to Dan. 'What have you done? Where is he?' She was screaming at him now.

Dan took her arm in a firm grip and bundled her into the car, slamming the door.

Everything was blurred as she felt the car move under his weight as he got into the driver's seat.

'Did you give him his inhaler?'

Dan took a breath in through his teeth. 'That message never got through, I'm afraid. My guy was a bit careless. And we couldn't exactly call an ambulance could we? But look at it this way, it's all the more to pin on Em.'

Rose looked ahead, her mind refusing to process what he was saying. She was in a dream. Any minute now she would wake up and this whole thing would never have happened.

Dan stared ahead. 'There's been a slight change of plan.'

'What? What have you done?' Rose approached him, her body shaking with fear and rage.

Dan sighed and shifted his weight on the seat. 'You see, the thing is, Rose, this whole thing hasn't been without its costs and I have people to reimburse.'

Rose stared at him, vaguely aware of her mouth hanging open.

'So there's the little issue of payment to consider.'

'What? We didn't discuss this!'

'Oh come on, Rose. You didn't think I would pay for all this out of my own pocket, did you? And what about all the risks I've taken? I could lose my job and be sent to prison. People like Sal don't come cheap. Surely even *you* are not that naïve.'

'You bastard! Bring Olly back!' Rose threw herself at him, pummelling his chest but it was like banging her fists against something solid and unmoving. Dan caught hold of her arms and held her away from him, his strength making her immobile.

'We haven't got any money!'

'Well, maybe you should have thought of that before.'

Rose could feel tears running down her cheeks and sobs forming in her throat. He was too strong for her – in every way. She felt all the energy leave her body and slumped against the seat.

'How much?'

'Let's make it a round £20,000, shall we?'

'But—'

'I know you don't think you can pay that, but believe me, you'll find a way. It's the only way you'll get Olly back.' When Rose didn't respond, he added, 'All you need to do now is act the distraught wife and stick to your story.'

'What? No! No. You can't do this.'

'Oh, but I can. And don't forget – you're responsible for the safety of your niece and nephew. Fern and Harry, isn't it? Nice names. Apparently they're cute kids.'

'I'll send the ransom demand to the local paper,' he added, smiling.

'And then, when it's all over, we can start our new life.'

Before Rose could respond, Dan turned abruptly, got out of the car, arriving at the passenger side before she could understand what was happening. He wrenched the door open and, grabbing her arm dragged her into a standing position. Rose leant against the car to steady herself, trying to make some sense of what was happening. Too late, she realised the car was moving, and unbalanced, she tumbled to the floor, vaguely aware of Dan's car disappearing at speed into a hazy distance. She had no energy to get up. She closed her eyes, never wanting to open them again.

Rose heard voices in the distance. 'Hello. Hello?'

She didn't want to respond, but her body propelled her towards consciousness and she opened her eyes.

She felt the ground, hard, beneath her and struggled to get up.

'Steady. Take it steady.' A hand on her arm helped her into a sitting position as the car park swam into focus around her.

'There you go.' A woman in a motorway services uniform was kneeling by her side.

'What—'

'You fainted, my love, but you're alright now.' She shifted her position on the ground. 'Here, have a sip of water.'

Rose obediently took a mouthful from the bottle the woman offered her. The cold sensation in her mouth bringing her back to reality. She looked over to the vacant space where Dan's car had been and knew she was back in the nightmare again. She groaned, putting her head in her hands.

'Do you think you can stand up if I help you?'

'I'll try.' Rose levered herself unsteadily to her feet with the help of the woman. She swallowed down the nausea that threatened to overwhelm her.

'That's it. Well done. Let's get you inside.'

'Thank you everyone. She'll be fine now,' the woman said firmly as Rose became aware of a small group of people hovering nearby.

'She went down like a rag doll. Just crumpled.' Rose heard an older woman's voice. 'It was something to do with that man who drove away. You mark my words.' There was a note of excitement as the voice rose in pitch and volume.

'Come on, Mum, let's go. She's okay now.'

'You keep well away from him, lovey. That's my advice.'

Rose was too busy trying to get her body to function to look at the speaker. She found herself putting one foot in front of the other as she was firmly steered towards the service station building.

Once inside, she was taken to an office where someone made her a cup of tea. The very smell of it turned her stomach.

'Do you have coffee?' she managed.

'Of course. No worries.' The woman seemed relieved that she was recovering and hurried to make a fresh drink.

As Rose sipped the drink and ate part of a biscuit, the woman busied herself at a nearby desk, no doubt writing up a report of the incident.

The woman turned to her and asked, 'What's your name, love?'

'Emily Totton.' Rose spoke without hesitation. 'Double T,' she added, putting the paper cup down. 'I need to get going.'

The woman looked doubtful. 'Are you sure you're okay? You can stay here as long as you like.'

'No, honestly I'm fine now.' Rose picked up her bag that someone had put beside the chair.

'I would see your GP just to get checked out, though.'

'No, I do faint sometimes. It's nothing to worry about.'

The woman seemed reassured. 'Well, mind how you go.'

Rose stood, willing her body not to sway. 'Thank you so much for your help.'

'No worries. Take care, Emily.'

Chapter Twenty-Seven

Rose waited for the automatic doors to open at their usual glacial pace before hurling herself through and racing to the double doors into the swimming pool.

The receptionist's, 'Hey. You can't just come in here!' echoing in her ears.

She scanned the area and saw Poppy at the far end of the pool with her over- sixties group.

'Poppy! Poppy! Oh my God!' Rose almost fell, slipping on the wet floor in her haste.

Poppy looked up open-mouthed. 'Don't run, slow down,' she yelled.

Rose forced herself into a quick walk as the class turned their heads in her direction.

Reaching Poppy, she grabbed her arm. 'I don't know what... Poppy, you've got to help me!' Rose was sobbing now, her knees buckling.

Poppy beckoned another member of staff over. 'Gus, can you just take over here for a few minutes?'

Once Gus had regained the attention of the gawping swimmers, Poppy ushered Rose through to the changing rooms, her eyes wide with fear.

'Sit down, Rose. Take some breaths.' She rubbed Rose's back. 'In...out...in...out.'

At last, when Rose was able to speak through the sobs, Poppy asked, 'What is it? What's happened? Is it Olly?'

'There's a ransom. I tried to get him back. I did everything he asked and now they want money and he hasn't got his inhaler.' Her distress poured out in a muddled mess.

Poppy leaned closer, scrutinising Rose's face.

'What? What are you talking about, Rose? Who wants money?'

'Dan.'

Poppy shook her head, trying to understand. 'Dan? You mean that policeman guy?'

Rose nodded, struggling to breathe through uncontrollable sobs.

'Did you—'

Rose turned, clasping Poppy's hands. 'It's all my fault. I've lost Olly. I don't know if he's okay or where he is.'

'But you just said...'

'It wasn't meant to happen. Dan was just going to keep Olly somewhere for a few days so we could frame Em for kidnapping him. And now I can't get him back! They want £20,000.'

Poppy sat up straight. 'Tell me this isn't true, Rose.' Her face paled as Rose's sobs returned. She put her arms around Rose's shaking body and held her tight.

'Have you actually seen Dan?'

'I went to hand over Em's DNA and he said...'

'Have you tried to ring Olly?'

Rose's eyes dropped to her lap. 'I've got Olly's phone,' she muttered.

Poppy took a breath before standing up.

'I need to get you home. We can't talk about this here. Give me a minute or two to organise things.'

Once Poppy had made them both a strong cup of coffee laced with a shot of brandy, Rose told her everything, Poppy stopping her every so often to double check what she was saying.

As she spoke, Rose felt the lightness of confession, and then a numbness crept around her body and suddenly all she wanted to do was sleep. What else was there to do? She could never get that sort of money.

She was shaken out of her stupor by Poppy.

'Rose. Rose, listen to me.'

Rose opened her eyes and looked out of the window. 'Rose, look at me.'

She dragged her eyes to Poppy's gaze. 'Do the police know about the ransom demand?' There was an urgency in her voice.

'Dan said he was going to contact the local paper.'

'What about Em? I'm guessing he will have planted the DNA by now, so maybe she's been taken in.'

Rose looked at the clock – 4 p.m. 'I guess...'

'Look at your phone. Are there any messages from the police?' Rose dug her phone out of the bag.

'Oh God, the police have tried to call me twice.'

'Okay, so that means they have something to tell you.' Poppy drummed her fingers on the arm of the settee.

'What should I do?' Rose felt that making any kind of decision was way beyond her.

Poppy took a breath. 'The way I see it, the best way to keep you in the clear is to stick to your story. How will they know anything different?'

'But what about Em?' Another thought struck Rose and she turned to Poppy. 'She knows who I am! She'll have recognised me in the photos in the house.' Rose couldn't stop trembling. 'Oh God! What if she says something?'

Poppy took a breath. 'Let's not worry about that for now. If she says anything, we'll cross that bridge when we come to it. Let's think about you.'

Poppy shifted on the settee, drawing her legs up and tucking them under her body.

She'd seen Poppy sit like this hundreds of times over the years – when they had shared school-days gossip, or secrets that only the two of them knew about. Inconsequential things, it seemed now.

She leaned towards Rose, their heads almost touching. 'Stick to your story.'

'But what if he tells the police I'm involved? And where would I even get that money?' Rose's voice shook. For the first time she was experiencing a visceral sense of fear. She could go to prison for a long time if Dan told the police about her part in this. But maybe that's what she deserved.

'I don't think he will – think about it. He would only be incriminating himself. And from what you say, he probably wasn't even in the police anyway. We'll just have to take that risk.'

Rose was shaking her head. 'I can't. I can't do this. I deserve to be punished. I need to go and tell them everything.'

Poppy grasped Rose's hands firmly and looked at her. 'Rose. This isn't just about you. Think about your family. What will it do to them if you are convicted of...I don't know what, and you get sent to prison? Think about Cutting It Fine. Shona's business will go down the drain.'

Poppy's words slowly filtered through the haze of panic and fear in Rose's head, and she knew she was right. This wasn't just about her. She had to think of others. People she cared about. She had to salvage something from this mess and it didn't involve the luxury of confession.

Replacing her mug on the table, she took a deep breath and re-clipped her hair. 'I'll ring the police and see what they've got to say.'

Rose tried to return the call, but her hands were shaking too much. Poppy took the phone and handed it back once the line was ringing.

'Hello, this is Rose Walker. Do you have news about my husband?'

'Hold the line for a moment, Mrs Walker, and I'll put you through.'

She looked at Poppy who was nodding in encouragement.

The calm and efficient voice of DC Brown came on the line. 'Mrs Walker. We've been trying to reach you.'

'Sorry I was asleep.'

'We've taken Emily Totton in for questioning. She's denying all knowledge of the kidnap of your husband but has admitted they were having an affair. She also claims to have no inkling that he was about to break it off, although she says she hasn't heard from him since Thursday.'

'Do you believe her?'

'Hard to say until we find your husband and unearth some evidence. I wanted to keep you updated. We are treating this as a missing person's case – possibly a kidnapping – and have deployed a lot of officers in the hunt for Olly. Don't worry, Rose, we'll find him.' Again, that rare softening of her tone.

Rose ended the call and relayed the news to Poppy. 'I don't think she's said anything about recognising me.' She exhaled a shaky breath.

'You have to wait now. Dan will have planted Em's DNA, given himself time to scarper and then he'll call the police, anonymously, with a tip-off about the location. I think it'll be soon – he won't want to drag this out. But...' Poppy tailed off.

'But what about Olly? He'll have taken him somewhere else.' Rose finished the sentence for her, a tinge of bitterness in her tone.

'Maybe you should phone your mum and dad and let them know.' Poppy looked at her, head on one side.

Rose sighed. The last thing she wanted to do was speak to her parents, to have to cope with their worry and concern, but she knew it must be done.

Poppy dialled the number before passing the phone to Rose.

'Rose! Are you alright?'

'Yes, Mum. I'm alright.'

Before she could say anything else, her mother said, 'Hang on, Rose, I'm putting you on speaker.' Rose tightened her grip on the phone.

'Right. What have the police said?' Her father's voice sounded calm.

Rose cleared her throat. 'They've taken in a woman called Emily Totton. It seems that...' Rose paused. She could do this. She had to force the words out. '...that Olly was having an affair with her.'

There was silence from the other end, and then some hurried whispering. Rose raised her eyes to the ceiling.

'Oh Rose...' she could hear the tremor in her mother's voice.

'Did you know about this?' It was rare for her father to get angry, but Rose could hear it in his voice now.

'I had a suspicion.' Rose decided to stick to the truth as much as she could. 'Actually, she is...was...one of my clients. Something she said made me suspicious.'

'So what's she said to the police?'

'She's denying it and is saying she doesn't know where he is. But they are pulling out all the stops now to find him, so that's good.'

Rose couldn't believe her voice was saying these things. These blatant lies. She reminded herself that she was doing it to protect them.

'I'm at Poppy's. I'll let you know if anything else happens.'

'Okay.' Rose could hear the hesitation in her mum's voice. 'We're looking after Fern and Harry today, otherwise we'd come round.'

Rose's breath caught in her throat, causing her to cough.

'Rose?'

'It's okay, Mum. Everything's okay. Keep Fern and Harry safe.'

She ended the call before they could respond.

'You're doing great, Rose.' Poppy hugged her again.

'What if something happens to Fern and Harry?' Rose's voice quavered. 'I'll never forgive myself.'

'They're safe with your parents. And nothing will happen while he's waiting for you to pay the ransom. Think about it. It's probably an empty threat anyway.'

Rose took a deep breath and closed her eyes.

'What about Em's socials? We should take a look.' Rose gave her phone to Poppy, who quickly scrolled through.

For the first time since the nightmare had begun, Rose wasn't interested in Em's life. It all seemed irrelevant now.

'Nothing. Not even about her hair appointment with Emmanuelle this morning.'

Rose took a look. Several regular followers were questioning where she was. And there were some more critical comments creeping in.

Very quiet, M. Everything okay?

You alright, babe?

Tell us more about Jay – we need all the info.

That photo behind you both says to me that Jay is spoken for. Were you actually in their house? What kind of a bitch does that?!

Accounts for all the secrecy.

Maybe she's done a runner with Jay. How romantic!

Come on, M, spill.

Do you think she's actually ghosting us now?

Considering some of these individuals followed Em's every move, it struck Rose that there was very little concern for their idol.

Chapter Twenty-Eight

R ose was almost relieved when DC Brown appeared on the doorstep later that evening. Already knowing what she was going to say, Rose steeled herself to act appropriately.

'Take a seat, Rose.'

Rose sat on the settee and waited, her hands palm-down under her thighs. She concentrated on the feel of the fabric, flexing her fingers against it, aware of concerned glances in her direction from her parents who had arrived a few minutes earlier.

'There's been a development. Em, or whoever has Olly, is asking for a ransom.'

'What?' It wasn't hard to make her voice tremble.

'£20,000 by noon on Monday.'

'I can't pay that! Where would we get that kind of money?'

'It's okay, Rose. We have protocols for dealing with situations like this.' DC Brown's calm acceptance of the situation was more than Rose could bear.

'It's not okay!' She heard her voice increase in volume and pitch. 'What about Emily Totton?'

'We had to let her go earlier, as we don't have enough evidence to arrest her, yet.'

'So what is the next step?' Rose's father intervened.

'We'll do whatever it takes,' her mother added. 'But we don't have that kind of money.'

'Our plan is for you to deliver a package which the someone will collect and then we will arrest whoever it is. You don't need to get the money. Chances are, if it's Em or someone like her, they won't have done this before and will make errors.'

'But—' Rose managed to stop herself just in time. She knew by now that Dan was no novice at this game.

'I'm not taking that chance with Olly's life...or this family's safety.' Rose stopped abruptly. She'd said too much. DC Brown looked up. 'What do you mean – the safety of your family? We've had no indication that the rest of your family is included in this demand.'

'No...I just mean all of us in general. Because you never know...' She tailed off knowing how lame the explanation sounded. 'Anyway, whatever, we need to get that money together.' Rose knew that if Dan didn't get what he wanted her family was in real danger. If only she could tell them and get them to understand!

'I think we should do what the police say, Rosy. They know what they're doing,' her father cajoled.

'No. We need to get the money!' Rose was surprised at the steel in her tone.

DC Brown got up. 'We have until noon on Monday, so I'll leave you to discuss it and we'll chat again tomorrow.'

Once Rose had seen DC Brown to the door, she hovered in the hall and took several calming breaths. She could hear her parents talking in low voices. She wanted to crawl into bed and shut everything out, she couldn't stand deceiving her parents any longer.

She went back into the room. 'Look, I'm pretty exhausted. Why don't you go home and get some rest. We can sort this out tomorrow.'

When they responded with worried looks and her mother began to protest. 'Rose, I—' Rose added, 'I just need some space,'

'Well if you're sure...' her mother glanced at her father who gave a brief nod. 'But we're at the end of the phone if you need anything.'

When she had eventually waved them off, Rose returned to the house and slumped against the closed front door.

Whatever happened, she needed to get that money from somewhere. She wasn't taking any risks.

After a night spent totting up where she could access money – including asking her parents – Rose knew she had nowhere near enough. She'd been onto the online banking site but any loan she was entitled to was too small an amount. She even investigated some dodgy no-questions-asked loan sites but the interest rates were exorbitant and she knew that she and Olly would never be able to meet the payments. But she bookmarked them anyway – as a final fall-back option if all else failed.

Looking out of the window, coffee cup in hand, she saw Harold sunning himself on Walter's front lawn and smiled as Harold appeared with a chair and sat beside him. As she watched, it seemed that Walter was having some kind of one-sided conversation with Harold who flicked his tail and yawned in reply.

Rose went out, feeling the warmth of the sunshine on her face. How could anything so dreadful be happening on a beautiful spring day like this?

'I see Harold is making himself at home.' Rose leaned on the fence, cup in hand.

'Indeed.' Walter lowered his voice. 'I wonder how I managed without him all this time, if I'm honest. But don't tell him, it'll only go to his head.'

Rose smiled. I think you and Harold understand each other perfectly.

Walter studied Rose for a moment. 'What's going on, Rose? Don't think I haven't noticed at the comings and goings. And I can spot a police officer a mile off.'

Rose looked across at Harold who apparently didn't have a care in the world and wished she could swap places with him – just for today.

'I—'

Walter took her hand across the fence. 'What is it, Rose?'

'It's Olly. He's missing.'

'Oh, my dear. How dreadful. And you have no—'

'And there's a ransom demand.' Rose cut across the question. 'There's no way to pay it.'

Rose thought she had exhausted her tears last night, but here they were again.

'Come in, come in and tell me everything.' Walter let go of her hand and walked carefully to his front door. Rose had no choice but to follow.

Once they were seated in his kitchen and Walter had provided a plate of biscuits, he said, 'Now tell me everything.'

Rose took a breath. She had to stick to her story. 'The police think that the woman Olly has been having an affair with – Emily Totton – has kidnapped him.'

'Why on earth would she do that?' Walter's eyebrows shot up.

'Maybe because Olly threatened to end it? She's one of these influencers who have lots of followers on social media and she couldn't afford to lose face. Her followers have doubled since she's been posting about her and Jay. That's what she calls Olly,' Rose added by way of explanation.

'You mean to tell me that she's been broadcasting the affair to all and sundry?' Walter put his cup carefully in the saucer. 'Oh Rose. I don't know what to say. I'm so sorry.'

'You know, I saw her here on Thursday evening. I'm guessing that was her.' He raised his eyebrows, questioning.

'Yes. That was her.'

'She left in something of a hurry around nine.' He cleared his throat. 'Do you think I should tell the police?'

I'm guessing they will be asking questions soon enough. 'But they already know she was here and left in a hurry because her sister was taken ill.'

'Oh dear! Do they believe her?'

Rose sighed and leant forward, her face in her hands. 'I don't know.'

'Now what's all this about a ransom demand?' Walter was using his Mr Powell voice.

'If it's her, she's asking for £20,000. We haven't got anything like that sort of money, and neither have my parents. I've been looking into loans all night trying to come up with something.' Rose clasped her hands and rested her head on them once more, elbows on the table.

'But surely the police have ways of dealing with this?' Walter asked gently.

Rose looked up. 'I'm not taking any chances with Olly's safety.' She congratulated herself on keeping to the story this time.

Walter levered himself up. 'This is something I can help with.'

'What are you doing, Walter?'

'Come with me.'

Rose followed him into the lounge where a laptop sat open on a desk. She gasped when she saw this new addition, but then she hadn't been into this room since Annie's funeral a year ago.

'I moved things around a bit after Annie.' Walter said in explanation.

'I didn't know you were even online,' Rose gasped.

'I took lessons. I needed to do something to keep the old grey cells ticking,' He tapped his head with a finger. 'Since you got my stick on Amazon, I've realised what I'm missing out on. I can't do much, yet, but I'm signed up for online banking.' He flexed his fingers, readying himself for the task. 'Now. I shall log in to my account and we'll work out how much you need. While I do that, you can go and get your bank details. He lowered himself onto the chair and Rose stood, open-mouthed. He waved a hand in her direction. 'Get along with you, then.'

'I don't need to go anywhere, I've got them in my phone.' Rose fished her phone out of her pocket. She was opened her banking app, aware of Walter's slow and careful typing.

'Right. I'm in. So you said £20,000, is that right?'

'Walter, no. I can't let you do that – it's too much.' A tingle of alarm travelled up Rose's spine.

Walter turned in the chair to face her. 'Look. I've got more money than I could ever need and there is no one to leave it too.' He glanced out of the window at Harold, still sunning himself on the lawn. 'And Harold would only fritter it away. So let me do this for you and Olly, Rose.'

For Rose, the thought of Walter helping her out with so much money when everything was based on a lie was hard to take, but she had to get Olly back, and if this was the only way, she had to accept the offer. They could always make it up to him afterwards when everything was sorted.

'Rose? Give me your bank details.'

Without protesting further, Rose recited the number which Walter entered with great care. Finally and with a flourish he pressed a button. 'There. Done!'

'Walter, how can we ever thank you?' The tears had reappeared again of their own accord.

Ignoring her, Walter was busy once more on the laptop. 'You can make a start by helping me with something.' He swivelled and looked at her. 'Draw up a chair.'

Once Rose was settled, Walter turned back to the laptop. 'With your assistance I'm going to do something I've been thinking about for a while. I need to look at mobility scooters – and that's something you can help *me* with. The stick is better than nothing but walking is still a struggle and I have to admit I've felt envious of the other old codgers whizzing about here and there, so I'm going to bite the bullet. So can you help me find out prices and what not?' He turned the laptop towards her. 'I'm not really clued in to these searching engines yet.'

Checking her phone once more for messages before replacing it in her pocket, Rose drew up a chair and spent the next half hour exploring the world of mobility scooters with her old headmaster. They found an outlet nearby and Walter booked a taxi to take him there the following morning.

'Are you sure about going on your own?' Rose asked.

'I know you'll be busy tomorrow, Rose and I can still do some things for myself, you know.'

Rose's phone pinged with a message:

Where are you?

She looked out of the window to see her parents already on the drive. 'I have to go, Walter, but thank you again.'

She gave him a swift hug and went to meet her parents, waving to Walter as she went.

Chapter Twenty-Nine

'We've been thinking.' Rose's mother said firmly, 'and we've decided to re-mortgage the house.'

Rose was horrified that her disastrous decisions might lead to her parents jeopardising their security and the house they had saved up to buy and had lovingly restored over the years. Shame burned deep inside, tempered by the relief that she had avoided involving them.

'You don't need to do that,' she said. 'I wouldn't want you to. I've sorted it and I can collect the cash from the bank tomorrow morning.'

'Oh Rosy, don't tell me you've done something stupid like taking out a loan.' Her father sighed and put his hands over his eyes and then pulling them down over his face.

'No, I haven't done anything *stupid*, Dad.'

Rose realised with a shock that she was sick of feeling like a child in her family and took some pride in the fact she had sorted out her mess without involving them. She pushed the thought that it was Walter (another adult from her past) who had come to the rescue and that it was all based on a lie, to the back of her mind.

'Walter is paying the ransom for now, and Olly and I will pay him back when all this is over.'

Rose waited for the response.

'Mr Powell? Oh Rose. You can't accept his money.' Her mother's body was rigid as she sat forward on the soft armchair while her father's eyebrows were drawn into an ominous frown.

'I've sorted this my way. I'm not a child.' Rose glared at them. 'Mr Powell...Walter offered and wouldn't take no for an answer and I accepted, because I intend to get Olly back in any way I can.' This was the first time she had ever defied her parents and Rose experienced a mixture of exhilaration and terror.

The tension in the room was broken by the sound of the doorbell. With relief, Rose got up to answer it and found DC Brown and another officer on the doorstep.

'This is DS Knight. He's a specialist in situations like this.' Rose nodded to him and ushered them in.

Once they were all seated, DC Brown turned her attention to Rose. 'Have you had any further thoughts about the ransom? When we spoke yesterday you were quite sure about paying it.'

'I still am, and I have the money – or I will have by tomorrow when I collect it from the bank.'

DS Knight leaned forward and rested his elbows on his knees. 'I know DC Brown has told you this isn't necessary but we will go along with your wishes. So this is our plan for tomorrow. The kidnapper has given us a time and place for the handover – it's the car park at Holton Country Park, twelve noon.'

Rose gasped. She couldn't believe Dan wanted to go back there. He was playing with all of them, but especially her, she knew it.

'Is everything okay?' DC Brown asked. 'Does that have some significance for you?'

'Only that it's somewhere Olly and I go quite a bit,' she lied. From the corner of her eye she could see the puzzled look on her mother's face and could only pray that she wouldn't say anything and hurried to change the subject. 'So do I take the money in a bag or something?'

DS Knight nodded. 'And you leave it under one of the picnic tables. Then you get in your car and leave.'

'Is that it?' Rose felt a wave of relief that she wouldn't have to see Dan. 'And then they'll let Olly go? Will he be there?'

'The usual thing is to get an anonymous call telling us where the hostage is. But we'll be following this individual as they might lead us to Olly.'

Rose thought of Dan and what he might be capable of. 'But what if they don't call? What if we don't get him back?'

'There is no reason for them to keep him any longer once they have the money. In our experience, kidnappers are usually only too glad to get shot of the responsibility.' Rose wondered how DS Knight could be so calm. What would he be like if it was a member of *his* family in danger?

'So what happens now?' Rose's father asked.

'Tomorrow you collect the money, Rose. I suggest someone goes with you and you have your car parked near the bank. Aim to get to the country park at about 11.55, place the bag under a picnic bench. Don't hang around, just drive away.'

'Maybe we could be there too, just having a coffee or something to see what happens?' Rose's mother clasped Rose's hand. 'We want to help.'

'No!' Rose swallowed and softened her tone. 'No, we need to leave this to the police, Mum. How do you know they won't recognise you?'

'Rose is right. You need to leave this to us. We will have surveillance of the whole site and won't leave until we know who collects that bag. You have my word.'

As she stood in the queue at the bank, Rose wondered how she had arrived at Monday morning. It had seemed an eternity away when DC Brown and DS Knight had left her house yesterday. The gap had been a yawning cavern of hours and minutes. Images of Olly gasping for air without his inhaler ran endlessly through her mind and her inability to help him until today had been almost unbearable.

In the end, she had persuaded Walter to bring his mobility scooter venture forwards and they had gone together yesterday afternoon. After an hour or so, Walter was the proud owner of a four-wheeler which was due to be delivered this morning, along with someone who would go through the workings of it with him.

As she moved closer to the counter, Rose looked at the time, 11 o'clock, and guessed the mobility people would be with Walter by now. When her turn came, she spoke in a low voice. 'I rang earlier to arrange to collect some cash?'

'Name?'

Once the teller realised who she was, she said, 'Come this way,' indicating a door at the end of the row of cashier windows. It had taken quite a bit of persuading to get the bank to release the cash, but in the end, a phone call from DS Knight had done the trick.

As she was shown into a side room, Rose unfolded the bag under her arm and held it out for the cashier to count out the money. She stared at the bundles of £50 notes. Rose had never seen that much real money. For her, money was mostly a figure on a screen, other than a few pounds and coins she kept in her purse.

Rose kept a tight hold on the bag as her father drove her home.

'It's not going to grow legs and run away, Rose,' her father teased.

Rose turned her head away without answering. When they arrived at her house she got out of the car in a rush and unlocking her own climbed in, putting the bag on the passenger seat beside her, throwing a belated 'Thanks Dad,' through the open window as she reversed out of the drive.

Once she was on her way to the country park Rose began to breath freely. Her parents were suffocating her with their endless advice and concern, even though she knew they meant well. But would they be as solicitous if they knew the truth? The pressure of not being honest was too much when she was with them.

As she approached the turning, Rose's heart started to race. Soon all this would be over, and she would have Olly back by the end of the day. Her thoughts turned to Em – the police had questioned her again and she was still denying all knowledge, claiming that she'd had a message to say her sister was ill and that she'd had to leave in a rush. Although Em claimed that when she'd arrived home, her sister had been fine. It seemed that the police weren't convinced as Em's sister was her only alibi. She sensed Dan's handiwork at play and wondered what Em must be thinking and feeling. She thought about Walter. Would the police question him? He could confirm Em's story.

Rose had been relieved that there had apparently been no mention of Em's hairdresser being Olly's wife. Maybe she was too embarrassed to reveal that someone as lowly as Rose did her hair, or maybe she simply hadn't noticed or realised who she was.

Rose pushed the thoughts away. She would not think about Walter or Em now.

Once at the site, she parked near the entrance, looking around for Dan's car, but it wasn't there. She retrieved the bag from the passenger seat and walked over to the picnic tables, wondering which of the people were undercover officers. She made herself look at the ground, feeling like a goldfish in a glass bowl, knowing that her every move was being watched.

Finding an empty table, she sat for a few minutes, kicking the bag underneath with her foot before getting up and returning to her car. At any moment she expected a helpful voice to carry across the carpark. 'Is this your bag? You left it behind.' But no one seemed interested in her or her bag and she heaved a grateful sigh of relief once she was back in her car with the engine running.

As Rose pulled out of the car park a police car turned in, sirens blaring, closely followed by an ambulance. Her heart lurched. This wasn't part of the plan. What was happening? The police were supposed to wait. For a panic-stricken moment, Rose thought about turning back to see what was happening, but she knew that would be madness, so she drove away. She resisted the urge to go straight to the police station and drove home – DS Knight had been firm about what she should do.

There was no sign of Walter or the mobility scooter as she opened the front door and let herself in. Everything in the house was just as she'd left it – as if nothing had happened – but Rose had a bad feeling. She was gripped by apprehension that things hadn't gone to plan. Something was wrong and that could only mean bad news for Olly. She sat on the stairs and clung to the banister.

Chapter Thirty

R ose had no idea how long she had been sitting there when the phone rang, but she was stiff as she shifted her position to answer it. When she took it out of her pocket, Rose realised it wasn't her phone that was ringing but the burner phone Dan had left her, chiming distantly in the kitchen.

She almost tripped as she got up in her haste, snatching up the phone from the drawer where she had hidden it on Thursday evening.

'Oh dear, Rose. You really messed that up, didn't you?'

'Dan? Where's Olly? I left the money. Have you got it?'

'Oh yes, I have the money, no thanks to you! What on earth made you think that involving the police was a good idea?'

Rose's head began to spin and she gripped the reassuring solidity of the worktop. 'But you messaged the paper and they contacted the police who already knew Olly was missing.' Rose stopped to gasp a breath. 'What did you expect?'

'I expected better of you. I thought you would have taken steps to throw them off the scent. I didn't think you would go along with their plan.'

Rose clutched her hair in a handful, pulling at it with her free hand. 'But how was I supposed to know—'

'Never mind.' Dan cut across her. 'The damage is done and now the outlook for Olly isn't good, I'm afraid. He'll get what he deserves. But look at it this way. You'll be free of him now, Rose. We'll be free to start our new life.'

Before Rose could respond, the line went dead. She flung the phone across the counter where it skittered onto the floor.

She felt herself go into freefall, as if someone had pushed her out of an aeroplane without a parachute. Everything was flashing by at break-neck speed and, as much as she tried to catch hold of things and understand them, they slipped away, the force of gravity pulling her downwards. She didn't understand anything anymore, only that Dan was mad. What more did he want? It never occurred to her to not listen to the police. He had told her to report Olly missing, point them in the direction of Em, and follow their lead. Hadn't he? Rose desperately thought back, second-guessing herself. Had she missed something? Some instruction he'd given?

Her phone rang on the stairs and Rose went answer it. It was if she was walking through a huge vat of treacle, every step an effort.

'Rose?' DC Brown was on the phone.

'Something went wrong, didn't it?'

There was a hesitation on the line. 'There was a hoax bomb scare and in the chaos of evacuating the site, someone picked up the bag and left with it and we couldn't see who. I'm so sorry, Rose.'

When Rose didn't respond, DC Brown said, 'Rose? Are you still there?'

Although Rose ended the call the phone rang again immediately. DC Brown was obviously determined to speak, so she answered the call, closing her eyes tight and leaning her head back against the uncomfortable banister.

'Rose, you didn't let me finish. We've had contact and, as DS Knight said would happen, they have left directions for finding Olly.'

Rose opened her eyes and sat up. 'Where is he? Is he...' She left the question hanging, not able to bring herself to form the words.

'We have a team heading there now. I'll be in touch when we know more. But this is good news, Rose. Olly will soon be back.'

'Okay.' Rose knew her voice sounded flat, but she knew more than DC Brown. She doubted that she would never have Olly back. It would be too late when they got there. She had no doubts that Dan would be as good as his word. How had she ever thought he would deliver Olly back to her? She had fallen for his reassurances but now she knew none of them were true. Dan never intended Olly to come back. He couldn't risk it. Olly might know too much, an inconvenient loose end. How could she not have seen that? She had traded his life for what? Just to get back at an airhead like Em?

Rose was silent as DC Brown perched on the edge of the armchair.

She had rung Poppy knowing DC Brown was on her way. Poppy knew more than anyone about what Rose had done and she needed her by her side. She couldn't deal with the police on her own.

'What about your mum and dad?' Poppy had asked.

'I can't face them,' Rose muttered into the phone. 'I can't do this in front of them.'

'Okay. I'll be there in ten.' Poppy had rung off and Rose heaved a sigh of relief.

'Have you found him?' Poppy asked now, holding Rose's hand.

'We have, but I'm afraid—'

'No! No!' Rose moaned, covering her ears with her hands. 'She didn't want to hear it.'

'Rose, he was in a bad way but he'll be okay.'

She became aware of Poppy gently moving her hand away from her head and squeezing it.

'Rose?' DC Brown spoke gently. 'Olly is alive.'

She felt some sensation return to her mouth. 'He's alive? But... Are you—' All thoughts of sticking to the story vanished as Rose tried to understand.

Poppy squeezed her hand again, cutting in. 'Where is he? Can Rose see him?'

'He's in a hospital in Nottingham. But you need to be prepared, Rose. He's been sedated until they get him stable. His oxygen levels were very low, and he has a number of broken ribs and a stab wound to the stomach. It looks like he's taken quite a beating.'

Rose squeezed her eyes shut to block out the picture.

'He's lucky to be alive,' DC Brown added.

'He didn't have his inhaler,' Rose said. 'He has asthma.'

DC Brown gave her a penetrating stare. 'Did you know he didn't have his inhaler, Rose?'

Poppy squeezed her hand again, harder this time. Rose resisted the urge to snatch it away from the, now painful, grip.

'I assumed he had one with him, there was always one in the car. But if his oxygen levels were so low – he obviously didn't have it with him, *did he?*' Rose heard her voice rise in pitch. Hysterical.

Another tight squeeze on her hand.

'The paramedics reached him just in time. It seems like he was also suffering from some kind of acute allergy.'

Visions of young, vulnerable Olly came into Rose's mind and her protective instinct returned, stronger than ever. Except this time, she couldn't blame bullies at school. This time, it was her fault. She felt herself physically drawn to be with him like iron filings to a magnet.

'We need to go.' Rose was already on her feet, wrenching her hand away from Poppy's grasp at last.

'I don't think you'll be able to see him until later, so maybe wait here for a bit?'

'I don't care. I need to be with him!' Rose was frantic.

'Where did you find him?' Poppy's calm voice stopped her in her tracks as she paused in the doorway.

'In a static caravan in Skegness.'

Rose suddenly thought about Em. 'Was it Emily Totton? Was she there?'

'No, but we suspect that she had been present. We have some items which we've sent for DNA analysis.' DC Brown stood and turned to Rose. 'So your hunch may have been right. She'll be brought in again for questioning – once we have more evidence.'

'But what did Olly say?' Rose needed to know everything, now.

DC Brown took a breath. 'I'm afraid he was unconscious when we found him, so we haven't been able to ascertain what happened, yet.'

'Let's go.' Rose started putting on her coat. 'I need to be there, even if I can't see him. I just need to be there.'

Poppy turned to DC Brown who was now also on her feet. 'Thank you for finding him.'

'I'm glad we have, and rest assured, I won't rest until I have found out who did this.'

Rose felt her face pale at the determination in DC Brown's voice. She suspected that she was one of those police officers who never gave up.

Chapter Thirty-One

'He's not answering.' Rose sighed as she put the burner phone down.

'Good riddance. He's obviously done a runner. Let's hope you never hear from him again – evil bastard,' Poppy hissed. 'It's probably better if he thinks Olly is dead.'

Rose wondered if that had been Dan's plan all along. Maybe he did think Olly was dead. She could believe anything of him now. His final sentence haunted her. 'We can start our new life together.' What had he meant by that? Surely he'd been talking about their separate lives – that they would never meet again. It had seemed an odd thing to say.

Rose eyed the array of unhealthy snacks in the hospital vending machine, resisting the temptation to buy a chocolate bar - the craving for the comfort of sugar was almost overwhelming. She chastised herself. She had almost caused Olly's death and was framing someone who was innocent, for his kidnap. How could she even be thinking about chocolate?

'Poppy.'

Poppy looked up from scrolling through her phone. 'Mmm?'

'It's not right. About Em. It's not right.' She spoke in a low voice even though the room was empty. 'She doesn't deserve this. She's got a sister who needs her.'

Poppy tightened her lips into a thin line, but didn't respond.

'Listen, Poppy. This is down to Dan, not her. I can't do this to her. We can still blame Dan – come clean and tell the truth. All of this is down to him. He's the one who should pay.'

'No. We agreed!' Poppy's voice was cold.

'I can't. It's not right.'

Before Poppy could protest again, a doctor dressed in blue scrubs appeared.

'Mrs Walker?'

Rose jumped to her feet. 'How is he? Is he alright?'

'Fortunately the surgery went well. The stab wound was millimetres away from his liver. The paramedics reached him just in time. Your husband is lucky to be alive. As well as the asthma, he's had some kind of severe allergic reaction. Does he have an allergy?'

'Yes, he's allergic to cats and dogs.' Rose hadn't thought about that.

'That explains it, then. The paramedics suspected as much as there were lots of dog hairs around the caravan.'

Poppy caught Rose as she swayed.

'Can I see him?'

'I would go home and come back in the morning – he's still sedated, as his body is recovering. But you'll be able to speak to him tomorrow, I'm sure.'

'Come on, Rose.' Poppy propelled her along the corridor. 'You want to be at your best tomorrow, don't you? The last thing Olly needs is to wake up to some bog-eyed hag tomorrow.'

Rose raised a faint smile. 'Okay. But I won't be able to sleep.'

As Rose and Poppy went down the corridor on their way to the exit, Rose noticed a uniformed police officer standing outside one of the rooms.

'Is that...'

'Just a precaution, Mrs Walker.' He smiled. 'I'll keep your husband safe.'

Rose glimpsed the prone form of Olly through the small window wired up to various machines, and her heart clenched with pity for him. She wanted to rush in and take him in her arms. To hold him and keep him safe.

She gripped the rim around the window with her fingers, bringing her face close to the glass for a few seconds before Poppy gently steered her away.

'I meant what I said, Pops,' Rose said as they reached the car park. 'I can't do this to Em.'

Poppy sighed. 'Look, let's just park that for now and see what tomorrow brings. What you need is a good night's sleep. Olly is safe now – that's the main thing. The rest can wait until you're rested and your head's a bit clearer.'

Rose replied, 'I guess...'

'Just focus on Olly for now.'

As they got into the car, Poppy said, 'Look. I need to get back to the kids. I hope you don't mind, but I rang your mum and your parents are going to come over and stay with you tonight.'

Rose groaned. 'For God's sake, Poppy! Why did you do that?'

'You can't keep them at arm's length for ever, Rosy.' She swallowed. 'They feel like you're being very distant and can't understand why. You need to let them in, because they feel they've done something to upset you.'

Rose huffed in irritation. 'For goodness' sake,' she muttered under her breath.

'This isn't just about you, Rose. Remember? As far as they're concerned, you've got Olly back in one piece and...you should be relieved and happy.'

As they drew up outside the house, Rose's heart sank when she saw her parents talking to Walter. Her face burned at the thought of the conversation they might be having.

Her mother rushed towards her, enveloping Rose in a tight hug. 'Thank God he's back!' she released her. 'How's he doing?'

'Yeah not too bad, considering the state he was in when they found him. He's had surgery but he's going to be okay.' Rose forced a smile.

'I'm so glad, Rose.' The genuine warmth in Walter's eyes made Rose feel even worse.

'Thanks to you, Mr Powell.' Rose's mother had never got out of the habit of the last twenty years and Walter no longer tried to correct her.

'I was more than happy to help.' Walter dismissed the subject with a wave of his hand.

'We've just been admiring Mr Powell's new acquisition, and I must say, it's pretty impressive.' Her father indicated the mobility scooter by the front door. 'And Harold obviously approves.'

Rose spotted Harold sitting, regal as ever, observing them from the basket on the front of the scooter. She smiled as she spotted the blanket Walter had provided for him to sit on.

Walter followed her gaze. 'He took possession immediately so the least I could do was make him comfortable. Harold doesn't seem enamoured with any of the things I bought him.' He gave a wry smile. 'Anyway, you must have a lot to talk about so I'll get on. It's just about time for my cocoa. I find these light evenings a bit of a trial I must admit. Odd how I never noticed it when I was working.'

Thank you again, Mr Powell, for all you've done for Rose and Olly.'

Walter waved his stick in reply as he headed for his front door, Harold jumping out of the basket and following him indoors.

'Mum! Can you stop thanking Walter. It's embarrassing!' Rose said as they got inside.

'£20,000 is a lot of money, Rose. It's not something to be taken lightly,' said her father.

'I know...I know,' Rose muttered as she put the kettle on. The business of making a hot drink was always something to do, other than simply standing aimlessly in the kitchen. Maybe that's why someone was always making cups of tea in a crisis – it was a default activity to fill a void.

'Rose, I know there's something you're not telling us.' Rose detected the concern in her mother's voice and immediately resented it. Why couldn't they get off her case? She wasn't a child anymore.

'Look, Mum, Dad.' She turned and looked at them, switching the kettle on with an irritated gesture. 'Whatever is going on is something that Olly and I have to deal with – it's not for you to worry about.'

'Of course we're going to worry – we're family, and you're my baby.'

'Oh for God's sake, Mum.' Rose slammed the mugs down on the counter.

'We know that you're not a child anymore, Rose.' Her father put a cautioning hand on her mother's arm. 'But you can't blame us for worrying.'

The tears that had appeared in her mother's eyes alarmed Rose more than any questions or words could have done. She had never seen her mother cry before. The Sugdens never made each other cry – at least, not once they were over the age of ten or so.

She dropped the spoon she was holding on the counter, coffee grains spilling everywhere and went to her mother and held her tight. Another thing that was different. Until now, it had always been one of her parents holding her. 'Mum, I'm so sorry.'

Her mother sniffed and blew her nose into a tissue which she held crumpled in her hand.

'I'm...I'm just a bit all over the place at the moment, what with everything.' She swept up the spilled coffee granules into a cupped hand. 'I'll feel better once Olly's well enough to come home. I'm just dead tired.'

'Maybe we're all a bit overwrought. We'll get out of your way, Rose, and you get some rest.' Her father ushered her mother into the hall. 'Let us know how Olly gets on.'

Before Rose knew it, they were gone.

Although she heaved a sigh of relief, part of her felt their departure as some kind of loss.

Chapter Thirty-Two

Rose was almost afraid to enter the room. She stood in the doorway listening to the beeps and hum of the machinery monitoring Olly.

'It's okay, lovey. You can go in.' The nurse stood beside her. 'I know it's scary to see him like this. It's always a shock.'

When Rose didn't respond, she stepped into the room. 'Let me see if he's awake.'

Leaning over Olly, she touched his arm. 'Olly? You have a visitor. Aren't you the lucky one.'

Rose saw Olly's eyes open but was rooted to the spot. It was like a bad dream where she couldn't move, however much she wanted to. The guilt and fear of facing him was overwhelming.

The nurse beckoned. 'Come on love. Come and sit here and hold his hand.' She moved a chair closer to the bed. 'I'm willing to bet that your presence will be more healing than any medication.'

Rose knew she had to face him. She couldn't not.

She stepped over and stood by the bed but couldn't stop the sharp intake of breath at the sight of his battered face, one eye, bruised and swollen shut.

'Hello Olly,' she said as tears appeared from nowhere – she hadn't expected them. 'Thank goodness you're okay.'

She grasped his hand and kissed his forehead.

'How're you feeling?'

Olly opened his good eye. 'Not bad. Not while I'm on all these painkillers,' he mumbled, his dimple evident as a faint smile hovered.

A rush of love filled Rose as she saw Olly. Her Olly. She had him back now and would do anything to keep him.

Rose knew, deep down, that she had to tell him the truth. If she was going to save their marriage, it couldn't be founded on a lie. But maybe now wasn't the time – she needed to wait until he was stronger.

'It was all my fault. I've been such a dick.' Olly winced as he moved one of his legs. 'I'm so sorry, Rosie.'

'Shhh. Don't worry, babe. You're safe. That's all I care about now.'

Rose rubbed her thumb across the back of his hand.

'It was her. I can't believe I was so stupid!' A tear trickled from the corner of his eye.

A week ago, Rose would have enjoyed his remorse, but that was then. Now it was like salt in her guilt.

'Rosy, I'm so sorry. I messed up...' Olly closed his good eye as another tear slid out from under his eyelid.

'Shhh. Whatever it is, it doesn't matter now. We can sort it.' Rose's heart clenched with love for him.

'But she took me...'

Rose couldn't help asking. 'Who took you, babe?'

'I smelt her perfume. I heard her talking to me. She wouldn't get my inhaler.' He took in a sharp breath through clenched teeth as if reliving the trauma.

'None of that matters now. I love you and I'm so glad you're back. Let's just put it all behind us and get back to being us.' Rose's voice was firm.

'You say that now. But it might be harder than you think.' She could hear panic and fear in his voice as he turned his face away.

'None of that matters now. Just rest.' She ran her fingers through his hair, just as she'd always done and within a few minutes he was asleep.

Rose tip-toed out of the room. She leant against the wall and tried to breathe. How could she tell Olly the truth now? Now that he thought it was Em. That's what he would tell the police. How could she contradict him?

No sooner had that thought formed than she saw the familiar figure of DC Brown coming towards her with another police officer she didn't recognise.

'Morning, Rose.' This is DS Torren. We've come to see what Olly is able to tell us. She went to push the door open. 'Is he awake?'

'Y-yes, he is. I've just spoken to him. But I think he might be asleep now.' Rose wanted to put the conversation between Olly and DC Brown off for as long as she could.

The nurse bustled over. 'Just a few minutes. He's already had enough excitement this morning.' She winked at Rose.

As the police disappeared into Olly's room, Rose took out her phone. She needed to talk to Poppy. Rose had never realised how lonely a lie – or several lies, come to that – could make you. She sighed in relief as Poppy answered immediately.

Poppy looked around the hospital restaurant. 'What a depressing place this is!'

Rose followed her gaze to the pre-wrapped, chilled sandwiches and the sugary drinks in the chiller cabinet. She stirred some sugar into her weak coffee.

'How's Olly? Have you spoken to him?'

'He-he's fine. But...' Rose rested her head in her hands, elbows on the tables. She looked up at Poppy. 'But he thinks it's all his fault! He's blaming himself for everything. He's sure it was Em.'

'Well...in many ways it is his fault, isn't it? He's the one who had an affair in the first place, for God's sake!'

Rose turned her head away from Poppy's anger.

'Come on, Rose. I'm right and you know it.'

'But I can't...I can't not tell him the truth.' She looked back at Poppy. 'Pops, I can't.'

'Didn't you say DC Brown was with him?'

Rose nodded.

'Well I think it's already too late then.'

Rose knew she was right. She'd known it already. But Poppy didn't seem to understand her anguish about the now, in-evitable, lie her life would become. She was the only person who could help her through this, and she didn't get it.

Someone with long, blonde hair caught Rose's eye. She would recognise those extensions anywhere. Em had her back to where Rose and Poppy were sitting, talking to the woman at the information desk.

'Did you—' Poppy followed Rose's gaze. 'Oh my God! Is that...'

Rose nodded.

They watched, transfixed, as Em became agitated, slamming her designer bag down on the desk, making the woman jump. The café and foyer area was too noisy to hear what was being said.

Eventually Em turned, tossing her hair over her shoulder, the woman thin-lipped with disapproval.

'Do you think she's actually got the nerve to come and see Olly?' Poppy whispered.

Rose didn't answer as Em fished her phone out of her bag and started talking, holding it up in front of her.

'*What?* She's actually making a live feed!'

'I'm not having this!' Rose went to get up, but just as Poppy put a restraining hand on her arm, DC Brown appeared with two uniformed officers.

Rose and Poppy watched open-mouthed, Poppy's hand still on Rose's arm As DC Brown, spotting Em, made a bee-line for her.

She produced a pair of cuffs and slid them around Em's wrists and appeared to be doing the anything-you-say, spiel. One of the officers relieved Em of her phone, switching it off and she was ushered out of the main entrance. A few onlookers watched, also open-mouthed, one having the presence of mind to start filming. He was spotted by the other officer and also relieved of his phone.

Within a minute, the whole area reverted to business as usual – Em's arrest apparently being a small blip in the hospital day. Rose noticed a satisfied smirk on the face of the woman behind the information desk. She let out a long breath as Poppy removed her hand.

'Did we just see that?' she whispered, wide-eyed. 'Yess!' She fist-pumped the air.

Rose didn't respond. She'd thought the sight of Em being led away in handcuffs would have left her jubilant. After all, it was what she's wanted out of all this, wasn't it? To have Olly back and Em out of the picture? On the outside?

But all she felt was an empty sensation as if part of her had been hollowed out.

It was definitely too late to change her story now.

Chapter Thirty-Three

T he next week passed in a blur of hospital visits as Olly got stronger day by day and his eye returned to normal, only a faint bruise any visible evidence of the beating he'd taken.

Rose sensed that things had changed between them as Olly was consumed with guilt about the affair and she herself was carrying the weight of a lie. They danced around each other in careful steps which Rose found exhausting. Although he was physically back, the Olly she'd known before hadn't returned.

By the end of the week he was more than ready to be discharged. He'd given his statement to the police and Em was still being held in custody, charged with false imprisonment and attempted murder.

Rose kept her focus on Olly and tried to put all uncomfortable thoughts about Em out of her head. There was one thing that wouldn't go away, though. Em's sister. What had happened to her? And however much she tried to not think about it, the fact that she was innocent in all this – more so than Em – couldn't be avoided.

How could she have thought that once Olly was back all her problems would be over? That it was just as simple as getting Em off the scene. Rose was astonished how naïve she had been only a few months ago. Poppy had tried to tell her but Rose hadn't been ready to hear it. And now she had never felt so isolated and ashamed. Caught in a web of lies that was too strong for her to break.

Once Olly was home, without the surrounding scaffolding of the life and routine of the hospital, the tension between them grew more oppressive. Rose tried to cook him nice meals – even getting her mother to drop round some of her famous casseroles. They watched their favourite films, did all the things they had enjoyed in their old relationship but now everything felt hollow and meaningless. Rose felt trapped and claustrophobic but stayed at home, trying to make everything right, until one morning, things erupted.

'For God's sake, Rose! Why don't you go back to work? You don't need to be here all the time. I can look after myself, you know. I'm not an invalid!' Olly levered himself up from the chair and began pacing around the room like a caged animal.

'But I've still got another week off. Now that you're feeling better, I thought we could have a few trips out. You know, go to some of our favourite places?' Rose knew that Olly would sense the pleading tone even as she said the words. She was grasping at anything that might rekindle their old relationship so that she could forget about the lie she had let Olly believe. But deep down, she knew it was gone forever and that soon she would have to face it.

'Rose. I just need some space, okay? Do I have to spell it out?'

Rose stared at Olly's flushed face, opened mouthed, as reality slapped her in the face. This was an Olly that didn't need her.

She stood up.

'Okay then, I'll head off to Paws for a bit.' She found herself walking out of the room and leaving the house without another word.

Paws was busy with the usual Sunday visitors and when Cath spotted her, she beckoned Rose over.

'Rose, thank goodness you're here. Can you show the Crawfords around the canine area?'

'Sure.' Rose put on her Paws fleece and led the family towards the sound of excited barking. Visitors always set most of the dogs off.

She was occupied for the next half hour introducing Cam and Annabel and their children to the quietest dogs.

'Oh can we have this one? Please?'

Marnie stroked a labrador lovingly.

'She's called Shania,' Rose told her.

'Hi Shania.' Marnie kissed her fur.

'For real? Shania?' Annabel gave a sudden loud burst of laughter which caused Shania to back away and growl.

Rose sighed. This was going to be a tricky task. 'I don't think Shania is ready for a new home just yet. Let's meet someone else.' Rose firmly steered them away, ignoring Marnie's protests.

She tried to think of a more suitable candidate as they walked. They stopped in front of a Westie who looked at them, head cocked to one side.

If anything said, 'Take me,' it was that.

'This is Brutus,' she said, opening the cage door and slipping a lead on. 'How about you take him?' She passed the lead to Marnie, Shania apparently having been forgotten. They walked to the field where Marnie passed the lead to her brother.

Rose sensed a rapport building and sat on a bench as the family took turns with their new best friend. She observed how they interacted, stooping to pet him and talk to him, giving him one of the handful of treats she had given them. Brutus was in his element and Rose felt herself relax.

She loved this place – her special place where she could be with the animals whose company she loved, who demanded so little and gave so much, many vulnerable to unscrupulous owners. When she'd first started volunteering after Poppy started working there, Rose had applied to the RSPCA, wedded to the idea of rescuing and nurturing ill-treated animals, true to her romantic nature. Rose sighed as she remembered the distress of dealing with aggressive owners, and animals that were beyond help. The job had been short-lived as Rose had despaired, feeling that there were more failures than successes. Her manager had gently suggested that maybe the front line wasn't for her and pointed her in the direction of volunteering at Paws instead.

Rose had trained as a hairdresser, where her caring nature and ability to put people at their ease had been put to good use. Aside from which, her technical skills had earned her the top of the class prize when she'd left college. She'd found her place in life and had been content – until a few weeks ago. In an hour or so she would have to go home. And she had no idea how that would go.

Eventually she could put it off no longer as Paws closed for the day.

Arriving outside her house, she paused in the car for a few minutes, taking deep, steadying breaths. There was no sign of Walter, Harold, or the mobility scooter, so no excuse to put off going indoors.

Olly was playing a video game as she sat beside him. 'I've decided to go back to work tomorrow. I'll take the extra week some other time.'

'Okay,' he muttered before putting the controller down. 'I'm sorry I was snippy.'

'It's okay,' Rose soothed.

'Look. We...us. I don't know how to do it anymore.'

Neither do I.' It was one of the few honest things Rose had said in a long time.

'So what do we do?'

Rose sighed. 'We try to get back to normal. I'll go back to work tomorrow, and maybe if the physio says it's okay, you could go back to the gym for a bit.'

'I don't think I can face going back there.' Olly stared at the motionless screen.

'But it's your job, babe.'

'I know, but everyone is going to know that I've been such a dick.'

Rose sat straight. 'No they won't. And anyway you're tough enough to brazen anything out these days.' She tapped the biceps on his upper arm playfully. 'You can do it. After the first visit, it'll soon get back to normal. You've got to take the plunge sooner or later.'

Olly sighed. 'Maybe after physio, I'll pop in for ten minutes tomorrow.'

'Good plan!' Rose took his hand. 'I don't know how we get back on track either, so we just take one day at a time, agreed? Things will sort themselves out in time, I know it.'

She felt the knots of tension in her stomach ease a fraction as Olly left his hand in hers.

'I thought you weren't back until next week.' Shona looked up as Rose opened the door.

'Thanks for the welcome. Now I feel really valued in the workplace.' Rose grinned.

'Well of course we're all thrilled to see you,' trilled Shona in an extra loud voice. There were murmurs of assent around the salon.

Shona drew Rose into the kitchen. 'How's Olly doing? I can't tell you how relieved we all were to hear about his return. For once the police got it right.'

'He's doing great but I need to come back, we're driving each other mad at home.'

Shona placed the back of her hand on her forehead in a theatrical gesture. 'I can't even begin to imagine me and Bob in the same house, even for a day.'

Rose laughed, already feeling better for being back in familiar surroundings where everything was carrying on as normal. No traumas here other than Mrs Scott spilling her tea.

'I thought I'd ring some of my cancellations and see if they could come in this week. Other than that, I'll do some tidying and cleaning.'

'Oh it's so good to have you back, babe.' Shona wrapped Rose in a sudden bear hug, knocking the wind out of her. 'Okay. Onwards and upwards.' She headed back into the salon, the door banging shut behind her.

Rose found herself spontaneously smiling for the first time in weeks as she followed Shona through, closing the door gently behind her.

At the reception desk, Abby was talking to a woman Rose didn't recognise as a regular. As she approached, Abby turned to Rose. 'I was just saying to...'

She turned to the woman, eyebrows raised. 'Angie.' The woman volunteered.

'...Angie, that we don't have space for anything other than dry cuts today.'

Rose smiled. 'It's okay, Abby. I can fit Angie in.'

Abby frowned. 'Are you sure, Rose? It's your first day back.'

'Yes, I'm sure. She gestured to Angie. Come this way and let's see what we can do for you.'

'Thank you so much. I've just moved here to look after my mother who's had a stroke. And what with getting everything scrted in the house, my hair has taken a back seat, I'm afraid.'

'Rose pulled her fingers through the curly, dark blonde hair. 'It looks like your hair has a life of its own.'

'You can say that again,' Angie chuckled. 'That's why I keep it short.' She sighed. 'I used to straighten it every day, but now I can't be bothered. It's not as if I need to look good for work anymore.'

'How about I just cut it into a style that's easy to manage? Something you can finger-dry?'

'That sounds just the thing. Thanks, Rose.'

Rose froze, startled by the use of her name.

As if reading her thoughts, Angie said, 'I heard the girl on reception call you that.'

'Oh yeah, of course. Okay let's get you shampooed and see what we're dealing with,' she said with false gaiety.

As she stood at the sink Rose's heart gradually settled back into a normal rhythm. When Angie had used her name, Rose had for a panicky moment thought that maybe she'd been sent by Dan. Or even Sal. Some kind of threat. She closed her eyes as she massaged Angie's scalp. Would she be looking over her shoulder for ever?

She knew full well that she had been the object of much gossip in her absence, as well as conjecture about Em. But everyone was careful to avoid the subject, for which she was grateful and by the end of what turned out to be a routine day at the salon, Rose had relaxed. There had even been minutes where it was as if none of the nightmare of the last few months had happened. She got ready to leave on more of an even keel, her more positive mood buoyed up by a new, happier secret.

When she got home, feeling pleasantly tired, Olly had cooked his special eggs and bacon on toast which they munched in silence in front of a rerun of an episode of Game of Thrones.

As they were washing up, Rose asked, 'Did you pop into the gym?'

'Yup.'

'And?'

'Yeah, they were all good.' He put the last of the plates away. 'I've agreed to go back next week.'

'Isn't that a bit soon?'

Olly gave an irritated sigh. 'I need to be doing something. I won't be working out or anything, just taking things easy. And I certainly won't be running the marathon with Mandy, or any marathons come to that any time soon.' He gave a wry smile.

'You will. You'll get back to it. I know you. You just have to want to do it.' Rose emptied the washing-up bowl and rinsed it out. 'I guess you're right about going back. I feel better for getting back to the salon.'

Some kind of normal service had been resumed.

Chapter Thirty-Four

'How are you feeling about going back to work tomorrow?'

Rose snuggled close to Olly enjoying the weight of his arm around her. Over the last week they had tip-toed their way back into some kind of normality.

'Okay, I guess.'

'It'll be good to get back to normal.' Rose sat up and looked at Olly when he didn't respond.

'I'll be sending good vibes,' Rose said half-jokingly. 'Not that you'll need them.'

Olly exhaled through his nose – a sign of irritation.

Rose experienced a now familiar feeling of panic. No matter what she did or said, she couldn't seem to get the old Olly back. It was as if the light had gone out. His body was doing all the things expected of it, but it was almost like a robot had taken over the essence of who Olly was. Just like one of the Sc-fi dramas they'd enjoyed together in the past.

She'd tried, over and over again to reassure him that his affair shouldn't be an issue between them, but she had come to realise he couldn't seem to forgive himself, and that anger and frustration was boiling over into their relationship.

'Fancy a coffee?' Rose headed to the kitchen, not waiting for an answer. Waiting for the kettle to boil, she gazed out of the window, watching a row of baby sparrows on the fence noisily demanding food from their harassed parents.

A week on, and the lies refused to retreat to the back of her mind - they lurked in her thoughts, especially when she was at home. DC Brown had been round and confirmed that Em had been arrested for kidnap and attempted murder, even though she was still proclaiming her innocence. Rose's stomach had somersaulted when DC Brown revealed that a witness – one of the staff at Weldon motorways services – had reported an altercation between Em and another man who they couldn't identify. Rose burned as she remembered using Em's name. She couldn't remember why she'd done it. It was just something that had come from nowhere. Some kind of reflex response born of not wanting to give her own name. Apparently Em was denying any knowledge of the encounter. It seemed that they hadn't questioned Walter.

Rose had dreamt of this time, when she and Olly were back together again and Em had been banished from their lives, but it wasn't working as she'd envisaged. What a childish idiot she'd been – to think that either of them could move on from this unchanged.

And there was something else she still hadn't told Olly – maybe now was the time.

When she'd missed her period a few times, Rose had put it down to stress, but the nausea she'd felt over the last few weeks drove her to get a pregnancy test. When the two bars had appeared, she stood looking at them – small lines with huge implications, this first sign of a new life.

A terrifying numbness had crept over her then. Deep down, Rose knew she wasn't a fit person to bring a baby into the world.

As she had settled back into life at Cutting It Fine, the numbness had receded and Rose had felt that maybe...just maybe...she could do this. She and Olly had always talked about children, and this could be the thing that could bring them back together again. A miracle baby. She had been waiting for the right moment to tell him. For once she had good news to tell. Something to celebrate.

She made the drinks and carried them into the living room where Olly was scrolling through his phone.

She sat beside him and tucked her arm through his. 'Babe, there's something I need to tell you.'

'Hmmm.' He didn't look up.

'I'm pregnant.'

Rose waited, holding her breath.

Olly swivelled his head and looked at her.

'Pregnant.' It was a statement rather than a question.

Rose felt the colour drain from her face. 'Aren't you pleased?'

Olly put his arms around her and pulled her close. 'That's great news,' he said without looking at her. 'Are you sure?'

She pulled back. 'I've done a test.' After a pause she added, 'Don't you want to know when it's due?'

'When's it due?'

'In around five or six months I think. But I'll know more when I've been to the doctors.'

Olly nodded. 'Have you told your parents?'

Rose drew back from him. 'No. I wouldn't tell them before you!'

'They'll be thrilled to bits.' Rose couldn't ignore the tinge of bitterness in his voice.

Something snapped in Rose and she stood up. 'For God's sake, Olly! Aren't you happy? Stop feeling sorry for yourself. Stop punishing me for something I haven't done.'

Rose bit her lip. She couldn't believe she'd just said that.

'We have another person to think about now. It's time we both grew up.'

In the doorway, she turned. 'We're going to Mum and Dad's and we'll tell them together before we go to Finn's gig.'

'But—'

Rose cut Olly off. 'Don't tell me you've forgotten. Just take some anti-histamines. I need to do this with you, not on my own.'

'Oh Rosy Posy! Oh that's wonderful!' Her mother released Rose from the hug and stood back, holding her at arm's length, observing her, head on one side. 'It won't be long before you're showing.'

'Mum!' Rose rolled her eyes.

'Humour me and let me enjoy this moment to celebrate my next grandchild.' She chuckled.

'Well done, love.' Her father gave her a wink. 'It's about time we all had some good news. Where's that champagne we had stashed away at the back of the cupboard?'

'Dad! It's there because no one likes it,' groaned Finn.

'We're going to open it and drink it anyway.' Her father was already on his knees rooting around amongst various bottles.

Once the bottle had been located and opened, they had a toast. 'Typical! I'm the one having the baby and I can't even join in the celebrations.' Rose pretended to complain.

'Cheers! Here's to better times.'

She caught Olly's eye and smiled. She appreciated the fact that he was doing this for her. Things were going to get better. It had taken a few weeks for her family to forgive Olly for the affair, but following Rose's lead, they soon dropped any grudge. She couldn't let them punish him because of her lies.

Jack and Jill jumped around, barking frantically at all the excitement, while Fern after a few minutes of thinking, came to a realisation. 'We're going to have a cousin!'

Rose had a glimpse of how the future could be. How she could be back inside the cosy blanket of her family again. They would see her differently now she was having a child.

'Okay, gang. I'm off to get ready.' Finn flicked his hair back in a nonchalant gesture, but Rose knew how nervous he really was.

'Go slay 'em little brother.' She nudged him before giving him a hug.

'We'll all be there, cheering you on,' her father added.

Finn shook his head. 'It's only a gig at the Red Lion. It's not exactly the Albert Hall.'

Once they were all seated with drinks to hand, Rose spotted Poppy squeezing her way through the crowded pub. She got up and went over to her, steering her away from the family.

'What's up, Rose?' Her eyes were wide with worry, and Rose felt a twinge of dismay at what she had put her friend through. But now that was all in the past and she could make Poppy smile again.

'Good news this time, Pops.' She stared meaningfully at her best friend before glancing at her stomach..

Then the penny dropped. 'Oh my God!! You're not...'

'Yup I am just a little bit pregnant.'

'Oh Rose!' She threw herself into Rose's arms. 'That's wonderful.' She drew back, tears in her eyes. 'This is your time, Rose. A new beginning. Everything else is behind you now.'

Rose glanced over Pete, sharing a joke with Olly who smiled and laughed in response. 'Do you know what, Poppy? For once I think you might be right.' She nudged Poppy. 'But I need to ask you a favour.'

Poppy's shoulders tensed and she put her drink down. 'What is it? Has something else happened?'

'I need to know if you are up to godmother duties.'

Poppy squealed as heads turned in their direction before hugging Rose once more.

As they made their way over to the family, Rose's mother stood. 'I'm guessing you've heard the good news,' she said to Poppy.

'Yeah. You and the rest of the pub,' Pete said rolling his eyes. Becca thumped his arm. 'Don't forget how you were when I told you about Fern. You actually ran out into the road shouting, "I'm going to be a father!"'

'Yeah, there was that.' Pete looked sheepish as Finn and the band stood to start their set, accompanied by whoops of support from the family.

Rose glowed with pride as each number was greeted with rapturous applause. She had never realised how talented Finn was, both as a musician and a poet. She closed her eyes and soaked up the atmosphere, the music, the cheers and whistles, her family around her and her best friend by her side. She had done it. The nightmare was over. She was awake now and this was her real life. The rest had just been a bad dream.

When Rose announced her news at the salon a couple of days later – glad of the distraction it provided from the events of the previous few weeks – she knew the reaction was of excitement tinged with relief that things were getting better for her.

There were hugs all round. 'Wow!' Shona held her hand to her forehead in mock panic. 'I'm going to have to let you have maternity leave, I suppose.'

'Rose laughed. I'm not planning to have too long off. My mum is falling over herself to babysit.'

'You say that now...' Shona said. 'But you'll feel different once it's born. Trust me.'

Marjorie was in her element. 'Didn't I say? I spotted it weeks ago.' She nodded importantly.

'I think an impromptu baby shower is called for,' Shona declared to a chorus of cheers.

The rest of the day passed in a pleasant haze as trips were made and clandestine parcels were smuggled through the salon, and by the time the final client had gone, later that afternoon, the salon was miraculously converted into a party venue within minutes.

Rose found herself smiling and laughing with her colleagues for the first time in weeks. Everything would be alright. It would just take time for Olly to adjust. The old Olly, she knew, would be thrilled about having a baby. And he was still in there somewhere.

Full of renewed optimism she left the salon but had only walked a few steps when she heard a familiar voice behind her.

'Hello Rose.'

Chapter Thirty-Five

S he froze for a second before turning around. She hadn't imagined it. Dan was standing behind her, frighteningly real.

'You knew I'd come back, right?'

Rose stared at him.

'Sounds like some kind of celebration going on in there.' He jerked his head towards the salon. 'So I'm guessing all's good.'

'Get away from me,' Rose hissed.

'Whoa! Just hold on a minute. After all I did for you? Putting my neck on the line. What kind of thanks is that?' His voice was menacing as he moved towards her. 'You got what you wanted. Didn't you enjoy getting revenge on that bitch?'

'Get away from me!' Rose spoke louder this time.

Dan looked over his shoulder and grabbed her arm tight. 'Not so fast, Rose. It's time for you to show some gratitude.' He hustled her along the pavement, away from the salon. 'Now if I recall, I did say I would come back so that we could start our new life together – and I've been pretty patient I think.'

So this was what he meant by 'our new life together.' He actually meant him and her...together. Rose's skin prickled at the thought of any kind of future with this monster and placed her free hand protectively over her stomach. 'You're mad! Do you think I would ever want to be with someone like you?' she spat. 'Especially now I've got Olly back. After what you did to him!'

Dan halted, still gripping her arm. Rose lost her balance at the sudden movement but his grip prevented her from falling. She winced at the pain. 'He's alive?' He was motionless for a few seconds before exhaling a sound that sounded half sigh, half hiss.

'We obviously weren't efficient enough. But hey! I guess it means he'll testify against Em. So all's well that ends well.'

He dragged her a few steps. 'Although that does create a complication, doesn't it?'

'What do you mean?' Rose's voice cracked.

'We'll have to finish the job. And then...my sweet...we'll head off for our new life together, just as we planned.'

'We? I didn't plan anything like that. You're mad!' She tried to drag her arm free and a searing pain shot across her shoulder.

'Oh you think I was just doing you a favour?' He gave a short laugh. 'Well, maybe it was all just business at first. But I soon realised that we'd make a good team. Under that sweet and innocent exterior, you are as ruthless as I am when it comes to getting what you want.'

Rose finally wrenched her arm away, clutching it with her hand. As she ran, she heard him calling, 'Where are you going to run to, Rose? You know what you need to do to keep your family safe. Too late to confess now.'

His voice faded into the distance as she ran.

Running up the path, she banged on the front door, not trusting her fingers to manage the keys.

'Olly!'

When he opened the door, Olly's eyes widened in shock. Almost faint with relief, Rose gave a fleeting thought to how dishevelled and wild she must look as she pushed her way past him into the hall, slamming the door behind them.

'Lock it!' she shouted.

Olly obeyed the command and then turned. 'What the hell's going on, Rose?'

The fear that one of Dan's people might have got to him before she could do anything, like last time, was more than she could bear.

She slumped onto the stairs. Now she had some time. Time to come clean. It was the only way to keep him safe.

Olly came and sat beside her, his arm around her. A few hours earlier, she would have been thrilled by the affectionate gesture, but now it made things worse because she was about to shatter the precarious world they had started to rebuild.

She savoured the final few moments, resting her head on his shoulder.

'I need to tell you the truth, Olly. The truth about what happened to you, because your life is in danger.'

'Are you okay, Rose? You look done in.' A look of genuine concern flashed across his face. 'Come on, let's get you into bed. You'll feel better after a nap. Maybe it's those pregnancy hormones kicking in.'

He went to get up but Rose pulled him back down. 'No, you need to listen.' She swallowed and took a breath. 'I arranged for you to be kidnapped. It was me.'

Rose felt the smothering silence envelop her, forcing all breath out of her body.

'What? Oh come on, Rose. We know who it was.'

'It wasn't Em. She's innocent.' Everything was coming out in the wrong order. Rose stopped to organise her thoughts.

'Look, I found out about you and Em because she was one of my clients. She couldn't stop going on about you.'

Olly made to interrupt but Rose carried on.

'So I followed her...and you, to see if it was true. I couldn't believe you would do that.' This time he didn't say anything.

'Poppy saw you and her at the gym and I followed you to that photo shoot. But when she posted a photo of you two together, I knew things were serious. So I decided to punish her. I wanted to get you back.'

'What the...'

'It was all pretty low-key at first – I imagined staging a burglary here and framing her by using DNA from the salon. But then I met Dan. And after that things got out of hand.'

'Who the hell is Dan?'

Rose forced herself to keep speaking and explained Dan's plan and how he had blackmailed her.

'I tried to get home to save you, but he was too quick for me. By the time I got back that night, you were gone. That's why I've rushed home now. He's coming for you, Olly.' Rose swallowed the sob in her throat – she had to keep going. 'It was him and one of his men that took you and hurt you.'

'But I heard—'

'Dan used AI to create Em's voice. I didn't know where you were or I would have come and found you. You have to believe me, Olly. I went to the police.'

'Did you tell them about Dan? Did you tell the whole story?'

Rose had no words. She couldn't meet Olly's gaze.

'I told them you were missing.' Her voice sounded small and far away.

The smothering silence returned, but thicker this time. Rose struggled to breathe.

Olly got up and stood at the bottom of the steps. He looked at her with an expression that froze Rose to the core. She didn't recognise his voice when it came. 'So you let me suffer. Not just physically, but you let me carry the guilt of having the affair. And you said nothing?'

'I—'

This time it was Olly who stopped her by holding up his hand.

'I don't want to hear your pathetic excuses. 'So now, thanks to you, this Dan is after me. Is that what you're saying? And, if that wasn't enough, you're happy to have let an innocent woman carry the can for *your* crime?'

'I'm not happy—' Rose tried to interject

'She's worth ten of you. In fact, I wonder if I've ever really known you at all.' Olly leant against the wall and closed his eyes.

Rose let the tears flow down her cheeks. 'Olly, I'm sorry. You've got to believe me. I never meant for any of this to happen.' She spoke between sobs as she held out her hand to him.

'Get up!'

'What?'

'You heard. Get up!' Olly's voice was rough.

He opened the door and grabbed the car keys. Indicating the car, he said, 'Get in. You're driving.'

Chapter Thirty-Six

'I 'm Oliver Walker. My wife wishes to make a new state-ment about my kidnap and the murder attempt on my life.'

The desk sergeant looked at Rose and she could see he recognised her. It was the same officer who had been on the desk when she had reported Olly missing the second time.

'Mrs Walker?' He looked from Rose to Olly, his eyebrows raised.

'Yes. I want to make another statement.' Rose's voice was growing stronger with the relief of confession. Of not having to carry the weight of a lie any longer. 'Also, I have reason to fear that my h— Olly is still in danger.'

'Take a seat and someone will be through shortly.' The officer picked up the phone and spoke in a low voice once Rose and Olly were seated. The hard plastic seats were not designed for comfort – just the thing before a confession. A comfortable seat wouldn't have seemed appropriate.

Olly didn't speak to her as Rose read the posters on the wall.

They didn't have to wait long before DC Brown appeared in the doorway.

'Mrs Walker. Come this way.' Her formality was chilling.

As Olly went to stand, she said, 'I need to speak to your wife on her own.'

'But—'

'If you could just wait here.'

Olly looked away as she was ushered through the door.

DC Brown showed her into a grey room containing a table and four chairs. The harsh lighting hurt her eyes. This time there were no pictures or plants – no suggestion of a welcoming environment.

Another officer came in and DC Brown introduced him as Detective Inspector Harmer.

Rose realised with a shiver that they were taking this seriously if a senior officer had been called in.

'I believe you wish to amend your statement about your husband's kidnap, Mrs Walker.' He put the file and pen he was carrying on the table and took a seat.

Rose nodded.

'Could you speak aloud for the recording, Rose?'

'Yes.'

The sudden switch to first-name terms threw Rose, nevertheless she felt herself relax a little bit.

'Where shall we start?' DI Hamer said, pen poised.

Rose started at the beginning and the truth followed easily. When she got to Dan's part in the story, DC Brown pushed a photo across the desk. 'Is this Dan?'

Rose recoiled at the sight of him. 'Yes, that's him.' She turned her head away. 'How did you...' she left the sentence hanging.

'When Olly was kidnapped our first thought was that he might have something to do with it. His MO is kidnapping and making victims suffer for the supposed crimes they've committed. He sees himself as a free-lance vigilante. But he has developed a side-hustle of demanding ransom payments. The only evidence we had was from the witness who saw you having an altercation with a man at the motorway services.'

Rose dropped her gaze to her lap.

'It was you, Rose, wasn't it?'

When she didn't respond, he pushed further. 'Why did you pretend to be Emily Totton?'

After a pause, he prompted her again. 'Rose?'

Under the table, she rubbed the skin on the side of her thumb. It had begun to heal and wasn't as sore now.

'I didn't plan it. It just came out. When she asked me my name, I just said it without thinking.' She moved to the edge of the chair, and putting her hands on the table leaned forwards. 'You've got to believe me!'

Without speaking. DI Harmer made notes, the sound of the pen moving across the paper, loud in the room.

Rose looked at DC Brown who was studying her as if trying to make sense of what she had done. There was an element of anger in her gaze. Disappointment.

Rose shrivelled inside. This was how everyone would look at her from now on.

'But he told me he was a police officer.' Rose dropped her gaze to the table. Was she really trying to make excuses for her behaviour?

DI Harmer made a dismissive sound. 'He was sacked from the force for gross misconduct – manipulating evidence – a few years ago. His real name is Michael Small. If he couldn't use the police force to punish what he saw as crime he resorted to doing it himself.'

'So why didn't you say at the time?' Rose looked up. Why hadn't they questioned her more closely? Maybe she would have told the truth if she'd felt safe, then all this wouldn't have happened.

'You didn't mention anything about the involvement of a man, only Emily Totton. If you'd have said we could have done something.'

Rose stared at the table. How could she have messed things up so badly?

'You've got to believe me about Dan's threat,' she said.

'Yes, we do, Rose. And now we know the truth, we have a lot of resources out looking for him. Tell us again what happened when he accosted you earlier.'

Rolling up the sleeve of her jumper, Rose showed them the red marks on her arm, bruises already forming. 'Like I said, he was there when I left the salon. He seems to have some mad notion that he and I had planned a future together.' She stopped, trying to resist gagging with a swallow. DC Brown pushed a glass of water across the table and Rose took a grateful sip. 'I never gave him any reason to think that. I think he thought that Olly was dead – he seemed taken aback when I said that he had survived. That's why I think Olly is in danger.' The last sentences came out in a rush. They had to keep Olly safe.

DI Harmer wrote some more notes. Watching him, she felt light-headed with relief that at last the truth had been told.

'What happens now?' she asked.

The police officers exchanged glances before DC Brown said, 'Would you excuse us for a moment, Rose?'

Rose imagined them discussing her case and whether to arrest her there and then. She gripped the sides of the chair with clammy hands wondering how many had sat here before her in the same situation.

When they returned, DI Hamer put the folder and pen down and leaned forward, his elbows on the table.

'Rose, the fact that you have come forward and told the truth will go very much in your favour when your case comes to trial, but we cannot ignore the serious offences you have committed.'

An arrow of ice shot down Rose's spine at the word 'trial' – suddenly it was all too real and now she had to face the consequences of coming clean. She would be going to prison. Her baby would be born in prison. She closed her eyes and took a shaky breath.

'But there is something more you can do to help us nail Michael Small once and for all, something which will go a long way towards a suspended sentence.'

Her eyes flew open and she leaned across the table. 'I'll do anything. I'm pregnant – I'll do anything to stay out of prison. Please. Anything I can do to put things right.'

DC Brown's eyes widened at this news, but neither officer commented.

'When Mich— Dan contacts you – which he will, would you be prepared to meet him wearing a wire so that we can get evidence that will make the case against him watertight?'

A breath caught in Rose's throat. She hadn't imagined having to face Dan again.

'I have a recording where he admits to the kidnapping. Would that help?' Rose moved forward to the edge of the chair once more, now desperate to help.

'When was this made?'

'I did it on my phone when I went to meet him to try and get out of the agreement. I thought it might be enough...' Rose trailed off uncertainly.

'So why didn't you bring it to us?' Rose flinched at the irritation in DC Brown's voice.

'I— I thought it might be illegal to record him like that. I didn't want to get into any more trouble. And I needed more evidence.' When neither officer spoke, Rose continued. 'He threatened my family so I thought I could sort it out myself.' She had run out of things to say.

'Can you play the recording to us now?'

Rose fished out her phone and fumbled her way to the recording app, closing her eyes and trying to block out the sound of her weak remonstrances to Dan as it played.

DI Harmer made several notes before sighing and looking up at Rose. His face stern. 'You should have brought this to us, but we have it now and need to move on. The good thing, however, is that this might go some way towards proving your resistance to the plan.' He made a few more notes. 'So, to return to my question. Are you prepared to meet him, wearing a wire?'

'We'll be right there and can pull you out if you're in any danger.' DI Harmer studied her.

She had to do this. She had to make sure Dan was never able to mete out his own form of justice by taking advantage of vulnerable people ever again. This was something she could do and she would find the strength from somewhere.

'I'll do it,' she said.

DI Hamer nodded. 'We appreciate the courage this will take and be assured, it will be impressed on the judge that you have tried to make reparation.'

A wave of exhaustion washed over Rose and she felt herself slump in the chair.

'You're free to go for now. It would be best if neither of you went home. Check into a hotel for tonight.'

Rose was suddenly filled with dread. 'What about my family? Will they be safe?'

'We have a police presence outside their homes and we will also be keeping an eye on Cutting It Fine. It might be an idea if you extend your sick leave.'

'But I've already gone back.'

'I'm sure you can think of something. We need to keep Dan away from the salon. Any place where you are, the people around you are in danger.'

Rose hadn't imagined she could despise herself any more than she already did, but now she wished she could curl up into a ball and disappear for ever.

'Get a good night's sleep, Rose and we'll be in touch tomorrow. If Dan makes contact, let me know immediately. 24/7.'

DC Brown handed Rose a card with her number on it.

When she reappeared in the foyer, Olly's face was etched with exhaustion.

'Your wife is free to go for now, Mr Walker, but as I've already suggested to her, it might be better for you both to avoid going home tonight.'

Olly nodded and stood to go. As she headed out of the door, Rose glanced back at DC Brown who gave her a brief nod and a smile.

She and Olly went their separate ways when they reached the budget hotel – there was an unspoken understanding. Although Rose had filled him in on what she had agreed to do to try and put things right, she knew that Olly would never forgive her. Neither of them were the people they had been when they'd first met as children.

Chapter Thirty-Seven

R ose saw Poppy showing a family around the canine area and marvelled that life could be carrying on as if nothing momentous had happened. People were still thinking of getting pets. Poppy was relaxed and doing the part of the job she enjoyed most – finding homes for the animals in their care. Rose watched the family spend a long time with Shania, petting and fussing her, and smiled. There were still good things going on in the world.

Once she had finished, Poppy waved and joined Rose in the makeshift coffee area. 'I think they'll be perfect for Shania. Did you see how she responded to them?'

Rose nodded. 'Yes, for such a picky dog, it was quite something.'

She'd wondered whether it was wise even to go to Paws with DC Brown's warning about her attracting danger ringing in her ears, but she needed to speak to Poppy and tell her what had happened. Surely it was safer here than at Poppy's house.

During the last few days hanging around in the budget hotel, Rose had had plenty of time to think about what this new, different life would look like for her. She had, at long last, let go of the notion that she and Olly could have anything resembling their old life and expected there was no form of relationship left for them that wasn't based on resentment and anger, even if it was unspoken. And there was no way her baby would be subjected to that. Rose knew she would always mourn what they'd lost and the old Olly, but she had seen, heard and done enough over the last months to learn that real life was a constant moving and changing thing and that to try and cling on to a past that no longer existed led to no good outcome for anyone.

So as she watched Poppy getting herself a coffee, she felt a curious lightness even though she knew there was a long journey ahead to make things right with the people she had hurt and lied to. But however rocky, she could see a way forward now that her life wasn't based on lies.

As Poppy sat, Rose said, 'Dan's back.'

Poppy turned, her face ashen. 'Oh shit! Have you seen him?'

'He was waiting for me outside the salon a few days ago and seems to have some notion about us going away together. He didn't know that Olly is alive, though.'

'Hang on, back up. You and him having a life together? Where did that come from?' She looked closely at Rose.

'Rose?'

'I've been to the police and told them everything. I had to, Pops. He was threatening to kill Olly. He's mad!'

'You've told them everything?'

Rose nodded. 'Yup. And it's a weight off my mind.'

'So they just...let you go? Are you under arrest? Oh my God, Rose!'

'They've let me go and I've agreed to do something for them. I'm going to meet Dan and get them the evidence they need to arrest him. He was sacked from the police for misconduct ages ago. His real name is Michael Small.'

Poppy's hand flew to her mouth.

'I'm going to meet him tonight—' Rose cut across Poppy's protest before she had chance to voice it, '—with the police monitoring everything. As soon as he does or says anything threatening, they'll move in.'

'Are you sure you can trust them not to mess things up like last time?'

'Yes. I have to be able to live with myself when all this is over, for this one's sake. And this is the first step in me putting things right.' Rose glanced at her stomach.

Poppy let out a deep breath. 'You've got guts, Rose.'

'Not really, I didn't confess until I was forced into it and Olly frogmarched me to the station.' Rose expelled a deep breath. 'By now, Em will know she's in the clear, thank goodness. What was I thinking?'

Poppy broke the silence. 'Look, Rose. I hate to say this, but what if Em goes to the salon or to your house even? Maybe she's the one bent on revenge now.'

Rose was stopped in her tracks before she thought. 'We've been told not to go home until Dan's arrest, and the salon is under surveillance as well, even though I've taken the leave owing me, so I don't think she'll get far.'

'But, don't you think online revenge might be more her style?'

'Well everyone will know, soon enough, so whatever she says can't make things worse than they're already going to be. Honestly, Pops, all I'm worried about at the moment is the safety of Olly and my family. I can't relax until he's caught.'

Poppy leaned over and gave her a tight hug. 'Proud of you, Rosy Posy.'

'I've been naïve and gullible. You tried to warn me, I know.'

'Maybe you had to learn it for yourself, though.' Poppy paused. 'You know I've always got your back, babe, whatever.' She sighed. 'And sometimes I need to see beyond my own issues.'

Rose returned the hug without comment.

'Right. That's enough therapy for one day. If you're finished, we have a collection to do. Up for it?'

Rose nodded. Collections were almost always difficult, sometimes with tearful, guilt-ridden owners, or worse, the discovery of cowed, malnourished animals who had long ago stopped trusting humans.

In the past, with memories of her brief employment with the RSPCA still traumatic, she had always tried to avoid these journeys, preferring instead to look after the animals who were already thriving at Paws – an activity that always lifted her spirits. But now she was a different, older Rose and would no longer try to imagine that the bad things in life weren't happening. She would face them head-on.

As they turned out of the entrance, Rose promised herself that she would teach her child to do the same – face things head-on.

Walter was kneeling in the garden when Rose drew up outside the house. As she climbed out of the car, he levered himself up using the handles on the kneeler he was using.

'Can't believe these irises are over already. Where has the time gone?'

His face registered alarm as she approached. 'Rose? What's happened? Is it Olly?'

'No, Olly's fine, but I need to talk to you, Walter. Can I come in?'

'Why, of course, my dear. Come in.' He brushed his hands on his trousers.

Rose's felt her heartbeat resonating through her whole body as she followed him into the house, bracing herself for his crushing anger and disappointment.

As they sat at the kitchen table, Harold taking up residence on a third chair from where he regarded her with narrowed eyes, Walter took her hands.

'What is it, Rose?'

She looked up at him, her heart breaking at the undeserved love and concern in his eyes. 'I've done a terrible thing, Walter,' she said, her voice trembling. She paused and took a breath. 'I've lied to you. The money you withdrew, to pay the ransom...' pausing, she cleared her throat.

'You didn't use it for that? Was that the lie?'

'No...yes, I mean I did use it to get Olly back, but it was my fault that he was kidnapped in the first place. I've lied to so many people that I love and made such a mess of everything.' A sob hovered in her throat and she couldn't speak.

'Tell me.' His tone was firm and Rose quailed inside. But she was no longer ten, she was a woman now and soon to be a mother. This was how she would start teaching her child how to live.

Rose explained everything to Walter and he listened without interrupting. When she had finished, she scanned his face, looking for clues as to what might come next.

Walter looked over at Harold, now in a crouching position, eyes closed, apparently unconcerned that Rose's life was imploding.

Walter sighed and put his hands over his face as Rose held her breath, bracing herself for what was to come.

In seemed like forever before Walter was ready to speak. 'Thank you for telling me, Rose. That was a brave thing to do, a step in the right direction, but...' he turned his gaze to the window. 'I can't deny that I feel betrayed. That the Rose Sugden I knew, who wouldn't hurt a fly, could do this.'

Rose felt every word was an arrow in her heart. She deserved no less. All she could do now was to try and put things right.

'I'm so sorry about the money, Walter. I'll pay you back, every penny.'

He stood and put the kettle on as Rose watched in silence, the hard lump in her throat making it imposible to speak.

'I always worried about your fierce loyalty to Olly.' He spooned out the coffee. 'I worried that it wasn't good for you...or him. But you were children then and I supposed that as you got older you would both find your own ways forward.'

He poured the hot water into the cups, a tremor still evident under the weight of the kettle. 'But I never imagined it would come to anything like this.'

He brought the cups to the table, rattling in their saucers. 'You poor girl. What a terrible time you've been through. I'm so sorry, Rose, that it has come to this.'

'Don't feel sorry for me, Walter. I brought this on myself and it's up to me to put it right. I'm just so relieved that Olly is safe.'

'Yes you made bad choices, Rose, and your loyalty to Olly led you into the clutches of a bad person. But don't forget that you are also a victim in all this.'

Rose took a sip of coffee and was silent for a few moments. 'It was like I became another person – I was still me, but a different me. Looking back on it now, it scares me that I was capable of doing those things.'

Walter took her hand. 'We all have a worst version of ourselves that can appear when we're under pressure and with the wrong people. And now you've experienced it you'll recognise the signs if you ever get in a situation that makes you feel like that again.'

Rose nodded. 'I'd like to think the real me is still a romantic, but maybe a more worldly wise one now.' She gave a wry smile.

Walter squeezed her hand in response. 'And do you know one of the best things?'

Rose shook her head.

'You *will* grow and thrive because of what's happened. You've taken responsibility head-on instead of becoming bitter and blaming others, reflecting only on your loss. I'm proud of you Rose, and thankful, for your sake, that everyone is safe.'

'There's something else, Walter.'

His hand stilled in hers.

'I'm pregnant.'

Walter looked at her for a moment, tears forming in his eyes. 'Oh my! Did you hear that, Harold? We're going to have a baby next door to fuss over.'

Harold licked his lips and made a purring sound.

'He's happy for you,' Walter said confident in his interpretation. 'We're both happy for you. And we're grateful for your thoughtfulness, that you brought us together. You did something good in the middle of your pain and distress. Hang on to that, Rose.'

Harold stood up and stretched before settling back on his haunches and purring in agreement.

Chapter Thirty-Eight

R ose checked her phone for the umpteenth time. Still no message and it was forty-five minutes past the time they were due to meet. The tension in her body held her upright and alert as she watched the comings and goings around her at the motorway service coffee shop. Dan was playing games – she knew that now. Probably checking for any police presence but also making her suffer the agony of waiting. However, this time they were ready, all exits covered and the fire alarm temporarily disabled with fire wardens primed to enable it if there was a real fire.

She thought about her family. She knew they were in a safe place but there was still a curl of worry that Dan might have outwitted the police once more and could be with them now – while she sat here, doing nothing.

The urge to get up and head back to her car was overwhelming and Rose was making a move to stand when she saw him. She watched as he made his way over, powerful, with his military gait. Clasping her hands in her lap she took deep breaths, reminding herself that this was the last time she would see him – as least, outside of a courtroom. She reminded herself that he was Michael Small.

'I thought you weren't coming!' Tension was evident in her snappy comment.

'Well, after the stunt you played last time, I had to be sure you didn't have company.' His slate grey eyes bored into hers and she looked away.

'I'm hardly going to risk my family, am I? I know what you and your cronies are capable of.' Rose exhaled a shaky breath. 'What do you want, Dan? You've got the money. Olly is alive, so you're at least not wanted for murder.' She was desperate to provoke him into some kind of admission so that this could all be over.

'Ah, but that's the problem, you see, Rose.' He leant back in the chair. 'Olly isn't supposed to be alive. He knows too much and he's in the way of you and me starting our new life.'

'You're mad! There is no us. No new life!' Rose spat.

'Well, the thing is, I've developed a liking for you, Rose Walker. Anyone who can do what you've done to get their own way is on my wavelength. Like it or not.'

Rose felt her insides turning to ice, the chill rising up into her chest. Was he trying to say that she had been a willing accomplice in all this? That she was like him?

'You're mad. You tricked me into something that was not...this!' Rose waved her hands around in the air between them.

'Well, whatever. We need to sort the Olly problem.'

Rose didn't reply, waiting.

'But I'll need your help.'

Again, Rose was silent.

'When he leaves Pro Fit might be a good time to catch him. Bundling him into a van is probably the way to go, and then somewhere remote. A shotgun wound...' Dan seemed to be thinking aloud.

'I know. Of course.' He leaned towards Rose, his eyes shining with an excitement that had something fanatical about it.

'Olly commits suicide. That's the way. Remorse over the affair, yada, yada.'

He smiled a complacent smile. 'Leave the details to me. All I need from you is to know his movements.'

Rose hoped this was all the police needed and prayed for them to appear and for this to be over, but there was no sign of rapid or sudden movement that she could ascertain around the coffee shop area.

She needed to get more. She had to lure him in.

'You were clever with that Em idea. Olly fell for it hook, line and sinker. He really believes that it was Em that kidnapped him. So why the need to get rid of him?' Rose couldn't believe she was actually uttering these words, but if that's what it took...

'Thanks for the compliment.' He inclined his head. 'I must say, I was very pleased about that. The AI voice worked perfectly. Lots of scope there for future projects. But I don't leave loose ends.' His tone darkened.

'And if I don't agree?' Rose felt this was the last throw of the dice. Thankful that he didn't know anything about the pregnancy.

'Rosie, you know what happens if you don't agree,' his voice was wheedling, patronising.

He sighed. 'The police might think they have your loved ones safe, but I know different.'

Rose said nothing and bowed her head. If he was right... It was all over. For a panicked moment, she believed him. That the police had messed up again. But then her head jerked up at a sudden crash and the sound of running footsteps.

Rose had never felt more relieved to see DC Brown advancing towards her. She went to stand. She felt Dan grabbing her arms before she saw him reach across the table. He gripped her tight.

'You bitch! If I go down. You're going down with me. I'll make sure of it!' he snarled between clenched teeth.

Rose had no recollection of what happened next except the sensation of the grip on her arms releasing as Dan was dragged away from her. Her shoulders burned from the way they had been jolted at the sudden force.

Sitting in the back of an ambulance, Rose sipped the hot, sweet chocolate drink, her body still trembling.

'It's okay, Rose. You're safe. We've got him. You did a wonderful job. I know how hard it was.'

Rose felt that DC Brown didn't know the half about how hard that had been for her, but she nodded anyway.

'Let's have a look at your arms.' The paramedic came over and turned them over gently. Angry red marks had already formed. 'You'll have some bruises I'm afraid, but painkillers should take the worst of the pain away. And your shoulders will settle. The main thing is to rest.'

Suddenly she remembered she was pregnant. How could she have forgotten? 'The baby... is it...?'

'Let's give you a thorough check over, but I'm pretty sure your baby is safe in there.' The paramedic indicated Rose's stomach.

Once it had been ascertained that all was as it should be, all Rose wanted to do was to go home. Did she still have a home? Would Olly even let her in?

She leaned her head against the ambulance door in defeat. 'Can I go home?'

'Your parents are here, Rose. They've come to fetch you. But before you go, just to let you know we're going to release a statement that someone is helping us with our enquiries but we won't mention your name before the trial. If I was you, I would keep it like that. Your defence lawyer will give you advice on how to proceed.'

Rose was past embarrassment and humiliation, she was too numb, and when her dad appeared and put his arm around her, she meekly allowed herself to be led to the car.

Once she was settled in the back seat, her parents turned. 'We're so proud of you, Rose. And so glad that you're safe.' Her mother's voice wavered.

'Let's get you home.' As her father started the car, Rose felt safer than she had in a very long time.

Chapter Thirty-Nine

A fter a few days with her parents, Rose wanted to be in her own home. Olly had offered to move out, for which she was grateful, although when she had told Poppy, she had snorted and said, 'I should think so! After all, it's not him having the baby, is it? Don't forget he's not innocent in all this!' Rose had smiled on the other end of the phone. She knew that Poppy would always be Poppy, but she also knew that she spoke a lot of sense.

Things had not been easy with her family, Pete in particular had been cutting in his comments, angry that his children had been in danger, until, unable to stand it any longer, Rose had snapped.

'Look, I know I've made mistakes, and yes, I've made a mess and let you all down, but I'm trying to put things right! What more can I do? I can't keep apologising for ever!' The tears had streamed down her face.

Her father had put his arm around her. 'Well, I, for one, am proud of how you helped the police get that man. That took guts, Rose. And yes, you made some bad decisions, but which of us hasn't over the years? It was just that yours had serious consequences.' He'd glared at the family, daring them to defy him.

'Everything Rose did was to save her marriage – she meant well. She never meant any of this to happen and now, as she said, she's doing her best to put things right. Let's not forget that in many ways, she was the victim here. And there but for the grace of God, go any of us.'

There was silence after this unusually long speech from her father.

'And now we have a new member of the family to think about.' He brushed unaccustomed tears from his eyes with the back of his hand.

'Dad's right. I'm sorry Rose. Come here.' Pete held her tight and Rose's body relaxed with relief in his arms. Relief that she had been accepted back into the family and was no longer on the outside, looking in, burdened with secrets.

Finn smiled at her over Pete's shoulder. When Rose had apologised to him and tried to explain he had waved her angst away. 'It's behind us now, sis. No point in ifs and buts and sackcloth and ashes. Time to move on.'

Rose softened as she remembered the faraway look that appeared on his face. 'Sackcloth and ashes. A great name for a song.'

As he reached for his laptop, she'd put an arm around his shoulders. 'As long as it's not about me.'

He grinned. 'You'll have to wait and see. Now clear off before the creative juices dry up.'

'Gross!' Rose had grimaced before leaving him to it.

Once her parents had left and Rose was alone in the house, she looked at the stairs, reliving the last time she and Olly had been there together, the moment that the final strand of their relationship had snapped.

The framed photos documenting their life together looked back at her as she mounted the stairs, gazing at each one in turn. She wasn't ready to take them down yet, but as she patted her stomach, Rose knew they would eventually be replaced with images of a new life.

For the first time in months, she slept soundly that night and awoke ready to face the day and the challenge she had been putting off. Several weeks had passed since she had last been in the salon, and Rose had no idea how much everyone knew or what had leaked out on the grapevine. But of one thing she was sure, if there was talk, Cutting It Fine would be at the centre of it. The local papers had revealed the story of Olly's kidnap and subsequent arrest of Michael Small. There had been a brief mention of a woman who was helping them with their enquiries but the news had soon moved on to the threatened closure of the sandwich factory on the outskirts of town that employed hundreds of residents.

Sitting on the settee, Rose's finger hovered over Em's account. There was one more thing niggling at Rose, something else she had to do. She had allowed herself only one glance at Em's socials over the last few days and could see that she was milking her false arrest for all it was worth – she couldn't blame her for that. Poppy kept her informed and they were both relieved that Em had seemingly decided not to mention Rose's part in everything that had happened...yet. Poppy was firmly of the view that if she was going to drag Rose's name through the dirt, she'd have done it by now.

Taking a breath, she messaged as herself.

Hi M. There is something I need to tell you. Can you DM me?

Rose tapped the phone, waiting, and caught her breath when a notification came up on a messaging app.

What is it?

I need to tell you something. It's important.

Rose had expected Em to be late and wasn't surprised when she swung into the coffee shop fifteen minutes after their agreed time, phone in hand.

'Hi, thanks for coming.' Rose made her voice sound firm.

'You've got a nerve after what you did!' Em spat the words out. 'I can't believe I'm even here.' She put the phone down on the table and tossed her hair over her shoulder.

'You're not doing too badly from what I can see. Good publicity, right? Oh and I can vouch for Emmanuel, he does a great job with your hair.' Rose couldn't resist the dig, but immediately regretted the words. She had to be better than this.

A flush appeared on Em's face, followed by a frown. 'How dare you belittle what Olly and me have been through.'

Rose held up her hands in a conciliatory gesture. 'Okay, I'm sorry, I'm sorry. I shouldn't have said that.'

'So what did you have to tell me that I don't already know?' Em glared at her, stirring a skinny latte.

'I'm here to say I'm sorry about what happened to you. I don't know how much you know, but things spiralled out of my control after Michael Small got me in his clutches.'

'Don't even try to make excuses!'

Her heart thumping, Rose pushed on. 'Look, I'm not looking for your forgiveness. Let's face it, we'll never be best buddies, but I am truly sorry for what I put you through. At the end of the day, I want Olly to be happy, and if that's with you, I have to let him go.'

'Right.' Em's face was stony.

'There's something else.'

Em flicked her hair and sighed loudly. 'What?'

'How is your sister?'

The colour drained from her face. 'My sister?'

'Yes. It was easy enough to find out about Jen from your neighbours.'

'You spied on me?' There was acid in her words.

Rose looked down at the table. 'Yes, and I am sorry. Really I am. But I was worried about her when you were...'

Em's blue eyes were cold as ice as she finished the sentence. '...in custody? And you've got the nerve to ask how she is?'

Rose's resolve was faltering. 'Look, I hope she's okay, that's all.'

'Yes, she's "okay", no thanks to you!'

Rose clenched her hands under the table. 'Also, I'm pregnant.'

Em's carefully manicured eyebrows shot up. She took a sip of coffee before saying, 'What's that got to do with me?'

'Everything if you and Olly are serious about being together. You will be involved.' Several emotions flashed across Em's face as she processed what Rose had said.

'But the main thing is that...for our child's sake, you need to keep my involvement in what happened off your socials. You and Olly can say whatever, but it won't be about me, or our child, not in the public eye. Rather like you keep your sister a secret – I'm not sure why you do that, whether it's to protect her...or or maybe she simply doesn't fit in with your brand.'

Rose let the silence lengthen as Em regarded her through long lashes. Eventually, tossing her hair over her shoulder, she replied, 'Fair enough.' She closed her eyes and took a breath. Opening them, she fixed Rose with an icy glare. 'And just to be clear, my sister is none of your business.'

Rose managed a smile. 'You're right.'

Em fiddled with her cup, moving it in a circle on the table. 'And, yeah.' She swallowed. 'I'm sorry about the Emmanuel thing. That wasn't cool.'

Rose inclined her head in acceptance of the apology. 'I won't say anything if you don't. I think we understand each other. Can I ask you something else?'

Em stared at her.

'That night, when you went to my house...' Em dropped her gaze. 'When you saw those photos and realised who I was. Why didn't you tell the police when they first questioned you? Why didn't you point the finger at me?'

'Like you did to me, you mean?' Em looked up and sighed. 'I knew I was innocent and guessed the police would latch on to you sooner or later. Later, as it turned out. I want to have Olly in my life, and creating suspicion about you might have pushed him away from me – back to you. It wasn't worth the risk. I wasn't sure how loyal he'd be. And then it was too late – there was too much evidence against me.'

'Happy now?' She glared at Rose. 'I'll never forgive you for what you did to me...and Olly. Just so you know.' She leaned forward in a sudden movement. 'That troll was you, wasn't it? _az!' She spat the name and Rose recoiled at the venom. 'Oh yes, I guessed once I discovered your part in this. It was so obvious!' She gave a cold smirk.

Rose bowed her head. There was nothing to say.

'Saintly, wonderful, Rose. Who knew what lurked beneath! And to think that Olly actually felt guilty about us seeing each other. He was always going on about you before I even knew who you were.' She paused running her hands through the extensions that Rose had painstakingly inserted. 'It was nothing to do with me. If he felt guilty that was his stuff to deal with. But for what it's worth, I think he would have come back to you. He loved you.' She gave a theatrical sigh. 'But that was before he found out what the real Rose was capable of.' She tilted her head to one side and smiled.

Rose was numb, vaguely aware of Em picking up her phone and bag, getting ready to go. 'But don't worry. I'll keep your little secret – for *Olly's* sake. We're on a roll and I don't want anything getting in the way of that.' She threw the barb over her shoulder as she left.

As Em strode away, Rose remained motionless. Her body and mind numb.

When her brain eventually started to function she tried to process what Em had said. If she had talked to him... If she hadn't become obsessed with Em... If she hadn't met Dan...she could have got Olly back before things spiralled out of control. Instead she had ended up putting his life in danger and pushing him into Em's arms. She put her head in her hands to hide the tears falling onto the table. It was too late for ifs and buts. Her marriage was smashed to smithereens. She, Rose, had ruined any chance of a future for her and Olly and there was no going back.

Then another thought occurred to her. Was Em telling the truth? Or was this her spiteful way of making Rose suffer, making her pay?

She would never know. But one thing was for sure, she would never go down that road again – of obsessing whether Em was telling the truth. She knew where that led. It led to the worst version of herself.

Rose wiped the tears with her hands, lifted her head and smoothed her hair back into the clip. She had other priorities now, a different future. She had to be strong. Olly would find his own way – whether it was with Em or a different way, it was his choice and she had to let him go.

She stood up and headed for the door. The only way was forward – with their child.

Chapter Forty

F ive months later

Rose placed the flat of her hand on her stomach as she felt Evie moving and shifted her position as she scrolled through her phone, enjoying the familiar smell of her mother's cooking. She had got used to couple pictures of Olly and Em by now, but even so she still occasionally felt drawn to look.

As a couple, their following had sky-rocketed and Em was in the line-up for the next reality TV show. They had done well once the story of Olly's kidnap had been sold to the highest bidder. They were regular guests on other platforms and TV shows and had become a golden couple with their looks, and now, money.

Rose studied Olly and could see that he was happy. From an inauspicious start, this was the life that he seemed to have been born to. Rose still gave herself credit for getting him to where he was but knew now that he had grown in a different direction from the one she had planned for them. Em was his future now and she had to accept it. After all, hadn't she wanted Olly to be happy? It just hadn't occurred to Rose that the story might not have included her.

The one thing she had to thank Olly and Em for was that neither of them had mentioned her part in what happened. Em had been true to her word. Michael Small was firmly cast in the role of the villain, and hadn't been given a public voice since his arrest so was unable to dispute their account. Dan had pleaded guilty, all the while seeking to justify his actions, according to DC Brown. He would be put away for a very long time.

Rose would never forget the terror and humiliation of her own trial, and the relief when the judge agreed that she had shown true remorse and had eventually done the right thing in helping them catch Small. Rose wondered if she was a mother herself, as she'd said there was nothing to be gained by a prison sentence in Rose's situation. She had been given a suspended sentence.

A few weeks after the trial, Rose messaged Shona. She wanted to get back to work but didn't know how everyone at the salon would feel about that. There hadn't been a lot of coverage about her in the press as most attention was on the unusually hot weather and impending drought.

Much to her surprise, Shona was thrilled that she wanted to come back.

As she'd approached, Rose slowed. She could see the salon doors propped open in the late summer heat and from a few yards away could hear the usual background sounds of hairdryers and chatter spilling out onto the street. Edging forwards, she peered through the window, not wanting to be seen.

It was just another Friday. Mrs Moss was busy chatting to Adele, having seemingly switched her allegiance in Rose's absence. It seemed as if Cutting It Fine had moved on without her. Rose looked in from the outside wondering whether she still belonged there, and for a brief moment was tempted to turn away not having the courage to find out. But she reminded herself of the resolution she had made for herself and her child. She would face things head-on if she was to be any kind of role model.

Taking a deep breath and standing tall she'd approached the open doorway, hesitating for a moment as a wave of the familiar smells enveloped her. Shona had turned and spotted her, rushing over.

'Rose! Oh, it's good to see you!' She put her arms around her and gave a bear hug.

'Look everyone. Rose is back!'

Rose was taken aback at the warm reception – she'd steeled herself for silent judgement and rejection and her tension melted away as she was drawn back into her world.

Shona had put her arm around Rose. 'Not here, lovey. You're our Rose and we've got your back.' Rose had been overwhelmed by the tide of affection and love that came her way. The feelings that she didn't deserve such treatment were fading and she allowed herself to be cared about.

'That little madam kicking again?' Rose's mother came and sat next to her at the table, bringing her back to the present. 'That's everything in the oven. Fancy a coffee?'

'Thanks, Mum.' Rose put her phone down.

As she bustled around making the drinks and cutting two generous slices of cake, she said, 'I'm so glad you and Olly have sorted out arrangements for Evie. It'll be difficult for her to spend much time with them at first. Their lifestyle doesn't really work for a small baby.' Her lips tightened in disapproval.

'She'll be treated like a princess here and spoilt rotten while I'm at work.' Rose nudged her mum, bringing a smile to her lips.

She laughed as Finn came into the kitchen. 'She already has her uncle Finn wrapped around her little finger. How many Star Wars figures can one baby use?'

'It's never too soon to start a collection. She'll be glad of her Uncle Finn's investment one day. Thanks, Mum,' he said as she passed him a mug of coffee.

'I'm so glad everyone was okay with you when you went back to the salon,' her mother said. 'That took guts.'

Rose sipped her coffee. 'If I'd had guts, I wouldn't have got into that mess in the first place. But no, they were great once we got back into the swing of things. '

'Don't forget you were blackmailed, Rose,' her mother said sternly. 'Everyone understands that, so don't be too hard on yourself. At the end of the day you were trying to keep us all safe. I'm sure they understand that.'

'Even so, there's no getting away from my criminal record, even though I got a suspended sentence. Partly thanks to this little one.' She patted her stomach again.

'Remember that Michael Small is the real criminal. Thank God he's going to be banged up for years, after they found out he'd done this several times before – sniffing out people that were hurting and offering them readymade revenge.'

'I know. But still...'

'Your future is Evie, now, lovey. And you've learnt some difficult life lessons that will make you a brilliant mother.'

'Rosy Posy and Evie!' Her father came into the room and gave her a hug from behind. 'Don't get up.'

'You make us sound like a children's TV programme.' Rose laughed.

'The cot is assembled round at yours and ready for yours truly.' He indicated Rose's stomach. 'None too soon by the looks of it.'

'Thanks, Dad. What would I do without you?'

'I think poor Evie would have been sleeping in a drawer with your DIY skills.'

He sighed and smiled at Rose. 'It's so good to see you happier at last, Rosy Posy.'

Rose felt her eyes fill with tears. What had she done to deserve such a wonderful family? She shuddered at the memory of how alone she'd felt when she had kept them away with secrets.

'I think we're ready for any eventuality. And Poppy is on speed dial to take you to the hospital.' Her mother put her arm around Rose. 'I'm so glad you two have sorted things out. She's a good friend.'

'I know that now.' Rose levered herself up. 'She won't know what's hit her when godmother duties kick in. Right I'm off to inspect your handiwork.' She kissed her father. 'Thanks, Dad.'

As she reached her house, Walter was travelling along the pavement on his scooter. Rose smiled at Harold in his usual place in the basket, sitting on his haunches, tail curled neatly around his paws. They had become minor celebrities around town – everyone recognised Walter and Harold.

Gliding to a stop, Walter waved to Rose. 'Just back from bridge. I was a bit rusty at first, but I'm beating them all hands-down now. Everyone wants to be my partner,' he added with a grin.

'Time for a coffee?'

Rose nodded. 'Don't forget, I'm off coffee now. Peppermint tea would be good.'

'Of course.' Walter smiled before turning and unlocking the door. 'Lead on, Harold.' He made a sweeping gesture with his hand as Harold obliged, his tail in the air.

Thank you

My heartfelt thanks to Lindsey, Lorraine and Clare, for beta reading Cutting It Fine and ferreting out pesky typos and other errors. Thank for your time and attention to detail.

Also to Chloe M for sharing her invaluable hairdressing expertise.

To Kostis for yet another stunning cover design

As ever, thanks to my wife, Glen, for supporting me through the writing of another book and for always being there. Without her encouragement and patience Cutting It Fine would never have seen the light of day.

And finally, thanks to all my readers who make the whole writing experience worthwhile.

Sheena is writing...

Thank you for reading Cutting It Fine. I love to hear from readers of my books, so please get in touch with your thoughts at sheenaiswriting@vanstonepublishing.com or contact me via my shop sheenaiswriting.com where you can also find out about my other books, special offers and various other goodies.

Reading Group Questions

- What do you think of Olly? Is he weak? Is he smothered by Rose? Do you empathise with his anger towards the end of the book? I have deliberately left his character open to interpretation.

- Do you feel sorry for Rose or is she the architect of her own downfall?

- What do you imagine the future holds for Rose and Evie?

- Does Em have any redeeming features?

- What impact does Harold's presence have on Walter?

BV - #0189 - 090625 - C0 - 203/127/16 - PB - 9781739674380 - Matt Lamination